"You ran over my hedgehog."

Liz stared at the stranger—a very angry man with green eyes—who was pounding on her car. His words were muffled, but she wasn't about to roll down the window while he had a hoe in his hand. "What do you want?" she yelled.

He repeated his accusation and added, "Don't you know how to drive?"

"We have hedgehogs in Nevada?" she asked, turning to look where he was pointing.

He made a sound of pure disgust. "Do you see that flattened lump of muck? Moments ago that was a living, breathing plant. A hedgehog cactus."

Relieved that it wasn't the brown, furry little animal she'd been picturing, she didn't know whether to laugh or cry as she studied the bits of shredded bark and some greenish splotch that led straight to her tire. "I'm sorry. I really am."

"Tell that to the hedgehog."

"Oh, for heaven's sake. It was an accident. I'll pay you for the damn thing."

"Save your money for driving lessons," he added as he walked away.

Dear Reader,

THE SISTERS OF THE SILVER DOLLAR miniseries evolved from my Signature Select Saga novel *Betting on Grace*, which was released in November 2005. The books center on the lives and loves of four sisters of Romani, or Gypsy, descent. Grace, the youngest, set in motion certain changes that affected her whole family. Second-born sister Elizabeth, for example, lost her job, which put Liz's most treasured dream at risk. Some people might let that kind of blow pull them down, but not Liz. Liz is a true heroine, the kind who rises to any challenge—even falling in love with a man who is an impostor.

Every book I've ever written has been shaped to some degree by my experiences, observations and connections to the world at large. Sometimes—magically, it might appear—people enter my life at just the right juncture to supply me with facts and insights that I didn't even know I needed. So it was with *Bringing Baby Home*. As I was researching Liz's experiences abroad, my dear friend Reen Perkins returned home from her sojourn in India. She just happened to have traveled many of the same paths that Liz had on her life-shaping journey. Imagine that. So thank you, Reen, for being the beautiful, giving person you are and for venturing far beyond the comfort of my office.

I hope you'll look for Alexandra's story, *The Quiet Child*, in November. If you have any trouble finding any of the SISTERS OF THE SILVER DOLLAR titles, please contact me at my Web site, www.debrasalonen.com, or write to me at P.O. Box 322, Cathey's Valley, CA 95306.

All the best,

Debra

DEBRA SALONEN
Bringing Baby Home

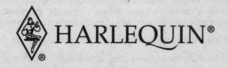

TORONTO • NEW YORK • LONDON
AMSTERDAM • PARIS • SYDNEY • HAMBURG
STOCKHOLM • ATHENS • TOKYO • MILAN • MADRID
PRAGUE • WARSAW • BUDAPEST • AUCKLAND

ISBN-13: 978-0-373-75130-3
ISBN-10: 0-373-75130-3

BRINGING BABY HOME

www.eHarlequin.com

Printed in U.S.A.

ABOUT THE AUTHOR

As a child, Debra wanted to be an artist. She saved her allowance to send away for a "Learn To Draw" kit, but when her mother mistook Deb's artful rendition of a horse for a cow, Deb turned to her second love—writing. She credits her success as an author to her parents for giving her the chance to realize those dreams. She and her high school sweetheart, who have been married for thirty years, live in California surrounded by a great deal of family, quite a few dogs and views that appeal to the artist still trapped in her soul.

Books by Debra Salonen

HARLEQUIN AMERICAN ROMANCE
1114—ONE DADDY TOO MANY*

HARLEQUIN SUPERROMANCE
910—THAT COWBOY'S KIDS
934—HIS DADDY'S EYES
986—BACK IN KANSAS
1003—SOMETHING ABOUT EVE
1061—WONDERS NEVER CEASE
1098—MY HUSBAND, MY BABIES
1104—WITHOUT A PAST
1110—THE COMEBACK GIRL
1196—A COWBOY SUMMER
1238—CALEB'S CHRISTMAS WISH
1279—HIS REAL FATHER

SIGNATURE SELECT SAGA
BETTING ON GRACE*

*Sisters of the Silver Dollar

Don't miss any of our special offers. Write to us at the following address for information on our newest releases.

Harlequin Reader Service
U.S.: 3010 Walden Ave., P.O. Box 1325, Buffalo, NY 14269
Canadian: P.O. Box 609, Fort Erie, Ont. L2A 5X3

For all the friends who play a vital part in my life—and my books. You enrich my days and my stories.

Chapter One

The stack of papers on the passenger seat of her Honda CR-V toppled sideways as Liz Radonovic turned onto the street leading to her house. The two-inch pile edged precariously toward the ridiculously messy floor, which was symbolic of her life, in general. Chaotic.

She slowed at the first of the newly installed speed bumps on Canto Lane.

"Ka-thunk," she said aloud in harmony with her car's rear suspension. She hated the four-inch hurdles that C.A.N., the Canto Association of Neighbors, had recently convinced the city of Henderson, Nevada, to install. There were two in the middle of her block—pretty much bracketing her driveway. She couldn't help but take their presence personally, even though the road committee had insisted this was for the good of the children.

"If you had kids, you'd understand," Crissy Montoya, mother of two and current president of the group, had told Liz while circulating a petition to enforce curb appeal. Buoyed by her success in curtailing speeders, Crissy was now on a crusade to make the four-block radius around her home more "charming."

Liz had been abrupt when confronted with the petition

and pen. Not because she didn't approve of curb appeal, but because the concept sounded like something that would cost her money.

And it had.

Crissy's project had been approved by the majority of homeowners and she'd hired a gardener, who was slowly adding plants, boulders and creativity to the otherwise boring tract houses that made up her subdivision. Nestled between Boulder Highway and the River Mountains to the east, the Canto development had sprung up when the line between Henderson and its neighbor to the north, Las Vegas, was still easily identifiable.

Liz hadn't met the man responsible for making all these decorative changes, but she'd seen him several times from a distance. Tall and lanky, he usually wore a wide-brim hat with a sort of curtain that covered the back of his neck and shoulders. Shirt, pants, hat—all tan. The color of the desert. He almost looked as though he was deliberately trying to blend in.

But he was good at what he did, she had to admit, smiling at a cascading bridal bouquet of a mature yucca. She had to respect a man who could transplant succulents and keep them from dying in this climate.

She figured her place was next, and the thought of an additional outlay of money—cash she couldn't spare—was enough to make her stomach heave.

"You need to be more proactive," her sister Alex had told Liz recently at one of their weekly roundtables. "You shouldn't let that Crissy woman boss you around. Tell her you're between jobs and can't spare the cash. She should be able to understand that, shouldn't she?"

Between jobs. Liz wished it were that simple. She had lost her physical therapist job after the administrator and several of the doctors at the private hospital where she'd been working were arrested. That had been one of the many repercussions the Radonovic family had suffered after Liz's youngest sister, Grace, blew the whistle on old family friend Charles Harmon, a lawyer and casino owner who had broken too many laws to count.

Liz had never had any trouble getting a P.T. job anywhere in the world. Until now. Either there was a glut of applicants in Vegas or her name carried some invisible black mark. Liz didn't know which and wasn't sure she cared. In a way, every closed door seemed to be a sign. She was ready for a change and knew what she wanted to do—help people stay healthy instead of trying to fix the body after something went wrong.

She was Romani and came from a long line of healers—women who knew which herbs could ease a tummy ache, help prevent arthritis and steady nerves in difficult times. During her stay in India, she'd been exposed to a different kind of healing—Ayurveda, the oldest medicine in the world. She hadn't stayed there long enough to become proficient in the practice, but the knowledge she'd garnered had fed a need in her soul.

Was there a market for herbs, teas and therapeutic oils in a city like Las Vegas? Liz was pretty sure the answer was yes. She'd recently started offering a few small-batch teas for sale and had heard only glowing reviews. The patrons at her sister Kate's restaurant, Romantique, had gone from ordering her three-mint blend from the menu to demanding tea bags to take home with them.

Could she make a living selling specialized teas? That was the real question. And how would opening a new business affect her other goal? Her most important goal—adopting Prisha.

Prisha, whose name meant God's gift, was the abandoned infant Liz had fallen in love with at the ashram where she'd volunteered in India. Underweight, with an obvious birth defect—her little feet were both turned inward—Prisha was one of the lucky ones. Her maternal family had cared enough to drop off the tiny baby at the ashram when the mother decided she couldn't care for the child.

Normally, the ashram didn't handle children with severe birth defects, simply because it wasn't set up as a nursing facility. But Liz had convinced the staff that daily, gentle therapy on Prisha's legs might be enough to correct the problem. She'd been wrong. A visiting doctor had confirmed her secret fear that Prisha was going to need more extensive care, including surgery, if she ever hoped to walk. And Liz was certain the only way that would happen would be if she adopted Prisha and brought her home to the United States.

Starting a new business and adopting a child from a foreign country at the same time probably didn't make sense, but Liz had no choice. Prisha needed her. And as long as the bank approved her application to refinance her mortgage, she'd have the money she needed to start the adoption process.

She eyed the sliding papers. Everyone was refinancing these days. Why shouldn't she? And surely her reason was valid. She wanted to make a home for a child who desperately needed one. Prisha was nearly a year and a half old. She should already have started undergoing the surgeries that would allow her to develop normally—and, eventually, to walk.

Liz shifted her gaze to the twenty-year-old house that she'd bought upon her return from India. Nothing special, really. Affordable. A good starter home, the agent who'd handled the deal had called it. Three bedrooms with a nice-sized backyard. Room for a child to romp and play.

"And if there's any money left over, I'll be able to pay for my front yard's facelift," she murmured.

Between making and trying to market her herbal teas, plus doing side jobs like helping at Alex's child-care center, there hadn't been time for landscaping.

As she slowed in preparation of the left turn into her driveway, she made a detour around the primer-gray pickup truck parked in front of Crissy's place, which as luck would have it was right next door to Liz's house.

She looked around but didn't see the owner. The tailgate was down, though, and an obviously homemade ramp was angled against it. She took the turn extra wide, to be safe.

The rear tires of her compact SUV bounced over the curb, lifting the car cockeyed, which made her papers slide to the floor.

"Damn."

She jammed her foot on the brake and leaned over sideways to collect the collated homework assignment in which the bank had asked for her life history, projected income till death and purchasing habits. She returned to an upright position and checked to see if anything besides dust had attached itself to her pristine pages.

Rap, rap, rap.

The aggressive sound of knuckles on glass made her jump. Her heart rate spiked. Adrenaline poured through her veins, bringing with it memories she could normally suppress. War sounds. Cries of pain. The harsh, acrid taste of blood and sweat and fear. Her armpits tingled. A sharp pain twisted across her brow.

"Hey, open up. Don't you know how to drive? You just killed my four-year-old Echinocereus triglochidiatus."

As her panic receded, Liz forced air into her lungs. Her vision cleared. She wasn't in Bosnia. She was in her car, in Nevada. She was home.

And some stranger—a very angry man with green eyes and an artificially black mustache was pounding on the window. His words were muffled, but she wasn't about to open the window while he had a hoe in his hand. "What do you want?" she yelled.

He gestured toward the road. "You ran over a hedgehog cactus."

"A hedgehog?" she asked, turning to look where he was pointing. "We have hedgehogs in Nevada?"

The idea made tears rush to her eyes. She wasn't exactly sure what a hedgehog was, but she pictured a little animal. Brown and furry. Maybe some relation to the groundhog?

The man made a sound of pure disgust and stormed away.

Liz watched him march to the rattletrap truck and toss his hoe in the back. He paused a moment and pulled a navy cotton handkerchief out of the back pocket of his one-piece jumpsuit and used it to mop the sweat from his neck and brow.

"You're too young to wear jumpsuits," she wanted to say. But she didn't. As her sisters would attest, Liz was no arbiter of fashion. If clothes fit and were clean, she was happy. But still, the guy was in his early forties or late thirties. He was tall, lean and—from the parts she could see, namely his arms—well muscled.

And he was also still worked up. She could tell by his body language, which, odd as it seemed, intrigued her. He was a living, breathing contradiction. She couldn't see his hair because of the hat, but his skin coloring belied the dark mustache. Liz was of Romani, or Gypsy, descent. She was surrounded by swarthy men with Mediterranean complexions. This guy's mustache didn't go with the rest of him. Nor did his eye color work for her. The green was too green.

Liz loved puzzles.

After stacking her papers neatly on the seat, she picked up her cell phone and got out of the car. She kept her thumb poised to call for help if he tried anything, but daylight and the peace of her neighborhood gave her the courage to approach him—from a distance.

"Hey. What was that all about? What did I do?"

He ignored her.

"Excuse me, sir, but didn't anyone ever tell you it's ridiculously impolite to pound on a woman's window then stalk off without any explanation."

"I told you."

His voice was deep. Liz didn't think she'd ever heard that rich a bass before. The lush tone drew her closer.

"Well, I was too freakin' scared to understand the words. I thought you were attacking me."

He made another sound of irritation and stuffed his hanky back in his pocket. "Just forget it. You wouldn't understand."

Now that was one charge Liz didn't take lightly. In her family, Liz was considered the empathic one. The person most likely to give a damn. Didn't two tours to Bosnia count for anything? Hadn't she opened her home to Lydia and Reezira, the two young Romanian prostitutes who'd been caught in an immigration nightmare after their "sponsor," the deceitful snake, Charles Harmon, was arrested?

"You're wrong. You don't know me, and you sure as hell don't have any right to condemn me without giving me a chance to defend myself. Where's the justice in that?"

"Justice." The mocking tone came through his laugh. "There's no such thing as justice."

He hesitated a moment then pivoted and started toward her. Liz tightened her grip on her phone. It wasn't much of a defense, but it was more than she'd had the last time a man attacked her.

When he was a foot away, he stopped. Without a car window separating them, Liz had a better look at his face. And it confused her. Mustache aside, the rest of the pieces were quite ordinary. Masculine nose—not too big, not too small. Nicely shaped eyes with pronounced crinkles that were tanned from his job, she guessed. A good-sized mouth and really excellent teeth. He was a decent-looking man, but, again, she had a sense that all of the features were slightly off. As if she were looking at one of those children's books in which the reader turns a section of the page to change the facial features and create a different character.

He gestured toward the street, impatiently. She looked where he was pointing.

"There. Do you see that flattened lump of muck? A minute ago that squished piece of debris was a living thing. A cactus. The word triglochidiatus defines it as a three-barbed variety. Its common name is the hedgehog cactus because early Europeans thought it resembled the little animal they remembered from home. Others call it a claret-cup cactus because of the beautiful ruby-red flowers that this one will never bear."

She studied the triangle-shaped planter at the corner of her driveway and the communal sidewalk. It hadn't been there when she left the house that morning. Two other plants—neither of which she could name—had survived, but bits of shredded bark and some greenish splotch led straight to her tire. Proof of her vicious, although unintentional, assault.

She honestly didn't know whether to laugh or cry. So she did both. She laughed until she tears started running down her cheeks. "I'm sorry. I really am," she sputtered, trying to explain that she wasn't laughing at the man or his dead plant. "It's just that this is so typical of the way my life has been going lately. I'm running around like a crazy person trying to keep all these balls in the air. And why? I can't even be trusted to keep a hedgehog cactus safe—how could I possibly think I…"

She didn't finish the thought. Adopting Prisha—the goal she'd returned from India with—had never left her, but it seemed further out of reach than ever. And maybe there was a reason for that. Maybe the universe was trying to tell her something.

"It's telling you you're a lousy driver."

She startled. Had she really muttered her thought out loud?

"I'm usually a good driver. Unlike my sister Grace," she added, mostly out of habit.

"Tell that to my cactus."

"Oh, for heaven's sake, I'm sorry. It was an accident. I'll pay you for the damn thing."

He drew himself up proudly. Too proudly for a person who drove such a rickety truck, she thought. "Keep your money. Use it for driving lessons."

Then he left. Not a backward look. Not a by-your-leave, as her mother, Yetta, was fond of saying.

But Liz was not without resources of her own. She could probably get the man's name and number from Crissy, but that meant knocking on the door and actually talking to her neighbor—something Liz preferred to avoid. If there was another way to find out where he lived, she'd send him a check.

She used the pen clipped to the stack of papers and

quickly scratched out the guy's license plate number. On the first page of her loan application, she realized too late.

Yep, it was just one of those days.

DAVID BAINES only made it six blocks before he had to stop, get out of his truck and rehook the chain that kept the right side of his tailgate from working loose. He used his shoulder to shove the worthless piece of metal in place then hooked two links between the grooved notches that he'd rigged up.

His head was pounding, but at least his temper was starting to cool. He couldn't believe he'd actually yelled at a woman for running over a plant. Yes, he cared about his cactus and other seedlings, but only a madman—a crazy demented fool—would place a higher priority on cacti than people. What was wrong with him?

So many things he couldn't begin to count, but he knew to a day when this change in his personality had begun. August 21, 2001. The day he'd died.

He reached over the side of his truck bed and made sure the rest of his tools were accounted for. Shovels, rakes, edger. No mower. He did landscaping, not yards. He grew the plants that he transferred to people's raised beds and patios. He didn't call himself a landscaper, though. That sounded too presumptuous. He was a handyman/gardener. He felt the combination sounded innocuous enough. Certainly not the kind of job a person with three postgraduate degrees would be doing.

Once he'd started his new life, he'd had no choice but to learn a new trade. He'd ceased to be a scientist with credentials up the wazoo and had become a man who worked with plants. He grew them in his makeshift greenhouse at the rear of the oversize lot behind the house he rented from his elderly and slightly whacko landlady. Mimi Simms lived in the double-wide mobile home on the adjoining lot. Her late husband had spent his final years in the shack she euphemistically called the "guesthouse."

The rent was reasonable, so David couldn't complain even though the one-bedroom, one-bath residence was impossible to heat or cool. And in the four years that he'd been renting from her, he'd managed to grow a wall of hardy and unforgiving thorn bushes that gave him privacy and some illusionary sense of safety.

He realized that he was hiding behind the hedge. Like an ogre in some children's fable, he'd distanced himself from polite society, only venturing forth to fulfill his private vow to do good. He'd done enough bad to last a lifetime.

He no longer made "better living through chemicals." He made a better world through plants. This time, on a very small, humbling scale.

Which partly explained why he lost it when someone destroyed one of his plants. Or so he wanted to believe, but he was too honest to place the blame for his temper tantrum on the lovely shoulders of the woman he'd just yelled at. He'd been in a funk for over a week. Happened every year around his daughter's birthday. Memories would slip past his defenses. Despair would fill the hole in his heart like air in a balloon—until he blew up.

This time, at a woman. He'd terrified her. And made her cry.

But she'd laughed, too, he reminded himself. As if his attack had been that of a crazy person. And she was right. Sane people didn't explode over little things. He owed that poor woman an apology. It wasn't her fault she'd smashed his cactus on a bad day. A day when the past couldn't be denied.

Today was Ariel's birthday. Number nine. No doubt she would celebrate with a party, friends and gifts galore. She was probably four or five inches taller than the last time he'd seen her. Maybe she had a retainer or braces. From what he'd gleaned from his clients with young children, orthodontists were starting earlier these days.

He tried not to think about Ariel.

She wasn't *really* his child, after all. He'd married her mother when Ariel was a toddler. Ariel's real father was a rat-bastard who had abused Kay and neglected their baby daughter and twins Jordie and Randall who were two years older than their sister. The man's only response to his wife's request for a divorce was his fierce refusal to pay child support.

David hadn't wanted his new love to be tied to a man like that in any way. He had a high-paying job with a billion-dollar pharmaceutical company. He could certainly provide for his new family. And he had—until Kay, the children's mother, left him for another man. A neighbor who was home when David hadn't been.

The timing, it turned out, had been providential. Kay and the children were safe from the fallout created by David's losing favor with his boss, a megalomaniac named V. A. "Ray" Cross. Born Vincente Aurelio Conejo, Ray went from being the first kid in his family to graduate from high school to the boardroom of one of the largest privately owned pharmaceutical labs in the country. His staff had often speculated about the number of bodies buried along Ray's remarkable climb to the top, and the closer David got to the man he'd at one time considered his mentor, the better he understood Ray's maxim for life. In Ray's world, only Ray mattered. The bodies, David feared, were real. And, in a way, included his.

He got back in the truck and drove carefully, never exceeding the speed limit. Faster cars passed him impatiently, but David was a follower of rules. Most of them, anyway.

"Thou shalt not kill"—unless you count poisoning thousands of unsuspecting consumers.

"Thou shalt not lie"—unless the truth means losing profits in any given year.

"Thou shalt not covet your neighbor's wife"—well, he could honestly say he'd never done that. His neighbor's life, maybe. All he'd ever wanted was a home and a family of his own. The kind he'd known as a child, before his parents were killed in a car accident and he was told he had to stay with his grandmother, who had considered her work over and done when the daughter she raised got married.

June, as his grandmother preferred to be called, did her duty. She even sent her grandson to the best college his inheritance money could buy, but it hadn't occurred to her to try to replace the love he'd known in his parents' arms.

He'd tried to find that as an adult, and thought he'd succeeded with Kay and the children. Until, fate ripped that family out of his hands, too. And seldom a night went by that he didn't think about the pain his "death" must have caused the children he'd called his own.

As he pulled into his driveway, he caught a glimpse of his landlady. Mimi Simms was eighty if she was a day. Her red hair was brighter than a poinsettia in bloom. She was an odd combination of nosy and antisocial. David preferred the latter. Once he'd made up his mind to speak out, to become a high-profile whistleblower, he'd had no choice but to leave the past behind and disappear.

For four years, he'd been lucky. He'd also never once had an altercation with a customer and drawn attention to himself. He could only hope that the beautiful lady with the kind eyes would shrug off his embarrassing faux pas and forget about him.

"You're a fool," he muttered as he pulled the truck to a stop in front of his little shack. "You had your chance at a normal life, but you chose to work for Ray Cross, instead. Now, you can't ever go back."

Nor could he start a new life with someone else. He'd made a vow never to put anyone through that kind of torture and distress again. His decision to give up his old life and enter the federal Witness Protection Program had been relatively easy—it was either that or wake up some morning with Ray Cross's gun in his face. The deputy U.S. marshals who had been assigned to his case had come up with an elaborate plan that included an inferno at the lab where David had spent most of his time. No body. No funeral. No fuss. Or so David had assumed. But apparently no one had informed his ex-wife.

Dying had been difficult, but it had been a lot easier on him than on his loved ones. He would regret that for the rest of his life.

Chapter Two

"Okay. Who wants to go first?" Alex asked, looking around their mother's table.

Alex, who was a year and four months older than Liz, often acted as the CEO of the Radonovic family. But beneath the businesslike facade was a gentle heart that made nearly every child at her Dancing Hippo Day Care and Preschool fall in love with her.

Neither Liz nor Kate volunteered. These weekly breakfast meetings just weren't the same without Grace, the youngest of the Radonovic sisters. She'd always shown up bubbly and full of topics for discussion. Sometimes Alex and Kate would share their problems, too, but nobody really expected Liz to contribute. She didn't dump. She preferred to keep her problems to herself. Things seemed to sort themselves out eventually without her sisters' help.

"Has anyone heard from Grace?" she asked.

Newly engaged, Grace had followed her fiancé, Nick Lightner, to Detroit, where she was settling in and planning their wedding, which was scheduled for next spring. But, in typical Grace fashion, she couldn't resist being an active part of Kate's recently decided upon nuptials, as well. "Practice makes perfect, right?" she'd told Liz on the phone a few days ago. "By helping to plan Kate's wedding, I'll know what mistakes to avoid."

Grace. Liz missed her—everyone did. Especially Kate.

"Here's her flight information," Kate said, handing Alex and Liz copies printed from the Internet. "Did I tell you she's having a costume made for Maya? Just like ours. Grace insists Maya will be ready to dance at my wedding. How? Are you teaching her, Alex? Because I sure as heck don't have time. And I know Liz is too busy."

"Liz is always too busy, aren't you, Liz?" Alex asked. "Too busy for anything fun."

Liz looked across the table at her older sister. As kids they'd shared a special bond. But the past few years had been difficult. So much had happened in both their lives that neither seemed able to talk about.

"I wouldn't make much of a teacher, even if I had the time," she said. "Do either of you want to try my new tea? I'm calling it Woman Power. It's better than coffee, Alex. And a heck of a lot better for you than soda, Kate."

Kate made a face. "I gave up sodas weeks ago, remember?" Kate's life had turned upside down when her ex-husband was released from prison on parole—just in time for his ex-wife's engagement to another man.

"Good for you. But you should try this. It has maté in it. A little pick-me-up without coffee's acid."

She poured them two cups and added a squeeze of honey from a bear-shaped vessel. "Where's Mom?" she asked.

"Airing out Claude's place. She hired a cleaning crew. Same people who did Romantique after the county boys got done with it," Kate answered.

Their paternal uncle had lived next door until Grace's hubby-to-be busted Claude and several other family members for their illicit business dealings with old family friend

Charles Harmon. The house was now empty, but with family coming to town for Kate's wedding, every bed would be needed.

"So, it's official? The Sisters of the Silver Dollar are dancing at your wedding?" Alex asked Kate.

Liz and her sisters had danced for their father as children, scampering after the coins he'd tossed their way. As they grew up, they'd taken the craft more seriously, incorporating the old steps into their routines. The name stuck, but the girls hadn't danced together since their father, Ernst, passed away. Until recently.

"Well, you know Grace," Kate said, sipping her tea. "Um, this is good, Liz. I told you your mint tea is a huge success at the restaurant. Maybe not being able to do physical therapy for a living is a good thing. Herbal remedies might be your true calling in life."

Her sister's praise was nice to hear, but Liz hadn't given up the thought of being a physical therapist completely. P.T. wasn't her first love, but it paid well. Starting her new tea business, which she'd decided to call Tea for Me, with a "T4Me" logo, was a terrifying leap of faith, but she'd really had no choice when every other avenue seemed closed to her.

Liz would never go back to WorldRx, a Doctors Without Borders kind of group. She'd been midway through her second six-month stay in Bosnia when she was brutally attacked and left for dead in a snowbank. When a patrol found her, they'd rushed her to the E.R. where she usually worked. The doctors sewed up her cuts, applied ice to her bruises and gave her drugs to protect against pregnancy and disease. But nothing had eased the sense of violation so traumatizing she'd spent three weeks in a farmhouse a mile from her station, refusing to return to her post until the men who attacked her were caught. An impossible task in a place devastated by war. As a friend later told her, "War doesn't bring out the hero in everybody. In most, it brings out the beast."

"Liz."

Liz startled. She felt her face heat up. She never let the past creep into her thoughts. She came from a long line of mystics and fortune-tellers. The last thing she needed was for one of her sisters to pick up on what had happened to her. She hadn't shared this particularly unpleasant experience for a reason. She was over it. Period. "What?"

"Well, don't bite my head off. I just asked if you could make a new tea for Jo. She's doing great since she got back from Stanford—she hasn't smoked in weeks, but the new medicine the doctor has her on is making her nauseous."

Jo Brighten was Kate's partner in the restaurant and mother of Kate's fiancé, Rob Brighten. Liz liked the frank, spunky woman a lot. She'd been battling what her doctors had thought was lung cancer, but after a trip to a specialist in California, Jo was told she had emphysema. The diagnosis had come as a huge relief to everyone, but she wasn't out of the woods, yet.

"I'll try to come up with something this afternoon. After I drop off my loan application at the bank." She took a drink of tea. "Boy, am I sick of those nosy jerks."

"So, why are you doing the refinancing?" Alex asked. "You've only been in your house a year or so. Do you have enough equity to make it worth the effort?"

Liz hoped so. The money, added to what she'd saved, would give her the initial application fee associated with a foreign adoption.

After her father's death, Liz had traveled to India to stay with a friend who worked in an orphanage. Liz had planned to volunteer her physical therapy skills at a nearby hospital, but she became so wrapped up in helping the children, she completely forgot about her original plan. The children, from infant to young adult, had seemed so grateful for every bit of attention she gave them. She'd seen enough death. She wanted to experience life. And then, one of the caregivers had handed her Prisha, and Liz's life was changed forever.

"I think so. I hope so," she added under her breath. And maybe all the landscaping by the homeowners association would work in her favor—increase the value of her home. If she ever saw that snarly gardener again, she'd thank him.

"It's true the price of real estate in Vegas has gone nuts," Alex added. "I couldn't believe what Rob paid for your new house, Kate. Not that it's not gorgeous. You're going to love living there, but…ouch. Glad I'm not in the market for a new home. I'm going to be stuck here in the Compound forever."

The Compound was what family and friends called the cul-de-sac where their mother's home sat. Uncle Claude's house was on one side, and his youngest son and daughter-in-law's place just one door down from there. Alex's four-bedroom, ranch-style home on the opposite corner had been converted to the Dancing Hippo. Some days it seemed as if you couldn't turn around without bumping into a family member.

Liz had looked in this neighborhood before she bought her home, but there hadn't been anything available. So, contrary to her family's wishes, she'd purchased a place in Henderson, twenty or so miles to the south—and was still catching flack for it.

"So, Liz, are you going to bring a date to the wedding?"

Alex asked. "One of my student's fathers—he's also a member of Rob's Dad's Group—asked me to go with him. I was so shocked I nearly dropped his kid."

"Um…I don't know. Probably not. Who would I ask?"

The only face that came to mind belonged to her irate gardener. She started to laugh.

"I told you something is wrong with her. She's giggling. Liz doesn't giggle," Kate said.

"Maybe it's the tea," Alex said, giving her mug a suspicious look.

"Liz, tell us what's going on. Should we be worried?"

Liz sighed. Maybe talking about the bizarre incident with the neighborhood gardener would help her let go of the nagging guilt she felt. Not from running over the cactus so much as from the impetuous call she'd made after he left the scene.

"Yesterday, I had a guy accuse me of murder."

"Murder?" Kate squawked.

Liz nodded. "The man who's installing some landscaping on the curbs up and down my block said I killed one of his cacti. Echinocereus somethingorotherus." She shrugged. "Come to think of it, he seemed surprisingly well educated for a gardener—knew the genus or class or whatever of the plant I ran over, but, I mean, come on. It was a cactus. They're a dime a dozen. And vehicular cactus-slaughter is not murder."

Alex shook her head. "He obviously doesn't know you—the Florence Nightingale and Mother Teresa of the physical therapy world."

She ignored the sisterly dig. Something about the guy had stayed with her long after the encounter. Maybe it was his compelling green eyes, she thought. Like icy fire or fiery ice. She couldn't decide which. "It's not like I did it on purpose," she said, shaking her head to stay focused. "I was reaching for my stack of papers. You know what the suspension is like in my car. Even mini-SUVs are a little top heavy, and I'd hit the curb while trying to avoid his truck. I really do feel awful, though."

"So buy him another one," Kate suggested.

"I would, but I don't know his name. Or phone number. Or address."

"Did you look in the phone book under *Mystery Gardener*?" Alex asked, laughing at her own joke.

"No," Liz admitted, "but I did call Zeke and asked him to track down the guy's license plate number."

Alex sobered. "You what?"

Kate sat forward. "That sounds a bit extreme. Why didn't you contact that pain-in-the-rear next-door neighbor of yours? She hired the guy. She must have his number."

Liz turned away so they wouldn't see her blush. She poured the last of the tea in her mug and said, "You know how much I dread talking to Crissy. She'd have made a big deal out of it, like I was going to undermine her authority or something."

When she looked over her shoulder, she saw her sisters communicating in silence. She knew what they were saying and hated the fact that they were right. Liz wasn't a coward, but for some reason she'd let Crissy—with her doggone Martha Stewart perfection—intimidate the heck out of her.

"What did Zeke say?" Alex asked.

"He gave me a hard time about not being on call for the Radonovic family, but he's hooked on my three-mint tea, so he said he'd do it."

Zeke Martini was their mother's undeclared beau. All of the sisters found this a bit surprising considering he'd headed the investigation that arrested Charles Harmon and brought the dogs of hell yapping at the heels of every Romani in town. No one—aunts, uncles and cousins, included—could seem to understand what Yetta, the acknowledged matriarch of the Romani clan, saw in the silver-haired *gaujo*—non-Romani—cop.

"Well, I'm sorry you had a run-in with the guy, but if you're that curious about him, I still say you should talk to that Crissy woman," Kate said. "I know how much you hate contentious situations, sis. But my wedding is in two weeks, and I need your complete focus."

Liz smiled. Kate was a self-disciplined go-getter who could multitask with the best of them. This blatant plea for help meant her sister was truly in over her head, which Liz probably shouldn't have found surprising given Grace's involvement.

"What do you need me to do?"

"Everything. Finish picking out the new furniture for the house. Find a hair stylist who can whip this mop into some kind of shape. Teach my daughter our old Sisters of the Silver Dollar routines. Make sure my future mother-in-law is taking her medicine. And anything else that crops up. Between the two of you, I'm sure you'll handle it. I'm going to my room and have a nervous breakdown. Bye."

She didn't leave, of course. And it wouldn't have done her much good, since her room was right down the hall. Kate and Maya had been living with Yetta since Kate's divorce. The arrangement had worked out well for everyone during the long, difficult time after Ernst's death. But, soon, Kate and her daughter would be living in a brand-new house not far from Liz.

"I'm happy to help. Keeping busy makes waiting to hear

from the loan officer that much easier," Liz said. Plus, cutting and curling her share of the skeins of ribbon Grace had shipped might take her mind off her mysterious cactus man.

But Kate was right. The person to ask for the name and whereabouts of the man in the tan jumpsuit lived right next door to Liz. So what if Crissy appeared to be living the American Dream—perfect house, two perfect kids and a perfect marriage? Liz refused to be intimidated.

"COME HERE, YOU DUMB BEAST. I'm not going to hurt you."

The cat, which David was tempted to call Ugly, switched his crooked tail and stepped behind the bags of soil additives stacked in the corner.

"Look. I bought you tuna. Not cat tuna. Real, recently-swimming-in-the-sea-meant-for-human-consumption tuna." He tapped his fork against the outside of the can. The tinny sound did nothing to lure the animal closer.

"Fine. Be that way. I have to leave in a few minutes and I was sincerely hoping we might settle the question about whether or not we need to get you fixed."

The cat was a strange color combination. Mostly gray with hair that was just a bit too long to make a clear call on the neutering situation. But he had two swatches of white. One under his belly and another from his foot to the top of his left hind quarters. He looked as if he'd slipped into an open can of white paint.

"Okay. We'll save that talk for later. But I really would like to get that cut above your eye looked at. Could get infected. Gonna leave a scar, that's for sure."

The cat suddenly sprang to the workbench where David potted his cacti that were sold at retail. "Scar. Maybe that's what I should call you. We both have them, you know. Yours are just a lot more visible than mine."

David dumped the fish into a bowl he'd taken from his cupboard. Nothing fancy. A set he bought at Goodwill right after he moved into his place. "I'm using the good china, so no inviting friends over while I'm at work, okay?"

He bent down and put the bowl on the floor. As soon as he was three steps away, the cat leaped down and attacked the meal. He acted starved, but David had left dry cat food out every day since the animal first appeared on his doorstep—exhausted, beaten-down and bleeding— David didn't have the heart to turn him away, even though he made it a point not to get too friendly with any living soul—man or beast.

It just didn't pay. Not when he might have to pick up and leave at a moment's notice. Nope. He didn't do relationships. Which was why he was stalling. He needed to get back to Canto Lane. Unfortunately, that carried the risk of running into the woman he'd yelled at the day before.

Granted their exchange hardly constituted a relationship, but she'd been on his mind ever since he'd driven away, and that bothered him. Generally, he was a master at living in the present—during the daylight hours, at least. Except on Ariel's birthday. Maybe that was why the woman with lush black-brown hair and eyes so dark they made espresso look watered down had stayed in his mind. He'd met her in a moment of weakness.

"Well, I'm not bringing in any money to buy tuna by standing here," he muttered, pocketing his keys. He rinsed out the can and put it in the garbage can under the sink, then walked to the door. A quick glance told him everything was in order. No telltale hint that might give away his true identity if someone came looking. The box with the only photo he had of his kids was carefully buried under a foot of potting soil. He was safe. For now.

Not that he had any reason to think Ray knew where to find him—or even whether he was still alive. For months, David had led a double life—working for Ray by day, helping the government build an airtight case against the man by night. The attorneys had assured David that the new life they'd chosen for him would be safe. But as a scientist, David left little to chance. He'd gone willingly into the federal Witness Protection Program, commonly called WITSEC. He'd watched the deputy U.S. marshals in charge of his relocation. He'd learned from them and done some investigation on his own. And a few months after his first rebirth, he'd disappeared again—without telling anyone.

WITSEC was entirely voluntary so David was sure the feds wouldn't bother looking for him. His flight might not have been the smartest thing he'd ever done in his life, but he knew Ray Cross. Ray hadn't reached the pinnacle of success by accepting anything at face value. Ray would dig into records—hell, he'd dig up a grave—if he thought there was any chance David, or Paul McAffee, as David had been known in his former life, was still alive. Because in Ray's book, death wasn't good enough for the person who betrayed him.

Ray—like the Grim Reaper—was coming. It was only a matter of when and where.

Chapter Three

"His name is David. Not Dave. He was quite firm about that."

"David what?"

"I'm not sure."

Liz couldn't tell if her very blond neighbor was being purposefully evasive or if she honestly didn't know. She and Liz hadn't connected on any level from day one. Crissy had ambled next door just moments after Liz's two large, swarthy cousins backed a rented trailer into the driveway and started carrying boxes inside. Hand-me-downs. A few antiques. A treasure or two brought back from her travels. A far cry from Crissy's place, which—just glimpsed through the window—looked like a page in some home-interior catalog.

"How is that possible? You pay him, don't you?"

"In cash. It's a big pain with the association's two-signature system, let me tell you. I just know someone is going to accuse me of embezzlement because I have to make the check out for cash."

What a drama queen, Liz thought. They weren't talking six figures here. "How do you contact him?"

"I leave my number with an answering service that's listed on a flyer he had up at the market. He usually gets back to me in a day or two."

"That seems like an odd way of doing business."

Crissy shrugged. "This is Vegas."

As if that explained everything. And maybe it did. People came to Vegas to leave their old lives behind, whether for a weekend or for good.

"Can I have that number?"

Crissy crossed her arms just under her perky bosom. Blond, size zero, always perfectly dressed, the woman was so the opposite of Liz it was no wonder they didn't get along. "What for?"

Like it's any of your business.

Liz shrugged. "He left a hand trowel here yesterday."

"Give it to me. I'll see that he gets it."

Damn. No wonder I never lie. I'm really bad at it. "I also want to talk to him about doing something different with my front planter." *Not.*

Crissy leaned forward to glance at Liz's house. "It could use a fresh look. Just a minute."

"It could use a fresh look," Liz muttered under her breath. Was Crissy's world really that small that she only cared about the outward appearance of the houses in her neighborhood? Liz recalled the expression on her neighbor's face at a community meeting when Liz suggested the money the association was spending on speed bumps and beautification might be better served on a skate park for kids like Crissy's stepson. Crissy had actually blanched at the idea and intently argued that sort of thing was Parks and Rec's responsibility.

Later, after the meeting was over, a lady from down the street had pulled Liz aside to whisper that Crissy's stepson was a thorn in his stepmother's side. "Eli chooses to live with his mother in Phoenix for a reason—Crissy. Make that two reasons. Apparently his ultracute little sister can do no wrong."

That hint had been the first—and only—crack Liz had seen in her neighbor's picture-perfect facade.

"Here's the number," Crissy said, returning a moment later. "But you're probably better off grabbing him when he's in the neighborhood. That's how I pay him. Just watch and wait."

Like I have nothing better to do than stalk a man. Liz thanked her and left. She had a small window of time to work in her herb room before the heat of the day turned her garage into a sweatbox. After she made the tea she had in mind for David-not-Dave—her way of apologizing for yesterday's fiasco—she would phone Zeke and call off the hunt for information about the man her sisters were calling the mystery gardener.

Maybe *David* wasn't so mysterious. He was just another Las Vegan doing his best to fly below Uncle Sam's radar.

Two hours later, Liz sealed the last of the tea bags containing her newest blend. The steam from the iron, which she used to run along the edges of the preformed bag, added to the ovenlike atmosphere in the garage. She used her sleeve to erase the mustache of sweat below her nose.

She was very happy with this mix, which was specifically designed for a man who spent a great deal of his day outdoors in the sun. She could only guess at David's age. Early forties, maybe? He'd had the look of a person who knew more about life than he cared to reveal.

"Takes one to know one," she muttered.

She pushed back from her workbench and looked around. She'd converted one corner of her garage into a small herbal pharmacy. She'd used a roll of thick opaque plastic, which she'd stapled to two-by-fours held upright by diagonal cross members. She stored her herbs in the house to protect them from the heat, but this area provided space and fresh air while mixing them.

The oscillating fan at her feet helped stir the hot air. Her morning visit to her mother's had cut into her cool time. She shifted her shoulders to catch the caterpillar of sweat inching down her neck. Usually, she didn't mind the desert climate. She'd traveled on four continents and had grown pretty flexible when it came to hot, cold, rain and snow.

"Leez," a voice called from the door leading into the house.

One of her roommates. Lydia, she guessed. "Yes?"

"The man. Dig in dirt. Now."

Lydia and Reezira, who had been living with Liz since the day Charles was arrested, had spoken practically no English when she'd met them. Television, the Internet and the Clark County library system had changed that. They now knew lots of words. But putting the hodge-podge vocabulary into complete sentences was another challenge.

"Thanks. I'm almost done here. Keep an eye on him for me, will you?"

"One eye? Or two?"

Liz turned back to her mix so Lydia wouldn't see her smile. "Your pick. I'll be there in a minute."

"O…kay."

Liz had no idea what was going to happen with her young friends. The police had finally tracked down an interpreter who got their story. It wasn't a pretty one. Orphaned at very young ages, both girls, who weren't related, had turned to prostitution for survival. Prisha might find a similar fate awaiting her if Liz wasn't able to rescue her. Although in Prisha's case, her physical handicap might make any future questionable.

The thought strengthened her resolve to do whatever

was necessary to procure her loan. She planned to turn in her application as soon as she was done making amends. She'd acted like a nincompoop yesterday when the gardener yelled at her. She should have apologized and insisted on paying for the plant right away. Laughing had no doubt added insult to injury. Being rude and insensitive wasn't her style. Self-control and kindness were her trademarks. She planned to prove it.

THE DRY HEAT was a stark change from what David was used to in northern Virginia. It had taken some getting used to, but the vastness of the desert more than made up for the weather. The second half of his childhood had been spent in his grandmother's claustrophobia-inducing brownstone in Pittsburg. She'd believed in keeping the curtains, which in later years were thick with dust whenever he visited, closed. Maybe that explained why he liked his sky—and his life—uncluttered.

Another aspect of his adopted city that he approved of was how easy it was to remain anonymous. That could be true of all large cities, David thought as he worked a second cup of fertilizer into the soil he was preparing for the next planting on Canto Lane. He'd already replaced the flattened cactus that he'd lost his cool over yesterday.

He glanced toward the house where the woman he'd accosted lived. Her car was gone. But there was some kind of activity going on in the backyard. Music emanated from behind the stucco fence.

The pushy one wouldn't like that, he thought.

Crissy Somethingorother. He'd known a number of women like her in the pharmaceutical industry. Aggressive, focused and intensely concerned about keeping all their boats in the water and at the front of the armada at all times.

Kay, his ex-wife, had been just the opposite. Gentle and kind. Too forgiving for her own good. She'd forgiven her ex-husband over and over—until he took a swing at one of the boys.

He rocked back on his heels and reached for the succulent he'd brought from his greenhouse that morning. A hearty survivor. Like him.

"Hello."

He nearly dropped the plant. The woman from yesterday. But her car… He glanced at the driveway.

"My sister has my car, if you're wondering why it isn't in the driveway. Her fiancé bought her a new SUV as a wedding present, but it was missing a couple of bells or whistles. I'm not sure which or how many. I followed her to the shop then she dropped me off. Getting ready for a wedding is no easy task, you know."

He didn't say anything and she gave a little laugh. "More information than you needed, as they say. But you looked curious."

"When?"

"When what?"

"When did I look curious?"

"Just now."

He gave her a look that usually made people take a step back. "What are you? A mind reader?"

To his immense surprise, she smiled and nodded. "Um…I have my moments. My mother is a bona fide Gypsy fortune-teller and most of the people in my family think I'm next in line to fill the role of Puri Dye."

Pure what? Gypsies? Did she think he was an idiot as well as an antisocial caveman?

"You think I'm making this up, don't you? Well, it's no big deal. I don't usually mention my background because people have all kinds of misconceptions about the Romani, but you don't strike me as the kind of person who would be prejudiced."

Why? He wondered. Because he was a day laborer. Because he drove an old truck and worked with his hands? He didn't ask. He had no intention of allowing himself to be drawn into a conversation.

"Well, whatever," he muttered and returned to his work.

"I came outside to offer you a glass of cold tea."

"Not necessary."

He leaned over to position the plant correctly. Placement was everything in the landscaping business. Put the wrong plant in the wrong location and you wound up making work for yourself a few years down the road.

"I know it isn't necessary. I didn't run over that plant on purpose. But I don't want you to think that I'm a heartless fiend who purposely mows down defenseless succulents."

"It was a cactus."

"Don't be obtuse. I'm trying to apologize here."

He leveled the dirt around the base of the plant then stood up. She was a good foot shorter than him, but she seemed taller. Maybe her no-nonsense attitude gave her added height.

"As you said, no apology is required. I don't like losing plants, but, hey, sh…stuff happens."

Liz was amused by his attempt to watch his language. She'd traveled with legions of men who'd cursed a blue streak regardless of the women and children in their company.

"Listen, we got off on the wrong foot. I like what you've done so far on the street, and I wouldn't mind picking your brain about how to make some cheap improvements to my landscaping. Key word in that sentence being *cheap*." If her refinancing went through, she'd need most of the money for India, but she had to do something to keep the garden zealot next door off her back.

He tugged on the brim of his odd hat. The gesture was less of escape from the sun as it was escape from her gaze. Why, she wondered? What does he have to hide? Her Romani sixth sense began to tingle. Not in a get-out-of-here-fast way, but in a this-is-intriguing way.

"Please," she said, giving him a smile she'd seen work for her sister Grace. "Just a glass of tea on my front porch. Surely, you're entitled to a little break. The association is paying you by the job, not the hour, right?"

He nodded in answer to her question, but still hadn't agreed to join her for a cold drink. "It's my own herbal blend."

His brows, which were two shades lighter than his mustache, moved together in question. "You grow herbs?"

"No. I buy them from a wholesale distributor. Some are from India and some are Western."

"This is your business?"

"One aspect of it. I'm a licensed physical therapist, but lately, I've started leaning more toward holistic healing—for a number of reasons." *Again, I'm giving him more information than he needs.*

"Come on," she said, "you can be a taste tester for a new blend. I'm calling it Please, Refresh Me." She felt her cheeks heat up. "A play on an old Engelbert Humperdinck song title. My mother was listening to a CD of his greatest hits the other day and the tune got stuck in my head. When it came time to name my tea…well, you get the idea."

She trotted ahead of him once she was certain he was following her. Unlike most of her neighbors' more traditional homes, Liz's house had a covered overhang that stretched from the wall of her garage to the corner of her living room. The house had been built on a concrete slab, of course, so this nook was nothing special, but she'd added some white pickets between the columns to give it a cottage feel.

"Morning glories," he said, lingering by the single step that led to her front door. "You don't see those much."

"My mother gave me the seeds. She grows everything in her backyard. She has the only green thumb in the family. Have a chair. I'll be right back with your tea."

David started to protest. He was dusty and grubby and her white plastic lawn chairs, though inexpensive, looked well cared for. Everything about the place, from the white rock borders to cobweb-free rafters said someone who lived here cared.

He respected that. Too many of the people he worked for never seemed to enjoy the elaborate living art, which is how he thought of his masterpieces, once they had them. The landscaping was for their neighbors' benefit, not their own. He would have resented their attitude if he hadn't been the same way…in his old life. Too busy to see the roses, let alone smell them.

"Here you go," she said, returning.

Elizabeth Radonovic. He knew her name from the roster of homeowners the head of the association had given him.

She handed him a tall glass filled with dark amber liquid. No ice cubes. He found that curious.

"I brewed this last night to test the blend and just finished putting the tea in bags. It's been chilling all morning. Ice cubes dilute the efficacy of the herbs. I hope it's not too sweet for your taste. The stevia leaf is one of my favorites, but it can be a bit much for some people."

She motioned him to take the chair in the shady corner of the overhang. To do otherwise would have been rude. His grandmother had stressed civility and manners above all else. He sat down, perching on the edge of the seat.

"You don't have to worry about getting these pads dirty. Nothing lasts long in the desert, which is why I don't spend a lot of money on outdoor furniture. Besides, my room-mates' cats love to sleep on these cushions. You'll probably be covered in cat hair when you stand up."

Cats. He'd never given them much thought until one adopted him. "What kind are they?" he asked, bringing the glass to his lips.

"The free kind."

Her grin truly was engaging and almost impossible to resist. He quickly took a sip of tea.

The cool, instantly refreshing liquid exploded in flavors he couldn't immediately identify. He ran his tongue across his teeth to recapture the taste. "Wow. This is great."

She blushed at the praise. "Do you like it? Really?"

He took another drink, savoring the way it soothed his parched throat. "You should bottle it. You'd make a million."

"I could use a million," she said softly. A sad look crossed her face.

David wondered, but he didn't ask. A person with se-crets didn't seek revelations from others. It just wasn't fair since no information could be offered in return.

She perked up a second later and set her glass on the little plastic table between them then she wiped her hand on her slacks and held it out between them. "I'm Liz Radonovic."

He had no choice but to shake her hand and say, "David."

"David what?"

Good question. "David Baines."

"Nice to meet you, David. I felt badly about our run-in yesterday and I wanted to call and apologize, but you're not an easy man to reach. How do you stay in business when you don't have a phone? Crissy gave me the number of your answering service, but don't most people in your line of work have cell phones?"

He shrugged. "I get jobs by word of mouth. And I sell wholesale plants to nurseries. When I have seedlings available, I call them. Everything is on a cash basis. It's simpler."

She smiled. "You're trying to keep off Uncle Sam's radar screen, huh?"

Someone's radar screen, that was sure. David didn't know if Ray had people looking for him or not, but he wasn't about to take any chances. Who would be the least bit curious about a handyman who grew cacti and succulents, minded his own business and rarely talked to anyone?

Until today, when he sat down to tea with a beautiful woman who reminded him of how much he'd walked away from. This was a mistake, he knew. Her smile was too normal, too inviting.

"I'd better get back to work," he said, standing up. He downed the last of his drink and wiped his mouth with the back of his hand. "Thank you. This was delicious."

She took the glass from him. "You're welcome. I'm glad you enjoyed it."

Reaching down beside her chair, she swiftly produced a small brown paper sack with a white label across the front. "Here," she said, holding it by the crimped top. "This is my way of apologizing for being such a ninny yesterday. Please take it. My conscience has been bothering me something fierce."

A gift? No one had given him a gift in so long, he took it without thinking. Without speaking.

Good Lord, he thought, as he hurried back to the safety of his truck, *I really am a mannerless oaf.*

Liz watched David Baines almost run back to this truck. He reached in through the open window to put her gift on the seat, then walked to the rear of the vehicle and lowered the tailgate. He leaned over to pick up a hand trowel before returning to where he'd been working when she'd interrupted.

He was intriguing. An anomaly. Refined language occasionally poked through an outwardly rough demeanor. At times, courteous and polite then moments later utterly lacking in finesse. His sandy brows that didn't match his dark burly mustache were just the tip of the incongruities where David Baines was concerned.

She heard the phone ring in the house behind her. Neither of her roommates would pick it up, she knew, so Liz got up and went inside.

"Hello?"

"Your mystery man's name is David Baines. No wants or warrants. A perfect driving record."

Zeke. Damn. She'd meant to call him and tell him not to bother. "Um…thanks. I'm really sorry to be a pest."

Zeke didn't say anything. The Rom in her told her there was more. "Hey, a clean driving record is a good thing, right? A girl can't be too careful these days," she joked. "You never know what kind of deviant might be lurking around the corner."

"I guess so," Zeke said. "But I'm always suspicious when someone just seems to materialize out of thin air. I think I'm going to probe a little deeper."

Liz could have protested, but most of the cops she'd met over the years followed their instincts and rarely took advice from civilians. Besides, the guy was interesting. If anything came of this attraction she felt, then maybe being forewarned of any skeletons in his closet was a good thing.

"WELL, LOOKEE HERE," a gleeful voice said. "The flotsam has finally surfaced. Your hunch was right, boss. Paul really did fake his death in that fire. Well, at least, it looks that way. Somebody is putting out feelers for information on a guy that sorta matches Paul's description. Same general age, height and weight. The hair and eyes don't match, but we both know how easy it is to change that," he added with a soft snicker. "Plus, it looks like he's got a business growing plants. Wasn't that one of the things you listed as a possible career choice if he tried to start over some place else?"

The man quickly scooted his chair aside to make room for another person at the computer.

"See?" he said, pointing to the monitor. "Those questions look a lot like yours. Might be a long shot, but I think your boy is in Vegas."

Chapter Four

Liz sat down at her laptop, which she'd set up on a make-shift desk in her bedroom after her "roomies" moved in. The two women had assured her they were comfortable sharing a room, but Liz preferred privacy over space, so she'd moved her office into her miniscule master suite.

She'd bought the house not for its spacious design or gracious perks, but because it was in her price range. The previous owners had just gone through a messy divorce and Liz had been at the right place at the right time. And, thanks to some first-time buyer tax credits and the fact that she had been bringing in a pretty respectable income from her job at the hospital, she'd been a loan officer's dream client.

Now her balance sheet didn't look so hot. A fact that could have a negative impact on both her refinancing and the adoption. A smart person probably would hold off on the latter until the former was squared away, she told herself. But mothers didn't always think with their heads, she'd heard Yetta say just recently to Kate.

Liz wasn't a mother…yet. But she felt like one. Even though her daughter was a half a world away.

She typed in her password then clicked on a shortcut link to her favorite place: Sha Navanti Ashram and Orphanage. Weekly, Jyoti, Liz's friend and mentor, e-mailed photos to the ashram's U.S. sponsors, who maintained the Web site and conducted fund-raising efforts on behalf of the children. Normally, the ashram cared for the children for the entire length of their childhood, giving them a loving home and an education in a group setting, without allowing for adoption. Parents of the children were welcome to visit at any time.

When Liz first arrived at the facility in the Haridwar district of India, some two hundred kilometers northeast of Delhi, she hadn't understood or appreciated the rationale behind the policy. But as she worked with the fifty or so children living at the ashram, she began to see that their parents had presented them with a chance to be healthy, safe and cared for in a warm, communal setting. The older children helped to care for the younger kids. All of the students learned skills that would benefit them once they reentered the real world.

Liz knew that she, a single woman of moderate means, would have had little hope of adopting a perfectly healthy India-born child. Even a special-needs child would be placed in a two-parent home first, but Liz had felt such a powerful connection to Prisha from the moment she'd taken over the infant's care, she'd begun to dream of bringing her home to the United States where Prisha could get the medical help she needed.

Liz knew that many babies were born with a slight intoeing—a condition commonly called "pigeon toes." But Prisha's metatarsus adductus was only part of the problem. Her left leg was shorter than the right and there appeared to be some internal tibial torsion, or twisting of the bone between the knee and the ankle. Without surgery, the little girl would never be able to walk normally.

By the time Liz left the ashram, Prisha was flourishing,

although she couldn't do many of the things babies her age were supposed to do. She could roll over, though. Quite a task considering only one foot functioned the way it was supposed to.

Liz had watched the tiny infant—she'd been a mere five pounds at birth—first with respect, then affection, then love. Prisha never complained. Rarely cried. And always accomplished what she set out to do—no matter how tough the hurdle.

Humming with anticipated joy, Liz quickly scanned the photos on the Web site. None included Prisha.

"That's odd," she murmured, switching screens to access her e-mail. Prisha was such a sweet-natured baby that all of the older girls loved to carry her with them, including her in their games, contests and even school lessons.

Twenty-nine e-mail messages were waiting for her. Not surprising since Grace copied Liz on every stupid joke currently surfing the Net. As usual, Liz deleted them without reading any. She did stop to check out any notes Grace included. One missive said: "Since you've turned into such a cat lover, I thought you'd like these shots."

Liz quickly scanned the attached photos. "Oh, Grace, you're such a soft-hearted boob." After a second of consideration, Liz selected two shots to print. They were cute photos, and Reezira loved kittens. Which explained how two felines had found their way into Liz's household.

Liz had never owned a pet of any kind as an adult. When you traveled as much as she did, the idea sounded selfish. She didn't plan to get a pet until after Prisha was completely and officially hers.

As the printer did its thing, she scrolled down the list of new messages until she found one from Jyoti. She clicked on it.

My dear friend, may all be well with you. I have news that will concern you, but please don't let it alarm you too much. Our darling Prisha is ill. A fever has been traveling through the ashram. It's accompanied by pain in the limbs and some vomiting. A volunteer doctor from Delhi has visited and declared that nothing can be done except to keep the children hydrated and warm. Which we are doing, of course. I will do my best to keep you informed of how she is doing, but for now I must rush away to help with the many. *Namaste*, J.

A chill passed through her. Her rational mind leapfrogged about: Kids get sick all the time. She'll bounce back right away. There's nothing you could do even if you were there. She'll be fine.

But dark thoughts quickly followed. Prisha was underweight for her age. She wasn't able to move around and exercise so her lungs weren't as strong as they should be. She'd been prone to sinus infections since birth. She needed someone to put eucalyptus oil in a vaporizer and rock her until her breathing eased. She needed a mother. She needed Liz.

"I brought your money."

David looked over his shoulder. He'd finished his work for the day and was just cleaning up his tools. He'd been so lost in thought remembering the slightly rueful twist to Liz's smile that he hadn't even heard the head of the homeowners' association walk up.

"Thanks."

"No problem. Well, it was some problem," she corrected herself. "I know you prefer cash, but the association works on a two-signature check system. The last time I did this, the bank objected to our making the check out for cash, so this time I had to get Roxanne, our treasurer, to make it out to me, then I cashed it. I just hope nobody accuses me of embezzlement."

He counted the twenties then stuffed them into the deep pocket of his coveralls. He'd first adopted the style of clothing as a sort of camouflage. Within days of his arrival in Vegas, he'd observed that a certain age group, namely men over sixty, favored the one-piece jumpsuit. He'd figured by assuming the dress code of the retired set, he'd look older. And be less visible. Since then, he'd discovered the clothing was also practical for the climate: loose fitting to allow for movement of air.

"I'll give you a receipt."

She actually looked relieved when he suggested it. Normally, he was reluctant to put his signature on anything, but he figured he could forge his made-up name pretty well after four years. Funny, he thought, how long old habits, like signing your name a certain way, stay with a person.

He walked to the cab of the truck and opened the glove compartment. The hinge was bad and its long, lingering squeak sounded like nails on a blackboard.

"Ooh, that's awful. You should oil it."

He knew that. But he figured the sound would alert him if anyone tried to poke around in his truck.

He pulled a pen from his chest pocket and opened his two-copy receipt book to a fresh page. After sliding the cardboard protector sheet into place, he printed the name of the association and the amount she'd given him, then shifted the tablet to the left to remind himself that the signature he was signing should read David Baines. He added just enough flourishes to render it virtually illegible.

"Here you go," he said, ripping off her copy.

She turned suddenly and with her back to David, yelled, "Don't be late, Eli."

David looked past her and spotted a kid peddling away as if the devil were on his tail. The boy, a hulky, wide-shouldered kid in his mid-teens, maybe fifteen or sixteen, was dressed in a black-and-gray football jersey and denim jeans that were easily three sizes too big. The kid's baseball cap was on backward. David couldn't make out the logo, but noticed it matched the color of his bike—bright red.

Crissy heaved a weary sigh. "My stepson. Lives with his mother in Phoenix, but his school is off-session, and she's working so we have the pleasure of his company." Her tone made it clear the pleasure was anything but.

"He was such a sweet kid when his dad and I first married. Then the evil teen fairy took away his brains and left a snarling, surly, hormone-driven mouth in his place," she said, laughing humorlessly at her joke. "I honestly don't know how his mother stands all that attitude and rudeness on a regular basis. A month is almost more than I can take."

He noticed her husband's name didn't come up. Probably because the guy was never around. Either he left before dawn and returned well after David was done for the day, or the gossips were right and the guy was a real jerk. David had overheard two women talking the day he was hired to do the landscaping.

Three board members had been required to approve his bid and sketches. When Crissy left the room to talk to her daughter—a fashionably dressed princess in pink at least five years younger than her half brother, he'd overheard the other two women discussing Crissy's family.

"That boy is a terrorist waiting to happen," the gray-haired woman in the Sam's Town Windbreaker had predicted.

"His father needs to step in now or they'll lose him to a gang. Too bad the man is always away on business."

David had never had the liberty of being a rebellious teen. His grandmother would have castrated him. Or kicked him out. Maybe people who knew unconditional love could afford to thumb their noses at the ones giving it, but that hadn't been his experience.

He started to clear his throat to get her attention back on the receipt he was still holding when a flash of purple caught his eye. He turned toward the house where he'd shared a glass of tea earlier. A slender woman in navy shorts and a royal purple tank top sprinted across the lawn and took off jogging down the street.

He used his sleeve to wipe a bead of sweat out of his eye. Running? In this heat? Was she nuts?

"Ugh," Crissy said, her gaze following Liz. "Self-discipline is one thing, but self-abuse? No, thank you."

When David didn't comment, she added, "Early evening is a terrible time of day to run. Traffic is bad. The pollution in the air is ghastly. And visibility is worse than at night. I sure hope she doesn't get run over."

David was surprised by her concern. He almost changed his opinion of her, until she added, "I don't know what would happen to her place if she were killed. Probably her family would sell it, but I suppose there's a chance she might have willed it to those *women* who are living with her."

Her disapproval of Liz's roommates was obvious. Curious, David asked, "You don't like them?"

She snatched the receipt from his fingers. "They don't belong here. This is a family neighborhood, not a refugee camp. Did Liz tell you what they did for a living before they snuck into America? They were prostitutes." She shook her head. "I can't believe I have prostitutes living next door to me. Not that I'm planning to sell, but can you imagine what that kind of information would do to the property values around here?"

Her tone positively dripped with repugnance.

He slammed the door of his truck with such force the bang made her jump. He didn't say anything. This wasn't his problem. Besides, he didn't know why he was surprised by her attitude. Snobs abound in this world, he thought, even in relatively ordinary neighborhoods like this one.

"Oh, I almost forgot, the association approved the extra expenditure for the vacant lot around the corner. I put together a couple of sketches of what I think might work. Do you mind coming in a minute?"

Yes, he did. But money was money.

Stupid. Stupid. Stupid.

The word repeated in her head every time her right heel hit the pavement. Only a stupid person would take off jogging at this time of day in this heat, Liz thought. If not for the wind, she probably would have melted into a puddle before she was ten blocks from home.

Normally, she ran in the morning. The earlier the better. But she'd overslept this morning and had had to race to her breakfast meeting with her sisters. Now she was running to get the frustration of not being able to help Prisha out of her system. So far away. So little she could do.

A soft cry escaped from her lips. Liz set her jaw and picked up the pace. Whimpering and moaning wouldn't help. Staying focused on her goal would. She'd made several online acquaintances who had undertaken a challenge similar to hers. One, a single woman like Liz, had recently celebrated her daughter's fifth birthday with a trip to Disneyland.

Happy endings do exist, she reminded herself.

There were differences in their cases, of course. Her friend was an executive with a prominent fast-food chain. Money was not a problem. Also, the child she'd adopted came from Calcutta, which didn't fall under the Central Adoption Resource Agency boundaries. That adoption had been faster than normal—a mere eight months, start to finish. Liz had been told to expect the process to last at least a year, if not two.

Liz could only pray that Prisha would survive that long. The child was a fighter, but how long could the spirit flourish when the body faced so many obstacles? If Prisha were here—receiving daily, one-on-one encouragement and treatment—her medical condition might not be life-threatening. But she wasn't here, and Liz couldn't do anything to help.

Her breath suddenly left her and she had to stop. Bending at the waist, she rested her hands on her thighs and tried to draw in enough air to keep her tears at bay. *Prisha will be fine. She'll get through this. And sometime within the next year, I'll be flying over there to pick her up and bring her home with me.*

"Hey, whaswrongwithyou?"

Liz lifted her head. Three boys on bikes. Not little boys. Young men, actually. They were too far away for her to see them clearly. Singly, none of the three would have appeared at all menacing, but as a group they gave off a sort of gangster vibe that made her wary.

Liz didn't answer. She took a breath and started jogging again, giving them wide berth. Unfortunately, she hadn't been paying attention to where she was running and had wound up in the middle of a large and completely empty church parking lot. She passed by the building nearly every day and there were always cars around. But not today.

"Damn," she muttered.

The church occupied about a third of a block and was surrounded by residential neighborhoods, but the closest houses were well out of shouting range. She headed toward the intersection where there was bound to be traffic at this time of day. People on their way home to dinner. Busy, hungry people. Lots of them.

"Hey, you. You're that Gypsy, ain't you?" One of the boys called after her.

There was no missing the kid's denigrating tone. *Gypsy scum*, she'd heard some boy say in the fourth grade. Her first introduction to prejudice.

Words can't hurt you, her mother had said when Liz came home from school in tears. But Yetta was wrong. Words could be the precursor to violence. Liz had seen firsthand the tragic repercussions of ethnic hatred. Death and destruction had left a lasting impression on her mind.

She stopped running. She hated confrontation of any kind. The smart thing to do was to walk away, but she'd learned the hard way that ignoring the problem often led to bigger problems.

In Bosnia she'd noticed the small group of surly, smoking, angry men that gathered every day at a certain street corner. Sympathetic to all the horrors and losses the locals had incurred, she'd never reported them—even when one or two made lurid comments and taunting gestures.

She'd paid a high price for minding her own business. These boys are young. Maybe, I can still reach them, she thought.

She turned around. She had to hop over a low, white

chain that directed foot traffic away from the newly seeded yard encircling the playground the church had recently installed. She could smell the scent of cedar from the red-orange shavings under the jungle gym.

One of the boys swung his bike around to face her. He was biggest of the three and something about him seemed familiar. *I've seen him before.* Which made sense, she realized. He must know who she was since he'd called her a Gypsy.

All three were wearing sloppy, oversized jeans that were belted almost below their butts. Their ball caps were pulled low over their foreheads making their chins, uniformly adorned with acne and half a dozen whiskers, their most prominent features.

The glare of the setting sun put them in shadow. She blinked and stepped to one side. She wanted to see their eyes when she talked to them. She wasn't afraid, even though she probably should have been. But this was broad daylight in a relatively public place, she reasoned.

Plus, after what happened to her in Bosnia, she'd learned self-defense. When she'd finally recovered sufficiently—physically—to travel, she'd gone to New Zealand to stay with a friend. The woman, a former relief worker Liz had met on her first tour in Bosnia, taught yoga and meditation at a youth hostel on the South Island. Her friend believed all women should know how to defend themselves.

As the boys murmured to each other, Liz unconsciously prepared—hips square to her body, knees flexed to take advantage of her lower center of gravity. She consciously braced her shoulders and said, "Is it Gypsies you hate or women?"

The leader slouched on the seat of his bike and grunted something she couldn't make out. The smaller boy fidgeted and looked ready to hightail it. All three were white. The bikes they were riding probably could have fed the children at the orphanage for a year.

"We heard about you—and the two hos you got livin' with you. You got some kind of kinky sex thing going?"

The last brought an edgy giggle from the other punks.

Yep, neighborhood kids, Liz decided. This one, at least. They probably overheard their parents gossiping. The idea made her slightly ill. She'd done a good thing by opening her home to two desperate young women. How could that possibly be cause for scorn and ridicule?

Anger made her take a step forward. "I know you, don't I?" she asked, pointing at the leader. "You live near me. I've seen you riding your bike around. What's your name?"

His barely audible curse wasn't anything she hadn't heard before. A small-minded bully with a trashy mouth. Nothing new there. She decided to ignore him. "Is that what you think?" she asked his two friends. "That because my family is Romani, I'm an inferior person? Well, I'm not the one standing in a parking lot calling people names, am I?"

The smallest boy, who was obviously younger than his friends, turned his bike in the opposite direction and took off peddling. The middle-sized kid groaned and tried calling him back. "Joey, get your ass back here, you coward."

Liz took a step closer. "He's not the coward. You are. All bullies are cowards deep down. They take advantage of someone else's weaknesses to harass them because it makes them feel powerful. Calling a girl names. Yeah, that's real brave."

The boy she'd been addressing flushed scarlet and looked down. His pal, the leader, shoved his bike to the ground and advanced toward her. Although not full-grown, he was several inches taller than Liz and a good thirty pounds heavier. And she could tell by the vitriolic flow of curse words that spewed from his lips, this kid was in a rage.

Whoever said rape was about anger, not sex, knew what they were talking about, her self-defense teacher had said. *If you keep your wits about you, you can use blind rage to your advantage.*

When he charged, Liz used his forward momentum to trip him. The kid did a sprawling belly flop on the pavement. His friend, who'd finally screwed up his courage, let out a cry of outrage and rushed to his buddy's aid. Together, they probably could have knocked her down and done enough damage to warrant a trip to the hospital—something she couldn't afford.

Liz turned to run, but the kid on the ground grabbed her ankle, twisting with both hands. His friend lunged at her from the side and latched on to her wrist. The sense of captivity triggered a memory so vivid it felt ripped from her womb. Old fear…and a burning fury that she'd tamped down for years surfaced, too.

"No," she cried, fighting them off with all her might. "I am not your victim, you snot-nosed little bastards. You're gonna think twice before you ever do this to another woman."

Chapter Five

David wasn't in a hurry. He had a cat to feed. Big deal. A solitary meal and some seedlings to replant. Another boring night in one of the hottest travel destinations in the world. The irony wasn't lost on him.

He slowed to a stop and looked in both directions. Just as he took his foot off the clutch, a kid on a bike shot out of a driveway and raced across the street as if the devil were on his tail.

By failing to step on the gas, David killed the engine. "Damn." He started the truck and eased forward, but a flash of color caught his eye. A commotion of some kind was taking place in the parking lot of the church. Curious, he turned to the right, instead of the left. The truck chugged slightly as he inched forward for a better look at what was happening.

Three people were involved in a confrontation. Two kids—big kids—and a woman. In a purple tank top…

He let out a curse and punched the accelerator. He didn't look to see if there was oncoming traffic or a curb. A thick white chain kept him getting as close as he would have liked.

"Hey, what's going on?" he yelled, jumping out of his truck.

Both boys turned to look at him then took off running. One was smart enough to grab his bike. The other clambered up a Dumpster to reach the top of a concrete block fence and slither into somebody's backyard. David didn't try to follow either of them. He'd gotten a good look at the big kid's face. The same boy he'd seen not a half hour earlier leaving his stepmom's house. He was Liz's neighbor.

"Liz. Oh, shit, are you okay?"

She was on one knee, leaning over, breathing hard. Her hair was half out of the ponytail she'd had it in. Her running clothes were a little scuffed looking, but fortunately she was still in one piece.

Or was she?

When she lifted her head, he saw the feral look in her eyes. The kindhearted healer he'd had tea with was gone, replaced by a stranger—a warrior who'd vanquished the enemy.

He watched her get to her feet, keeping his hands close to, but not quite touching, her shoulders. He saw a tremor pass through her body. Anger? Fear? Dread? He wasn't sure what.

"Liz," he said bending slightly to make eye contact. "Do you need a doctor? Do you have your cell phone with you? We should call the police."

He wanted to take back the words the instant they left his mouth. He didn't do cops. Good Lord, the last thing he needed was his name on some police blotter.

She didn't respond to his questions, but a quick scan of her body told him she wasn't carrying her phone. "Can you make it to my truck?"

His question apparently connected. She blinked twice then looked around, as if coming back to her body. Her hands returned to a clenched state. "Where are they?"

"Gone. You're safe." He gingerly took her elbow. "If I

hadn't shown up, I'm pretty sure you would have whupped their butts."

He wasn't sure that was true. There had been two of them, after all. But she didn't need to hear that. Not now.

She stopped suddenly and looked over her shoulder. "I…I wasn't expecting them to react like that. They were so young. I thought they'd listen. But then the bigger boy got in my face and this time sorta got mixed up in my head with the other time."

The other time? A sick feeling started to churn the acid in his stomach. "I'm going to take you home, and you can call the cops from there, okay?"

He wasn't sure if she nodded or not. Twilight was pressing in. A fleeting thought hit him. What would have happened if he hadn't come by? He swallowed hard to keep the bad taste from climbing up his throat.

He closed the passenger door and raced around to the driver's side, stopping only long enough to toss the abandoned bike into the bed of his truck. Yep, same bike he'd seen Crissy's stepson riding that afternoon. He and that kid were going to have words.

"Do you need to see a doctor? There's an out-patient clinic not far from here."

She shook her head. "I'm not hurt. Just embarrassed. I knew there was a reason I never preached from soapboxes—the fall from one hurts like hell."

He made her explain.

"I don't know what I was thinking. I've been called names before, but this time, something just sorta snapped. I honestly thought if I talked to them—made them see me as a person, not as a member of a minority deserving of their scorn—I might actually make a difference. As if lecturing kids that age would do any good. Am I a fool or what?"

"More idealistic, than foolish," he said. "But sometimes you have to put your foot down. Smart or not."

She took a deep breath and turned slightly to look at him. "You're right. Damn it. I was thinking like a victim. I did that once before and promised myself never again."

He was glad to hear the spunk in her tone. He nodded. "Well, if it makes you feel any better, from what I could see, you weren't behaving like a victim. Where'd you learn to fight like that?"

"New Zealand." She put the middle finger of her right hand up to her mouth and nibbled on what he assumed was a broken nail. "A friend of mine taught me self-defense and in return I did physical therapy on her shoulder. She'd been knifed as a teen. The tendons never healed quite right."

David knew there was more to the story but he didn't ask. They'd already reached the traffic bumps on her street and his tools in the back—along with the bike—rattled loudly. Liz flinched and pulled into a protective posture.

"We're here. Your place. You should be safe now." Unless the kid next door had something else on his mind. David planned to find out, after he helped Liz get settled. He didn't like bullies. And even though getting involved went against the basic code he'd adopted when he'd started his new life, David couldn't run the risk that the brat across the fence might be plotting some kind of revenge on the woman who'd refused to be terrorized by him.

HALF AN HOUR LATER, David was still sitting in Liz's living room. He'd walked her to her door, and had planned to disappear as soon as she was safely in the hands of her roommates, but when the two, highly excitable, non-English-speaking women appeared on the porch, he hadn't been given that option.

"You. Come in," the taller said, her tone less a command than a hopeful request.

"She need you," the shorter added.

He'd always been a sucker for a woman in need. Hell, he'd married one, right? He'd known from the start that Kay wasn't in love with him. He'd naively assumed that those kinds of feelings would grow between them. But they hadn't. Not really. Respect. Admiration. Friendship had blossomed. And their mutual devotion to the children had soldered their bond—for a while.

But love? He wasn't sure he even knew what that was.

"These are my roommates, Lydia and Reezira," Liz said, pointing to the tall one first. "This is David. He saved my life."

David tried to explain that that was an exaggeration, but neither of the pair seemed to get his meaning.

"I make tea," Reezira said.

"Taste bad. You like," Lydia added.

As they disappeared into the kitchen, which seemed to be just on the other side of the far wall of the living room where Liz was leading him. "If you have to run, don't worry about the tea. The girls love brewing it, even though they add so much sugar I nearly gag. Still, it's better than the sodas they'd seemed addicted to when they first got here."

"I'll stay a minute," David said, looking around as he sat down. Simple, uncluttered yet cozy. The decor had a personal feel. He was pretty sure nothing on the walls had been purchased to appease someone else's idea of style. This was all Liz.

"I get the impression you're ambivalent about calling the police. Can I ask why?"

"We Romani don't have the best working relationship with law enforcement," Liz said rubbing at the abrasion on her knee. Red, but not bleeding. "Comes from centuries of being picked on, I guess. All I know is my first inclination is to call my cousin Gregor. He has connections all over town. He could probably find those brats and put the fear of God in them, but that might only serve to escalate the bad feelings they have about the Romani."

"You're right. Disciplining bad behavior in teens isn't your job. Sometimes professional help is needed. What if harassing joggers is the first step toward becoming rapists?" he asked. Her flinch was too obvious to miss. Something had happened to her before this incident. Something he probably didn't want to know about.

"Hey, I'm not a big fan of the police, either, but this is the kind of problem they have the means and authority to handle."

Her roommates returned at that moment, each carrying an oversized mug. "No cops," Lydia said, in her heavily accented voice. She set her mug on the side table next to David.

"No good," Reezira chimed in, giving her cup to Liz.

Both were slim with wavy dark hair that fell almost to the waist. Their gaunt cheeks gave them a waifish look that many men probably found attractive. David preferred Liz's toned muscles and nicely rounded physique.

"Ban…bon…bondage," Reezira declared. She seemed a bit timid, but her concern for Liz's injured knee was obvious. She dashed away only to return a moment later with a box of adhesive strips and a plastic bottle of hydrogen peroxide.

Liz let the young woman attend to the wound then she asked Lydia to hand her the portable phone. David couldn't make out the conversation because a puffy beige cat distracted him.

The animal didn't seem to have limbs; it was a slow-moving tank of fluff.

"Baby," Lydia said, picking up the beast, which had to

weigh at least ten pounds. She buried her nose in the animal's fur and her whole face disappeared for a minute. "More tea?"

David hadn't tried it. He picked up the mug, which proclaimed, "Life is too short to dance with ugly men." His grin made it hard to drink. But he did. A large gulp. The powerful combination of minty sweetness brought to mind a candy he remembered eating at the movie theater with his dad.

He took a second swallow then said, "I'm good. Thanks. I should be going."

Liz, who was sitting in a navy blue recliner across the room from him, returned the phone to the end table and said, "Um…I hate to ask, but could you wait till my mom gets here? That was her on the phone. She wants to meet you. She loves a hero."

He'd waited long enough. That sixth sense of his that had kept him out of harm's way for four years was telling him to leave. Now.

"Well, that's not me." He stood up and turned to leave just as the doorbell rang.

Liz bolted to her feet. "They're here."

They? Already? How was that possible?

"Mom and Zeke were only a block away when I called. I'd forgotten that they'd planned an early dinner with my sister Kate and her fiancé at the Hyatt Regency Lake Las Vegas. They'd just finished when Mom got a feeling that I was in trouble. It's a Gypsy thing."

Gypsy? My God, she was serious about that?

Two people walked into the room. The woman, who—after hugging her daughter—advanced on him with a wide smile and friendly look in her eyes was definitely Liz's mother. Elegant. Dignified. Almost regal. She paused a foot away to scrutinize him with a frankness that made him squirm inwardly. But it was the man who followed a step behind that set off an alarm so loud David was surprised no one else could hear it.

Cop? Police? FBI? The guy belonged to some branch of law enforcement; he'd bet his life on it.

Damn. Why didn't I leave when I had the chance?

Liz kept the introduction short. "Yetta and Zeke, meet David. My knight-errant."

"David, it's very nice to meet you. Thank you for helping my daughter," Yetta Radonovic said. She shook David's hand firmly, and then turned to her daughter. "Are you okay, dearest?"

"Scrape on the knee. My neck is a little sore, but nothing a hot bath won't fix."

"Let me see."

Liz submitted to her mother's gentle ministrations because she knew there was no way to avoid them. She'd always believed that her leanings toward the medical field had stemmed from the time she'd spent at her mother's side—both in the herb garden and on visits to family members who'd needed help or were in pain.

"I'm fine, Mom. Honest. But I wouldn't be if David hadn't arrived when he did. The little brats had more energy than me."

"How old?" Zeke asked.

Although Liz might have preferred to discuss this matter alone—without presence of the police—that hadn't been an option since Zeke had been driving the car when Liz called Yetta.

"Early teens?" she postulated, looking at David for confirmation. "What's wrong with my mind? When I try to draw the whole thing up, all I can see are black hats and three pimply chins."

"Take your time," Zeke said, sitting down only after Yetta chose a spot on the sofa. "It'll come back to you."

"More like fifteen, sixteen," David said. "The biggest of the three was pretty hefty. Hundred and fifty pounds, maybe."

Zeke pulled a small, lined notebook out of the pocket of his black Windbreaker. The look he gave David was professional and...just a little intimidating. "Who are you again?"

Liz suddenly realized that Zeke would recognize David's name the minute he said it out loud because of the license plate search she'd asked him to run. Damn. She didn't want David to know she'd been investigating him. Not only did that sound intrusive, it made her look desperate. Or wacko.

"A friend," she said. "A very resourceful friend who was at the right place at the right time."

"Actually, I arrived too late to be much help. Liz already had the little hoodlums running home to their mommies. One of them was in such a hurry he left his bike behind. It's in the back of my truck. And I could be wrong, but," he hesitated before adding, "I think it belongs to the kid next door."

Liz let out an audible gasp. He was right. No wonder the boy looked familiar. Liz had seen him half a dozen times, although never as close up as this afternoon.

"Oh, my God," she exclaimed. "I didn't make the connection. That's how he knew I was Rom."

The realization sickened her. Her neighbors were bigots.

She had to force herself to focus on the discussion that followed. David's understanding nod almost brought her to tears. She knew he wasn't comfortable and wanted to leave. Badly. And her intuition told her Zeke was to blame. Even though no one had mentioned his profession, she'd noticed that Lydia and Reezira had made themselves scarce the moment the policeman walked in.

"Zeke, this isn't David's problem. I'll get the bike then we can decide how to handle things with Crissy, okay?"

She led the way to the door. Once they were outside on the porch where only a few hours earlier they'd shared a glass of tea, she said, "I'm sorry you wound up involved in this, but thanks for everything."

He had a serious look on his face. "You're a brave woman, Liz. But a word of advice—be extra nice to yourself the next few days. Post-traumatic stress syndrome and all that."

Although his demeanor was casual Liz heard genuine concern in his tone. She knew about P.T.S.S. and wondered if Davis's knowledge came from experience. But she didn't ask for details. "Good advice. Hopefully this won't start some kind of neighborhood war."

She followed him to the truck and watched him lift the bicycle from the back. He rolled it to her. "If they're any kind of parents, they'll want to do what's best for the kid. He's obviously got some problems and getting this out in the open right now might save him a lot of grief down the road."

"Yeah, the big *if*. The boy is Crissy's stepson. I don't think he and Crissy get along very well, but that's just the impression I got from something one of my other neighbors said."

He nodded and his funny mustache wiggled slightly telling her he was smiling. "I got the same impression earlier today when I saw the kid leave the house. Hopefully the boy's dad will step in and do the right thing."

She wasn't going to hold her breath, but maybe Zeke could persuade the man.

David walked around the truck, but didn't open the door. "I have a big order to fill for a greenhouse so I probably won't be around for a couple of days, but I have your card. If it's okay, I'll call you tomorrow to find out how everything went."

She nodded. "Sure."

He was parked directly under the streetlight. When he glanced at her neighbor's house, he said, "Don't let them intimidate you. If they give you any grief or don't believe your side of the story, I'd be happy to have a few… um…words with the kid."

A shiver passed down her spine. There was nothing intimidating in his words or tone, but she knew that was one talk Crissy's stepson would never forget.

She watched his taillights bounce over the speed bumps then disappear out of sight.

After a fortifying lecture from her mother and Zeke, Liz accompanied the detective next door. Although she would have preferred to file a complaint and let the police handle it, Yetta had convinced Liz that she wouldn't feel a sense of closure unless she participated in the meeting.

"Is this your son's bike?" Liz asked when Crissy opened the door.

"Oh, my gosh, you found it. I just called in a report to the police. Eli said he forgot his lock and someone stole it while he was in the library."

"The library?" Liz choked.

Crissy frowned and looked from Liz to Zeke. "Who are you? What's going on?"

Zeke showed his badge and asked if they could speak with her and her husband.

"I guess so. What's this about?"

"Is your son home?"

"No. He's spending the night with a friend."

Zeke didn't say anything, but his serious demeanor obviously unnerved Crissy. She ushered them inside and pointed toward the scrupulously neat living room. "Have a seat. Elijah's in the den."

Eli? Elijah, Junior?

Crissy returned moments later with a six-foot version of the boy who had started this whole debacle. Once the two were seated and introductions had been made, Zeke described the events of the evening.

"No way. Not Eli," Crissy's husband roared. The look he gave Liz clearly called her a liar. She had no doubt where his son's antipathy stemmed from.

"Are you sure it was Eli, Liz?" Crissy asked, her voice thin and whiny. "You don't really know him. You could be mistaken. Maybe the kid who stole his bike—"

She stopped, no doubt realizing how desperate and ridiculous she sounded.

"There's another witness who identified your son," Zeke said. "Let's get something straight here. Ms. Radonovic is the victim. She's well within her rights to press charges—and I've encouraged her to do so, but she's hoping to spare your son a trip to juvenile court. It all depends on how you handle this."

Crissy turned to her husband. His brow was crinkled and his expression fierce. Liz's intuition told her this man harbored a deep-set hostility toward women. He had yet to make eye contact with Liz.

"He's just a kid," the man said, his voice a deep rumble that was nowhere near as soothing as David's bass.

"A kid with a serious problem," Zeke added.

"I just want to see him get some help," Liz said.

Crissy's look seemed to say she agreed with Liz, but her husband was already making noises about hiring a lawyer to fight the charge. He even muttered something about proving Liz was to blame. "What do you expect from someone who has Eurotrash living with her?"

Zeke stood up and took a step closer to Crissy's husband. He didn't have a gun in his hand, but somehow he managed to look just as threatening without one. "Like I said, Liz is the victim here. The victim is the one who has all the rights, not your twisted little brat who doesn't know how to behave in polite society. If you were smart, you'd join him at the shrink's."

The man lost some of his bluster. "Kids are kids. They talk trash. It doesn't mean anything."

"Or maybe it does. Are you willing to take that chance? This might be your last opportunity to turn this boy around. Are you going to blow it because your ego is on the line?"

Crissy reached out and took her husband's hand. To Zeke, she said, "What do we do?"

Zeke sat down. "I'll tell you what's going to happen. Pay attention. If any of this doesn't get done, your son is going to find himself spending a night—maybe longer—in juvie."

Liz listened to the agenda Zeke laid out for the couple. Their son would apologize to her in the morning, face-to-face. He would give Zeke the names of his friends, whose parents would also be informed of their sons' activities. The three couples and their sons would visit Zeke in his office, no later than Thursday. At that time, they would give him an item-by-item accounting of what repercussions had been decided upon, in particular, what community-service projects and counseling the young men would be participating in. He ended his lecture with a warning. If Liz or her roommates were negatively affected in any way by this unfortunate incident, he would return…and he'd leave his good manners at home.

Liz kept her gaze on the ground as they left. She was glad to have the confrontation over. Despite Zeke's threat,

Liz would bet her relationship with Crissy—and the home-owners' association, which had elected Crissy president—was going to deteriorate. From bad to worse.

She closed the door behind her with a grateful sigh, but she knew the evening wasn't over yet. "It went better than I expected," she told her mother and roommates, who eagerly awaited a full recap of the confrontation. "Thank goodness Zeke was there. I don't think I had enough fight left in me to take on Eli, Senior. The smaller version was bad enough."

Her mother gave Zeke a smile that Liz hadn't seen in a long time—not since her father's stroke, in fact. The look in Yetta's eyes held a certain satisfaction, as if life were starting to make sense again and this man was helping.

The pounding in her head intensified. Liz wanted her mother to be happy, but she really couldn't deal with any more emotional upheavals tonight. She was too tired.

"Thanks for your help, Zeke, I'll keep you posted," she said, letting her mother know it was time to leave. "And for the record, I'd like you to call off your search for info on David Baines. He's a decent guy who went out of his way to help a relative stranger. That makes him okay in my book."

Zeke and her mother took the hint and left a few minutes later. Lydia and Reezira settled down in front of the television. And, Liz was finally free to escape to her room and her computer. To visit India and Prisha. Where her heart was safely waiting.

Chapter Six

"Dammit, Liz, if you don't get off your duff and get over here in twenty minutes, Kate and I are coming to your house to roust you out of your funk ourselves. And let me warn you, there will be blackstrap molasses and cod-liver oil involved."

Liz laughed out loud for the first time in a week. A week? She couldn't believe seven days had passed since her confrontation with her neighbor's son and his friends. "Isn't that what Dad used to threaten us with when we were slow getting up in the morning?"

"Exactly. Neither of us is sure how much of each to use or which end it goes in, but we're willing to experiment if it helps you get back on your feet."

She laughed again. "You're crazy."

"And you're not. So are you coming to Mom's?"

Liz considered the steps involved in that sort of undertaking: shower, finding and putting on clothes, lacing shoes, locating the key to her car, driving said car through morning rush-hour traffic…no, the whole thing made her slightly queasy. "Next week. I promise."

"Kate," Alex called to someone apparently well across the room from her. "You find the molasses, I'll get the cod-liver oil. See you shortly, sis." Then she hung up.

Liz groaned and placed the phone back on the receiver on the wall of her kitchen. Her roommates, who were eating breakfast at the table across from her, stared as they chewed their highly sugared cereal. Liz had done her best to try to introduce healthy food into their diets, but Lydia and Reezira possessed firm opinions about what was "good." Marshmallows and peanut butter were their favorite choices. The soy milk they poured over the brownish clusters was their concession to Liz.

"They come?" Lydia asked.

"I don't know. Maybe."

"Good," Reezira said. "They need shoot you." She demonstrated by holding a pretend syringe to her arm.

A shot in the arm. "Somebody should," Liz muttered.

She looked down at her pink Betty Boop pajama bottoms. She'd been wearing them for a couple of days now. Two? Three? She wasn't sure. With the curtains closed and twenty-four-hour cable, a person could easily lose track of time.

But she'd done more than watch TV. She'd filled out every page of the adoption application. She had researched several adoption agencies that had been recommended by some of her online contacts. She'd talked to Jyoti—even though the cost of a phone call to India was a luxury she really couldn't afford. Thankfully, Jyoti had eased Liz's worries. Prisha was doing better. Still not totally out of the woods, but she was breathing easier and sleeping through the night again.

If only I were. The nightmares that had troubled her immediately after the rape had come back. This time there were more men involved in the violation. Different ages. Different colors and nationalities. She fought them off valiantly and usually managed to wake herself up before anyone touched her, but the fear lingered.

"I guess I'll take a shower," she said, trudging down the hall to her room.

She was just tucking a gray University of Nevada, Las Vegas T-shirt into her shorts when the doorbell rang. Her sisters never rang the bell.

Her pulse quickened as she hurried, barefoot, to the foyer, where Lydia was standing with the door slightly cracked. She was talking to somebody. Liz couldn't see the person, but she could tell by Lydia's body language something was wrong.

She walked to the door.

"Oh, Liz, there you are. I was hoping you were home."

Crissy. No wonder Lydia was tense. "My car is in the driveway. Where did you think I was?"

Crissy glanced over her shoulder. "Um…yes, well, that's just it. Your car hasn't moved in days and I was worried. After what happened, I mean. You're okay, aren't you?"

"I'm fine. Just working from home. Was there anything else?"

She looked uneasy. "Um…no. Not really. Eli is back with his mother. Did your policeman friend tell you about the punishment we came up with for the boys? They worked all weekend at the church where the um…confrontation took place. Mowing, weeding, painting an old storage shed."

Liz had heard, but she didn't care. "That's nice."

"And we made Eli give his bike to Goodwill."

Liz recalled the moment when David passed her the bike. Their hands had touched for a brief second. She'd thought about him a lot since that night. He'd promised to call, but he hadn't.

"Um…Liz, I don't know if I said how sorry I am this happened. My um…husband has strong opinions about certain subjects. It's how he was raised. I…I don't always agree with him, but I've made it a point not to interfere with how he talks to Eli. I'm only the stepmother and—"

Liz cut her off. She was sick of excuses. "You could be a positive influence in your stepson's life. You could stand up for yourself, for women, for your daughter."

Crissy's face crumpled like a scolded child's. "But I'm not strong, like you."

"You're as strong as you choose to be." Why was she wasting her breath? Crissy didn't get it. Maybe she didn't want to get it. A sudden wave of fatigue made her sway.

Lydia reached around her for the door. "Go now. Leez busy."

Reezira helped Liz to the couch. "I bring tea. Your tea. Taste funny, but good for you," the earnest young woman said.

Liz was still sipping the strong hot beverage when Alex's car pulled into the driveway. The calming herbs had helped settle the jitters that made Liz feel like she might jump out of her skin. She was finally ready to admit that David had been right about post-traumatic stress. The confrontation with the boys had opened the door to the devastating memory of that night in Bosnia.

One brief but loud knock preceded the arrival of her sisters and their mother. "Whoa, she's dressed. Mom, you can put the fish oil away," Alex said, shedding her sun hat. She dropped her designer shades on the hall table.

Yetta, who was carrying a purse large enough to be called a carpetbag, set the heavy-looking thing down and rushed to where Liz was sitting. "I made them bring me. This is serious, dear. You're not yourself and I'm worried."

"Why? I was a little shook up. Surely that entitled me to a couple of days of doing nothing."

Reezira frowned. "She fights. In dreams. Bad."

Liz hadn't realized she'd been sharing her nightmares with her roommates. The fact caught her off-guard and left her feeling exposed. "The attack brought back memories. Bad memories. Something that happened when I was overseas."

Kate and Alex exchanged a look that Liz knew well. All four sisters at one time or another communicated without words. They were connected deeply, whether they liked it or not. Hadn't that been part of the reason Liz had fled to New Zealand after the rape? She'd known if she came home one or more of her sisters would have figured out what was bothering her. Her shameful secret would have come out.

Alex sat down beside her and took Liz's hand. "Tell us. We're your family. Your blood. You hurt, we hurt. Secrets are divisive. Didn't we learn that with everything that Grace went through?"

Liz looked into her sister's brown eyes, so like her own. "I was attacked in Bosnia. Two men. One held me down while the other…raped me. A patrol came by or the second one would have done it, too. I was dazed and bleeding. I had to crawl out of the ally where they dragged me. The military patrol didn't see me. I couldn't cry out because they'd bruised my windpipe. I would have frozen to death, but the Jeep backed up. I never found out why."

Unburdening herself turned out to be easier than she'd believed possible. In the company of five women—five very different women, she found sanity, sanctuary and compassion. The two women who had experienced the worst of men—and life—relayed their own horror stories. Not in a competitive way—"My wounds are deeper than yours." But rather the way good friends share problems and support each other—"I understand your pain because I've felt it, too." Her sisters cried. And gave Liz hell for keeping her secret to herself so long. Her mother, in her divine wisdom, stayed silent, her comfort reaching Liz on a deeply subliminal level.

"The bottom line is," Alex said later, when they'd switched from tea to wine, "you did the right thing last week. You stood up for yourself. For Romani and for women. You didn't let those little commando brats get off free."

Yetta nodded. "Alexandra is right, but you need to talk to Zeke. Find out if what that Crissy woman said is the truth. Were the boys punished and, more importantly, are they getting counseling?"

"What I want to know is, is the dad getting counseling?" Kate muttered. "Bigotry that deeply ingrained goes back generations."

Liz saw her roommates look at each other, and she realized she hadn't even considered how this ordeal might have affected them. They hadn't been outside lately, listening to their music and sunbathing—two of their favorite pastimes.

"All right, Mom, I'll go see Zeke at his office."

"Tell about black car," Lydia said.

"What black car?" Liz asked. The two woman were avid window watchers. Keeping an eye on what was happening on Canto Lane entertained them and made them feel safe. They knew the neighbors' vehicles and also knew when strangers came around.

"Two men. Black car. Look in old truck," Reezira explained.

Liz frowned. She'd had them keeping an eye out for David's truck and he hadn't been around in days. "Do you mean David's?"

"Night you and boys…" She made a fighting gesture with her hands. "David—" she stroked a pretend mustache above her lips "—inside with mean lady."

"Crissy?"

Lydia nodded. "We hear…" She mimicked the hideous screech the glove compartment door of David's truck made. "We look. Different man. No hair. Go in black car."

"Why on earth would anybody break into David's truck?" Liz wondered aloud.

Her sisters looked each other. "Doesn't he lock it?" Kate asked.

Liz pictured him reaching inside the open window on the day they'd had tea together. "His truck is so old I'm not sure it has locks."

Alex chimed in. "Even if a person wasn't worried about someone stealing his car, there's the whole identity-theft thing. Insurance papers could tell a lot about an individual."

Liz agreed, and suddenly got a nervous feeling in her belly. "That's a good point. I'll bring it up when I see him."

"Speaking of which," Alex said, grinning, "we think you should ask him over for dinner. I can't remember the last time Liz went on a date, can you, Kate?"

Liz ignored the pair's good-natured teasing. Every Gypsy knew that strange men in black cars were never a good omen.

"Whaddaya think, boss? It's him, right?"

The man behind the wraparound dark glasses surveyed the evidence laid out before him. He wasn't impressed. They'd gotten no fingerprints from the handle of the shovel their operative had taken from the gardener's truck, and the envelope stolen from the glove compartment had only revealed a post office box registered to one D. Baines. Their lab guys had managed to pull a partial off it, but the similarities in the sworls of the supposedly late Paul McAffee and a man named David Baines were far from conclusive.

David Baines had moved to Vegas six months after Paul

McAffee died in an explosion that destroyed an empire. *My empire*, the man in the sunglasses added under his breath.

Was there anything about this coincidental timing that linked Baines and McAffee? Not really. Logic said such a leap seemed extreme. Foolish.

But Vincente Aurelio Conejo had never allowed logic to blind him to possibility—even after he changed his name to Ray Cross. If he had, he'd still be selling bootleg prescriptions out of the back of his van. No, Ray was a go-with-the-gut kind of guy. He took risks and followed his instincts. He never played by the rules, unless the rules worked in his favor. His renegade attitude had helped him amass a fortune.

The only time he'd gone against his gut he'd paid heavily for it. He'd trusted someone dear to him. So dear that Ray had begun to think of Paul as the son he'd never had. He'd opened his heart to Paul McAffee. Shared his secrets. His hopes. And, his idea for a drug that would make them both richer than any oil sheik.

"What do people desire more than money? More than sex? More than a luxury vehicle in the driveway of their five-thousand-square-foot house?" he'd asked the chemist he'd taken under his wing right out of college.

"Eternal youth." That was the answer. Give them something that slowed—possibly even reversed—the aging process and people would gobble it up like candy. They'd mortgage their children's inheritances to pay for it.

True, there had been setbacks in the development. A few tragic losses during the experimental tests. But a certain loss-to-benefit ratio was to be expected. Everyone knew that. How could Paul not have seen that the overall benefit outweighed the risks? Why hadn't Paul trusted him? Believed in him?

Paul, the scientist, had read the research data differently. He'd theorized that the drug would be responsible for more birth defects than thalidomide—horrible, multi-generational birth defects that ultimately would cost the company every penny the drug earned and then some.

"We'll be paying for this forever," Paul had cried.

Forever?

How stupid was that? How could Paul have failed to see that the initial gain would have given them nine months' worth of profit before any supposed birth defects showed up? It would have taken another three to five years in litigation before any court proved their drug had been responsible for the birth defects. Even if the Federal Drug Administration took their miracle cure off the shelves, the world market and black market would have continued to line their pockets with gold. In the time the courts would have taken to find either of them personally responsible, Ray and Paul would have reaped fortunes that could easily have insulated them from any fallout. They could have lived like kings in places that had never heard of their drug.

But Paul hadn't seen it that way. He'd gone to the government with his research—the proof, he'd claimed—that the test results the company had provided the FDA were falsified.

Betrayal came in many forms.

As did retribution.

"Prepare the jet. I want to check this out myself. I would recognize Paul no matter what he did to disguise himself."

Chapter Seven

Liz was glad Zeke had suggested meeting for coffee, instead of at his office. She didn't carry the same antipathy toward law enforcement as some members of her family did, but she didn't want to make a big deal over this. She'd done her part by reporting the incident, right? The rest was up to the families of the three boys who had hassled her.

"So, what happened to them? Some public service, I hear."

They were sharing a table near the back of the room. No window seat for Zeke. From the first day she met him, she'd privately likened him to an old-West marshal. Not that he resembled one—his close-cropped hairstyle was very modern, but he carried himself with a certain dignity that went with a badge and a gun.

"Lip service for the judge's benefit. Junior is a piece of work, just like his old man. The other two snots left my office crying. I'm pretty sure I got through to them. That Eli kid, though? I have a feeling I'll be seeing him again."

She watched him drink from the clunky white mug he'd asked for. Despite its trendy name, the Bean Pod wasn't a hip place with forty versions of some microclimate coffee. It was a coffee/donut/sandwich shop that was popular with members of the police and fire departments.

"You know, I blame myself for this. I should have kept walking, but I sorta…snapped. Something happened to me in Bosnia, and I guess I've been harboring a lot of anger." She gave him an abbreviated version of the incident, but she had a feeling Zeke could supply plenty of details on his own.

He set down his cup and let out a sigh. "If these kids fail to comply with our agreement, I'm filing this complaint. It would be up to the D.A. to decide if Eli gets tried as an adult. A trial could get ugly—for you. And we'd probably need to subpoena your friend."

Your friend. Would David call himself that?

"Speaking of David, I need to get in touch with him and he doesn't have a phone. I don't suppose you still have his address, do you?"

Zeke's look said he saw through her overly casual tone. She didn't know whether to mention the black car or not. What if David was behind on his credit-card payments or owed some bookie money for a bad bet on the ponies?

She realized anything she shared with Zeke came down to trust. She and her sisters had adopted a sort of breathless wait-and-see policy where Zeke and their mother were concerned. Yetta deserved to move on with her life, but could they trust a *gaujo* cop to fit into their world? The jury was still out on that one.

"So, you need his address." It wasn't a question. "That's why you called me."

"Y-yes. And Mom suggested I talk to you about the incident so that I could get some closure. W-was that the wrong thing to do?"

He took another drink of coffee and let out a sigh before answering. "No, not at all. I was just a little surprised when you called. I know your family doesn't reach out to the police easily, despite—or maybe because," he added with a faint grin, "of what happened with Grace. But, I guess, I might have been hoping this was a social call, too."

"Because of you and Mom?"

He nodded. "I like your mother."

"I know you do. I think she likes you, too."

Neither said anything for several moments, then Zeke said softly, "She invited me to Kate's wedding."

Liz hadn't heard about that. She wondered if her sisters knew. Zeke obviously found this a significant development, and no doubt the rest of the Romani family would, too. She wasn't sure what to say, so she went with her gut. "I'm glad. She'll enjoy herself more with a date. Wish I had one."

That almost-grin returned. For a second. Then he took his notepad, scribbled something and ripped out a page. He hesitated just a second before placing the note, facedown, on the table between them.

Liz reached for the paper, but he kept his index finger on it until she looked up to meet his gaze. "Before I give this to you, I want you to understand a few things. This man is not necessarily who he says he is. For one thing, he seems to have materialized out of nowhere four years ago. There are a number of possible explanations for this— mostly, bad."

"How bad?"

"Anywhere from escaped felon to someone hooked up with WITSEC. That's what most people call the Witness Protection Program. But I checked and David Baines is not on any list that I could find. Hell, for all I know he's a dead-beat dad on the lam from child support payments or a mental patient who walked away from the funny farm or a serial killer…"

Liz's heart stopped for half a second then she laughed

out loud. She couldn't help herself. She let go of the paper and patted Zeke's hand. "Zeke, one thing you should have figured out by now about my mother is her ability to read people. She's had a couple of misses over the years—Kate's ex-husband, for one—but I guarantee you that she would have picked up on anything that awful about David."

He didn't say anything, but he did push the note a little closer. "I hope you and Yetta are both right about this guy. But I want you to promise you'll be careful. David Baines is a mystery, and mysteries don't always work out the way you want them to."

"SCAR, IF YOU DON'T stay out my way, you're going to end with even more cuts."

In a week, the beast had gone from wary to pest. As if he'd made up his mind that David—purveyor of fine fish and kibble—could be trusted. Now the foolish animal wouldn't leave him alone. A dangerous situation when David was hacking apart boxes with a very sharp blade.

Whisk. Swish. The box cutter sliced through the cardboard.

He tossed the excess pieces into a pile he'd later recycle or shred for mulch. He'd been to seven stores in the area earlier that morning to collect boxes after stopping for a quick bite at his favorite deli. For the first couple of years after he'd moved to Vegas, David had made a point never to frequent any particular store, bar or restaurant too regularly. Lately, he'd slipped into patterns that might spell trouble if anyone was looking for him.

The waitress at the deli knew him by name. A couple of guys in the neighborhood pub had recruited David for their dart league. He was on a nodding basis with a number of store clerks. He'd gotten comfortable.

So far, that hadn't been a problem, but this past week he'd started feeling a growing unease. He couldn't decide whether it was from fear of discovery or dissatisfaction with his life in general. He'd thought about Liz Radonovic a lot. Too much. He hadn't seen her. Partly because he was no longer working on her street. He'd moved on to a new neighborhood.

But he couldn't stop thinking about her. Was she okay? Had she bounced back after her altercation that night? How was she handling contact with her neighbor? He'd called the next day, as promised, but her roommate had told him Liz was asleep. He hadn't left his name or tried again.

Cowardly, he knew. Certainly nowhere near as brave as Liz herself. She was a fighter. She didn't turn tail when faced with a couple of loudmouthed punks. She stood up for what she believed in, what was right. She'd confronted the parents even though she'd known that she would have to live next door to them. He'd also stood up for his principles, but in his case, fleeing had been his only option.

Or was that a lie he told himself to assuage his ego? He'd asked himself that question a million times over the years. *What if I'd stayed?* Would the police have been able to protect him during the course of a trial—if they'd been able to find Ray, his former boss and mentor?

He was haunted by what-ifs. But even the bravest among us have their demons, he reminded himself. He'd caught a glimpse of Liz's when he'd driven her home that night. Like him, Liz had secrets and she kept them well hidden.

"Meow."

"Scar, has anyone ever told you that you have a really horrible voice? That is the most mangled meow I've ever heard."

"Meow." Louder this time.

David gave a full-body shudder and pocketed his box cutter. "Fine. I'm done with the prep work. I'll feed you before I start loading up the plants."

As he'd told Liz, he had a big order to fill for one of his largest nurseries. The company had recently started an online operation in addition to the local retail store and was planning to feature exotic cacti for an entire month on their Web site. Not only were they buying the plants from David, they'd hired him to write little blurbs about each variety. Not cut-and-dried facts, but the history and/or myths surrounding the plant. Since he didn't have a computer, he'd had to type each factoid on a recipe card using the manual typewriter he'd found at a thrift shop.

The cards were stacked on the front seat of his truck. The extra two hundred bucks the store was paying him for the cards would come in handy since a couple of days earlier he'd noticed that one of his caps was loose. He ran his tongue over the tooth in question as he selected a can of cat food.

"Meow."

"Worse than fingernails on a blackboard."

He'd just started turning the manual opener when he heard the buzzer that he'd rigged up across his driveway go off. The noise happened so rarely that he reacted unconsciously, dropping the can and grabbing the box cutter from his pocket. Scar yelped and disappeared under the workbench.

David hurried to the single window of the potting shed, which sat at a right angle to his greenhouse. His cottage was directly across from him. He had no trouble making out the car that pulled to a stop in front of his porch. Liz's little, dark green Honda SUV.

His racing heart returned to normal as he let out the

breath he'd been holding. He retracted the blade and set down the cutter then brushed off his hands and jeans and walked outside.

"This is a…surprise," he said.

Liz, who had one hand raised to knock on his door, gasped. She turned to follow his voice. "Oh, there you are. I saw your truck by that building back there, but I didn't want to just wander around looking for you."

He watched her walk back down the steps then come toward where he was standing. He'd never seen her quite so polished. Khaki crop pants. A butter-yellow tank top with a vibrant beaded necklace that looked like she might have brought it back from some exotic land. Her same hippie sandals, in black.

She brushed a lock of hair out of her eyes and smiled. "Sorry to barge in like this. Am I catching you at a bad time?"

Yes. A bad time in my life. "I have a big order to get out today."

"Oh, that's right. You mentioned that the last time we talked. Um…do you need some help? I'm free until three-thirty. Then I have to meet with a loan officer. I think she's going to tell me I don't qualify for my refinancing."

She sounded pretty down about that. He'd owned a house once. *I wonder what Kay did with it?* He'd never changed his wife's name as sole beneficiary if anything happened to him. She was also executrix of his will.

"All I have left to do is load up," he said, starting toward the greenhouse. Maybe if he kept things chilly between them she'd take the hint and leave.

"I'm stronger than I look." She followed after him. "And I know how to lift without compromising my lumbar muscles."

Her upbeat tone was so cheerful and inviting that David's

immediate inclination was to ask her to stay. But he knew he had to end this—whatever it was—between them before somebody got hurt. He stopped abruptly. Without his sunglasses, the bright desert sun was punishingly bright. "Listen, Liz, I don't know why you're here, but…"

"I owe you."

"No, you don't."

She crossed her arms. "I'm not talking money. I don't have a dime to spare. But you helped me last week and—"

"I'm not the hero you're trying to make me out to be."

She made a wobbling motion with her hand. "I don't mean you saved my life, exactly, but the situation might have gotten out of hand if you hadn't shown up. Plus, you reminded me about post-traumatic stress. This has been a rough week. The incident with the boys dug up a memory of something I thought I'd gotten over."

He wasn't surprised by her admission. He'd seen how vulnerable she'd looked, how haunted. "I'm sorry."

"I'm not asking for sympathy. I'm feeling better now. But visiting that dark hole reminded me that we never really escape the past. Not completely."

He had to work to keep from shivering. Her words sounded ominous.

She went on. "My sister Kate is a perfect example. I probably mentioned that my family background is Romani. My mother has a gift, and many people trust her to make predictions about their futures. When we were kids, she claimed to see a certain prophecy for each of us girls. Kate's was something about trying to outrun the past. I can't remember the exact wording, but when she met her fiancé—about the same time as her ex-husband got out of jail—the prophecy seemed to make sense."

"What's yours?"

Her gaze dropped to the ground. "Mine's already happened. Well, the first part of it, anyway." Her usual animation was replaced by a look of such despondency he almost reached out to comfort her, but she rallied before he could react. "The only reason I mentioned this is because I think things happen for a reason. You and I have a connection. Maybe it's as simple as you helped me and I'm supposed to help you in return. I don't know, but I can't just ignore it."

"Maybe you should." He turned away and resumed walking. He was a scientist. He didn't believe in preordained fate. But even if he did, what kind of perverse cosmic devil would weave a plot that removed him from a family he loved and dropped him in the desert to fall for a beautiful Gypsy—only to have to leave her, too?

"I'm not interested in a relationship, Liz," he said. Blunt and brutal. Not his usual style, but still…this was the way it had to be.

"Me, either. Lord, if you could see what I have on my plate at the moment, you'd think I was some kind of masochistic freak. But I…um…I did something that might… well, I…"

He stopped abruptly. He'd never seen her at such a loss for words. "What?"

"After we met—when you bawled me out for running over your cactus, I called Zeke—the detective who came to my house the other night—and asked him to get me your address." Her cheeks flushed with color. "I…uh, gave him your license-plate number."

David's stomach turned over.

"I know that was wrong. Zeke scolded me, but he… well, he did it, anyway."

"Why would you do that?"

She blushed.

"It was an unforgivable intrusion into your privacy. You intrigued me and I was trying to avoid talking to Crissy—which I ended up doing anyway. Nuts, right? Juvenile. I really am sorry."

She seemed as repentant as she was embarrassed. "What did Zeke tell you?"

"That you have a very good driving record," she said brightly, then her gaze shifted to some point over his shoulder. "For the four years that you've been in Nevada."

"And…"

"And there appeared to be some, um…inconsistencies in your past."

Inconsistencies? Of course there were inconsistencies. The real David Baines, grandson of one of his grandmother's friends, had died at age eleven. David didn't know why he'd never forgotten the kid's name, but when he decided to create a new identity, that was the name that popped into his head. Borrowing the dead boy's social security number, place and date of birth had proven fairly simple to do.

He couldn't stifle the curse word that slipped out.

"I'm sorry, David. I acted impulsively and I shouldn't have. I treasure my privacy, yet didn't think twice about invading yours. I really can't apologize enough."

He could tell she was sorry, but there was something else bothering her, too. "What else?"

She swallowed. "I don't know if the two things are connected. There's probably no reason they should be, but we don't get much crime in our neighborhood, so when my roommate said she saw somebody poking around your truck last week, I got this uneasy feeling in my stomach." She tried to smile. "Quantum leap, right? But, I mean, who would rob your truck?"

They both turned to look at the vehicle in question. Primer paint and dents too numerous to count. The beat-up Chevy wouldn't have interested the most desperate of junkies.

"Lydia just mentioned the black car this morning. I don't know if the two things are connected, but like I said, I got a very bad feeling about this when she told me."

His instincts told him to run like hell, but he'd learned from the pros. An ill-planned escape was worthless. He remembered one federal agent telling him, "A tracker can read the clues left behind and make it to your next destination before you even decide where you're going." He had to cover his tracks, and to do that right, he needed money. Which meant he had to deliver these plants and collect his fee.

"Probably just an addict looking for something to steal."

"Maybe." She didn't appear convinced.

To distract her, he said, "Okay. You can help me load the truck. The sooner I get this order filled, the better." *The sooner I can disappear.*

She lit up with a relieved smile. "Great. I'd be happy to, but could I use your bathroom, first?"

He'd never taken anyone inside his house. Maybe this would be a good test. If Ray's goons had found him, they'd be inside his house soon enough. Were there clues he'd overlooked? "My house is kinda hot," he said, leading the way. "The window unit is in the bedroom and it barely works."

"No problem. I'll be as fast as I can, then I'll help you load your plants."

DAVID HADN'T LIED about his overly warm home, Liz thought a few minutes later. The windows and shades were closed and a ceiling fan was roaring overhead, but the heat—like the tension between them—seemed tangible.

"You really keep your place neat," she said.

"Sloppy men are a stereotype perpetuated by television sitcoms. My grandmother made sure I had my clothes picked up and my bed made every morning before I left for school."

He also took off his cap when he entered a room, she noticed. Without his funky cap, she had a good look at his hair and face. It was a nice face. And his blondish brown hair was thick and wavy.

"You're right. That was a sexist comment. I'm a bit of a neat freak, but that was the only way to keep my *stuff* intact around three sisters."

They were standing quite close. He smelled like dirt and fresh air and some deodorant with a macho name.

"The bathroom is over there."

His tone was curt. She could tell he was upset about her poking her nose into his driving record. He probably thought she was some kind of kook, too. Why had she blabbed about her mother's prophecies? She never discussed that sort of thing with outsiders. People rarely believed her so why bother? David had seemed just as skeptical as all the rest. "Thanks. I'll only be a minute."

She headed in the direction he pointed, but paused to glance into the tiny kitchen. An old-fashioned typewriter—the kind she vaguely remembered seeing at her grandparents' house as a child—occupied one end of a painted wooden table. A half-empty juice glass and rumpled paper napkin sat at the other.

"I was in a hurry this morning," he said, scooting past her to carry the glass to the sink. "Do you want a drink of water or anything?"

"I'm fine, thanks."

She quickly made use of the facilities. The tiny bathroom was tidier than the one at her house—her roommates weren't big on neatness—and as impersonal as a motel's. She washed her hands and returned.

David was standing by the front window, gazing toward where her car was parked. She used the time to look around his home. Three *National Geographic* magazines on a low table beside a recliner that was shrouded in a dark blue throw. Mismatched lamps. A lumpy-looking beige-and-rust plaid couch.

The only clues to the man himself were his plants. Four or five pots with clever arrangements. She walked to a gallon-size pot stuck in a rusted pail. The cactus was one she'd never seen before. Tall, slender arms with hooked barbs. "Cool plant."

"Thanks."

"How long have you lived here?"

"A couple of years."

She started to ask why there weren't any family photos on display, but she didn't get the chance. "If you're done, I need to get back to work," he said, starting toward the door. "The nursery pays by check and I want to cash it at the bank before the drive-up window closes."

The word *bank* reminded her of her own appointment. "You're right. Let's get those plants loaded."

She opened the door and stepped onto the tiny porch. The house was old. Stick built with narrow siding and peeling paint. She had a sense that this entire area might have been a farm at one time, but she didn't ask. He'd said he was renting and he probably didn't care about the place's past.

"Didn't I hear you say you have a cat?"

He nodded. "Sorta. A stray that thinks he lives here."

Liz had noticed an impressive stack of canned food on the counter. She was relieved to know that wasn't David's dinner.

"My roommates' cats came from a little girl with a box in front of the grocery store. I hadn't really planned on getting pets before...well, so soon, but Lydia and Reezira adore them."

They walked across the empty expanse to where his truck was parked half in, half out of the weathered shop she'd noticed when she drove in. The ground was baked hardpan, cracked and dusty. Miniature whirligigs blew up in the wake of their steps.

He wasn't happy to have her there. She wasn't normally so pushy, but she'd missed not seeing him this week. True, she wasn't in the market for a boyfriend, but she liked this man.

Plus, she needed a date for the wedding. How better to get to know a person than by spending time with him under the scrutiny of her large and meddlesome family?

Now, if she could just work up the nerve to ask him.

Chapter Eight

"So, when did you know you were a horticulturalist?" she asked, once her eyes became accustomed to the hazy light inside the Quonset-shaped building that had obviously served multiple purposes over the years. One faded and rusted sign used to patch a hole in the tin siding said Mel's Garage.

He'd tossed a bunch of empty boxes into the back of his truck and moved the vehicle to the long, rectangular greenhouse, pulling partway into one of the open bays. She noticed that only some of the space was used. One area appeared to serve as a storage area for someone's junk. She was pretty sure the stuff, which included a dust-covered motorcycle circa the 1970s, didn't belong to David.

"I'm not one. I grow cactus. That's it."

And quite well, she noticed. Special lights were suspended over trays of loose, porous-looking soil. Juvenile plants, incrementally ranked by height, were situated beneath roughly framed skylights made of clear plastic. Larger pots containing grayish green mounds with inch-long spikes lined the front of the building, taking advantage of the direct sun.

"Why cactus?" she asked, using her teeth to extract an almost-invisible sticker from her thumb. She'd accidentally brushed against an innocent-looking plant with thick blondish foliage—which had turned out to be needle-sharp barbs.

"I find them interesting. You've got to admire a plant that can not only survive but bloom and thrive in some of the harshest climates on the planet."

She heard passion behind that rather eloquent statement. And something else, too. Sadness? She didn't ask. Instead, she said, "I have to admit, I've never thought of cacti as beautiful. Mom's always grown flowers outdoors, and she has orchids and violets and green plants indoors, but no cactus."

He put on a leather apron that tied around the neck and waist, a pair of clear goggles and gloves that reached almost to his elbows. "Understandable. They're not for everybody, but in the past few years, there's been a lot of interest in plants that don't need a lot of water—or maintenance."

"Makes sense. And the combinations you've put together on the curbs are really beautiful. Simple yet eloquent."

David looked at her and tried to decide if she was buttering him up for some reason or actually meant what she said. Her smile seemed sincere. But she had an agenda, too, he decided.

He turned back to his workbench where he'd assembled his delivery. Squaring his hips to the waist-high trestle-type table that he'd constructed of used lumber, he reached around the first box that he and Liz had assembled and pulled it in to better distribute the weight. The tailgate of his truck was down. All he had to do was carry each of the boxes six or seven steps to the truck. No problem. He'd hauled heavier loads.

But two of the boxes he was using today were larger than usual. He'd driven to several convenience stores trying to find the right size, but had finally given up and taken what was available.

"I could take one end. I'm stronger than I look."

He decided to try the first one on his own. As he lowered the box to the bed of the truck with a soft "Umph," he felt a muscle in his low back complain. He stretched to push the box all the way to the front then went back for another. "I'm curious about these prophecies of your mother's. How come yours was a two-part prophecy? Have any of the others come to pass?"

"Well, yes, actually. Grace was told she'd marry a prince, but first she had to save him," she said, ignoring the first part of his question. "Or something like that."

"Your sister is marrying a prince?"

"Um…well, in Grace's opinion, he's practically regal."

He couldn't help but smile. "I see."

"Actually, Nikolai's birth father, Jurek, is a distant relation. Mom calls him a cousin, but according to Jurek, it's more like second cousin twice removed, or something. Anyway, Mom says we share a family legend that says we're descended—on the wrong side of the sheets, of course—from royalty. I have no idea what kind of principality we're talking about, but I'm pretty sure it's not one you've ever heard of. Probably the fairy-tale kind."

He started to pick up the second box but noticed that one corner of the cardboard was ripped, so he stopped to find the masking tape he usually kept nearby. "So, how did your sister save this so-called prince?"

"She stepped between him and a bullet."

"Ouch. Is she okay?"

She nodded fervently. "She's fine. But be forewarned, if you're ever around her, don't ask to see her scar. Her husband-to-be is both jealous and a cop. Plus, she tends to embellish things a bit. There was only one shot, okay?"

He chuckled. He couldn't help it. He'd always envied

people with large families and with colorful relatives. He'd wound up with a grandmother who had managed to piss off most of their relations, so they never got invited to group functions.

"I'll remember that. Now, what about your two-parter?"

She looked toward the ceiling. "Like fortune cookies, prophesies are often ambiguous and open to interpretation."

He finished taping the corner then looked at her until she made a face and recited in a singsong voice, "A man of shadows, a child of light. You will only be able to save one."

A shiver passed down his spine.

She gave an exaggerated shrug and added, "My dad was the sun in the center of our universe—until his stroke. Then a shadow fell over our family. I worked with him every day. Strengthening exercises in the pool. Therapeutic massage. I'm a physical therapist. This is what I do. I save people who are close to giving up and help them find the will to live. I tried my best with Dad, but…I failed."

He stopped what he was doing and took a step closer to her, compelled by the stark look of grief that changed her face. "He's the man of shadows?"

She nodded.

"And the child of light?"

She didn't answer right away. When she did, her voice had changed. It was softer, happier. "Her name is Prisha. She's not yet two. She lives in an orphanage in India. I fled there after Dad died. I'm going to adopt her. Well, I'm going to try."

You can only save one. Adoptions take money. The bank. All the little clues she'd dropped were making sense.

"Are you going to let me help you carry that?" she asked.

He rearranged a couple of the smaller pots to keep them from tipping over. "I've got it. I'm fine."

He bent his knees and put his arms around the box, being careful not to squeeze too hard. His last-minute adjustments meant the weight wasn't quite as evenly distributed, but he tried not to let on. He didn't want Liz getting dirty before her important meeting with the bank.

"Um, I know this is going to sound kinda crazy, but my sister—the one with the crossroads prophecy—well, she's getting married on Saturday, and I was wondering if you might be free to go with me? It's more like a party than a wedding. Nothing big. Lots of food. Music. If I don't have a date, my great-aunts will give me all kinds of grief."

Step. Step. Bend. Drop. Twinge. "Sorry. Can't."

"Oh. Previous engagement? I meant to ask you last week, but then that whole incident with the kids came up. Confrontations aren't my thing. I read somewhere that second-born children are the peacemakers. I don't know why, but that's me. I used to hate to be around when Alex and Dad butted heads. And Mom and Kate are always arguing. Nothing hostile, just…family stuff."

He'd never known that kind of family *stuff*. He went back to the counter for the next box.

"Do you have siblings?"

"No."

"Are your parents alive?"

"No."

She gave a little snicker. "You've really got that word down. Kinda like my four-year-old niece."

David blocked a grin by taking a deep breath and picking up the next box. Too heavy, dammit. But he was committed. He walked slowly over the uneven ground and carefully eased it down.

Everything was fine until he let go and stood up. A

muscle in his midback suddenly went into spasm. David grunted in pain.

"Whoa. What was that?" Liz pushed off from the post she'd been leaning against. "Are you okay?"

Sweat broke out on his upper lip. He couldn't answer because that meant letting go of the breath he was holding. Movement of any kind produced pain. Excruciating pain.

"Oh-oh. Let me guess. Midback?"

He nodded a fraction of an inch. Lightning rods shot sideways around his gut.

"Okay. Not good, but not unfixable. Can you turn around? Slowly. Very slowly."

She moved in close enough to act as a crutch as she helped him toward a four-foot-high stack of fertilizer bags. "I want you to lower yourself down across these, but let's take off your apron first."

His welder's apron. He found it really helped protect against cactus barbs that worked their way into his clothes.

"Good thing you're wearing a regular shirt today instead of those coveralls, isn't it?" she asked as she rose up on tiptoes to pull the loop over his neck.

He'd chosen jeans and a button-up shirt since he was going into town after his delivery. And yes, he thought, it was a good thing he was in street clothes since he usually wore nothing but Jockeys under the one-piece suit.

With her help, he managed to shed the heavy leather gloves. He'd already tossed his goggles onto the tailgate. "Let me unbutton that for you. You focus on breathing. I don't suppose you have any ice out here, do you?"

He started to shake his head but stopped. She got the message.

A part of his mind registered the fact that a beautiful woman was undressing him. Her scent was very pleasant.

Intriguing. It helped take his mind off the pain…until she eased him forward.

"No. Stop. That hurts. Why don't I just take a couple of aspirin and wait for the pain to go away?"

"Because the muscles that you tweaked need help now, and covering up the problem won't fix it. Here. Let me put your shirt and apron over the bags first. Now move incrementally. Nice and slow."

He appreciated the fact that she hadn't said, I told you so. He should have let her help him move the flats in the first place.

"Let it go," she said, softly, her lips close to his ear. "Tell me if this hurts."

She put some pressure on the exact place that burned. Then her fingers shifted. He felt a tingle all the way down the inside of his leg to his arch. It didn't hurt exactly, but he felt it. "What are you doing?"

"Pressure-point therapy. Just try to breathe naturally, but concentrate on letting the pain leave your body with each exhale."

He focused on his breath and slowly he felt the pain subside. The pulsing beat in his eardrums lessened. He shifted his hips slightly. Not bad. He lifted up just a bit, being careful to use his stomach muscles. No knifelike slice in his lumbar.

"Wow. You're amazing."

"Right place. Right time. Most people try to ignore the pain and it only gets worse. Swelling and inflammation create more problems. You really should get an ice pack on that ASAP. And no more lifting." She looked at the remaining pots of cacti.

"I—" he started.

"Can't lift," she repeated. "Nothing heavy, anyway. So,

instead of going the macho weight-lifter route, we'll break up the boxes. Fewer pots per trip mean more trips, but think of all pain you're saving yourself. Do you have an extra pair of gloves?"

"Over there."

"Good."

It took them twice as long as it should have to complete the transfer, but David's back, though sore, didn't experience any more spasms. Liz closed the tailgate while he hooked the chain through the V to keep it secure. "Thanks. I couldn't have done that without your help."

She took off her gloves and handed them to him. "You're welcome."

"Water?" he asked.

He kept a carton of bottles under the workbench. The concrete floor kept them surprisingly cool.

She accepted his offer and quickly downed a long, thirsty drink. "Wonderful. Well, I'd better get going." She looked at him. "Will you be okay?"

"I'll be fine, thank you. There'll be people to help me unload at the greenhouse."

They lingered in the shade a moment. David had a feeling there was something she wanted to say. He wished she'd say it quickly—before he kissed her. Her lips were wet from the water. Lush and naturally dark red. Her nose was slender and long. Her cheekbones strong, like her jaw. Her beauty came from her lineage, he decided, her exotic past.

She let out a sigh. "Okay."

The sun was intense and neither of them had sunglasses on. David wondered if he'd ever see her again. Maybe he'd just blown the only opportunity he'd ever have to kiss her. But that was a good thing, right?

She took a step toward the strip of bright sunlight

streaming through the open garage door, but hesitated and turned around to face him. "Um, maybe I'm totally off base here, but I feel a connection between us." He didn't refute her claim. He was many things but not a liar. "Normally, if a guy made it clear he wasn't interested, I'd let it go. But, the Rom in me says we're not done with each other yet." She blushed. "Darn. I'm really bad at this. I wish Grace were here."

"What do you mean?"

She hesitated. David could see an ongoing debate in her eyes. "I'm the healer in the family, not the seer. Mother's sight became compromised after Dad's death, but Grace appears to be heir apparent to those abilities. She...um...sees things."

"What kind of things?"

"Well, she says she saw the gun that our cousin's wife pulled on Nikolai. And she saw blood—she just didn't guess it would be her own." She grinned sheepishly. "Like I said, prophetic interpretation isn't exactly an exact science."

Could she tell me if Ray's still alive and hunting for me?

"She's coming home for your other sister's wedding?"

"Yes. This Saturday."

"At a church?" He hadn't been inside one in years.

"No. It's going to be held in the backyard of Kate and Rob's new house. Very casual. No suit required." She blushed as if mentioning his wardrobe might embarrass him. "The food will be fabulous. Did I tell you Kate and her future mother-in-law own a restaurant? It's called Romantique. They're both pretty amazing chefs."

One night in public. He'd leave the next day.

Her brows came together above her nose. "Are you reconsidering my offer?"

He knew what he should say, what he intended to say, but what came out of his mouth was "Yes."

"Really?"

Impulsively, he was sure, she suddenly propelled herself across the distance between them, and kissed him. A quick, friendly peck at the corner of his mouth.

But he instigated the kiss that came next. Her lips were soft and lush and inviting. Her scent curled into the recesses of his sad, empty life and made him desire every drop of goodness she could give him. Hope, kindness, love…yes, even love. A fool's dream, of course. But for a few minutes on a sun-drenched afternoon…he'd play the fool.

She moved closer and put one hand on his shoulder— to steady herself or to push him away, he wasn't sure. But the little sigh that hummed between them sounded happy and content. She turned her head slightly and pressed closer, her tongue finding his.

The first touch sent a shiver through him as crisp and potent as an electrical shock. His blood raced, making a high-pitched sound in his ears. He hadn't felt this sort of passion dance through his veins in so long he thought he might embarrass himself.

"Wow, where'd that come from?" Liz asked, lifting her chin, eyes still closed. Her voice was husky, sexy.

"I don't know, but it was probably a mistake." *Probably?* He knew without a doubt any kind of connection was out of the question. What the hell was he thinking?

He stepped back, causing her arm that had been resting on his shoulder to drop between them. Instead of arguing with him, she grinned. "Absolutely. But it was sweet, just the same. Thanks."

He blinked and shook his head. "Thanks?"

Her smile made him want to grab her hand and pull her into his hotbox of a house. He was pretty sure they wouldn't notice the heat.

She touched her fingers to her lips. "It's been a while. But that was really nice. Made me remember what I've been missing. Now that might not be a good thing, but the kiss was worth it."

He knew exactly what she meant. And she was right. The memory would come in handy when he was running for his life.

Chapter Nine

A wedding. His swan song—of sorts. His backpack was fully prepared with the desert-survival gear he'd gradually accumulated over the past four years. His funds were diversified—one-third in the form of a cashier's check made out to his new name and mailed to a post office box that he'd opened in L.A., another third was in a Vicks jar in his backpack and the last third was buried in two waterproof containers under a cactus that he'd planted on Canto Lane. Inside his billfold was a note to his landlady instructing her to sell his remaining plants and personal belongings if he failed to return from his excursion into the desert. He was ready. Almost.

First, he was giving himself a gift. Tonight, he'd pretend he was a normal person. He'd brush off those sorely neglected manners and social skills he'd acquired in his past life and enjoy himself. That required mingling, David thought as he strolled around the large, lush backyard.

The grass—clearly sod—was so thick and cushiony it felt like expensive carpet. The landscaping was bland, but, as Liz had explained on the drive, her soon-to-be brother-in-law had only recently purchased the house, and most of his efforts since moving in had gone into preparing for the wedding.

Three tents were strategically situated to take advantage of the setting sun. The smallest held an altar adorned with flowing ribbons of red and gold that danced in the early-evening breeze. Two crystal champagne flutes bracketed a thick Bible, which sat beside a thick purple pillar candle flanked by twin white tapers in ornate silver candleholders.

Bouquets of balloons tied with bright ribbons of every color in the rainbow were affixed to the pristine stucco wall that surrounded the yard, as well as to the backs of chairs and at regular intervals along the railing of the multilevel deck.

"Well, what do you think? A bit over-the-top?" the woman standing beside him asked.

"I've never seen a wedding with as much color," he said after taking a sip of the wine he'd been handed the moment he'd entered the yard. "I don't find it garish at all. Just… festive."

"Grace will be so happy to hear you say that. When she was describing what she had in mind, Alex and I told her it would look more like a Byzantine marketplace than a wedding. She said that was exactly what she wanted." Her laugh sounded amazingly carefree. "I told you she was a character, didn't I?"

He and Liz had arrived a few minutes earlier, and so far, he'd met both Alex and Grace. Alex, he knew, was the eldest of the sisters. She was also the tallest. Thin, but beautiful. Grace, who moved so fast she made the people around her appear to react in slow motion, had stopped long enough to shake his hand.

"You're David?" she'd asked, her tone skeptical. "Really? Has anyone ever told you that your name doesn't fit you?"

David's advance warning system had sent a burst of panic through his veins, but, fortunately, she hadn't waited for an answer. "I'm really glad to meet you. Liz never dates. She's the serious one. Well, Alex is serious, too, but she was less serious before Mark broke her heart. Liz has always been serious."

She'd flashed him a high-wattage smile then given him a quick hug before dashing off. "Gotta go check on the bride. See ya."

The bride. Kate. He hadn't met her yet. Which wasn't surprising. Although this wedding seemed a bit unconventional in some aspects, he was sure certain protocols would be observed. "How come you're not one of your sister's attendants?"

Liz, who looked so dazzling David could barely keep his gaze off her, smiled. "She isn't having any. Maya, her daughter, is the flower girl. That's it. Oh, and both mothers are lighting candles. The minister is a friend of Rob's…or rather, she's the sister of a friend. Kate and Rob wrote their own vows. Should be interesting."

He'd wanted to write the vows he and Kay spoke when they got married, but she'd been against the idea. She'd insisted she wasn't eloquent enough to put her thoughts into words. In hindsight, he suspected she hadn't wanted to look too deeply at why she was marrying.

"What's that tent for?" he asked, nodding toward the middle-sized structure. Because it was enclosed on three sides and draped with yards of diaphanous material—gold, silver, purple and red—one almost expected to see a sheik's harem sitting on the piles of cushions set about along the walls. A wooden platform of some kind occupied the center.

"Ah…that's where we'll dance."

He looked around. "I don't see a DJ."

"There's one coming. After dinner, which will be served

in the main tent. But at some point, my sisters and I are going to perform a couple of traditional, and some not-so-traditional, Romani dances. We haven't done this in ages—not for a large crowd, anyway. When we were younger, we danced at all the family parties. Our dad called us the Sisters of the Silver Dollar, because he'd toss us coins when we did well."

"Interesting. I can't wait to see you perform."

She rolled her eyes. "I can."

"You don't enjoy dancing?"

"I love music and I love to watch dance, but I'm not a natural at it, like Alex and Grace. Kate and I usually stay in the background and let the two hams fight for the spotlight, but this time Kate won't be with us. Maya is taking her place, and she's only four and a half."

He looked her over, starting at her toes. He'd never seen her wear high heels before. They accentuated the curve of her calves. She wasn't wearing hose, not needed in the still-warm evening. Her dress, a sheath of wine-colored silk, fell just above her knees. Her perfect knees. The deep V neckline showed plenty of skin. Skin that begged to be touched.

"I bet you're better than you think," he said softly.

Peeking through her thick black lashes, she made a moue with her lips. "It's been a while. I'm afraid I'll be even worse than I remember."

"I'm sure all the moves will come back to you."

"I'd feel more comfortable if I'd had a chance to practice a couple of times before this."

A tingle of sexual awareness danced through his extremities. Were they talking dance? Or something else?

"I'll cheer for you. No matter what."

She leaned in closer, as if drawn by his smile. Was she

remembering the kiss they'd shared? Lord knew he'd been thinking of little else, despite his methodical preparations for his impending departure.

One kiss does not a relationship make, he reminded himself.

"Hi, Liz," a voice called. "How are you?"

She jerked back sharply. A ruddy blush deepened the makeup dusting her cheekbones. Pivoting too fast—her heels apparently imbedded in the soft soil—she swayed unsteadily. David caught her elbow and stepped close enough to stabilize her.

Their bodies fit nicely together, he thought, as his hand settled casually at her waist.

"Gregor," she exclaimed. "Hello. MaryAnn, it's so good to see you. Come let me introduce you to David."

Two of the many cousins she'd predicted he would meet tonight, he gathered. He hadn't planned on trying to keep the names straight. Why bother, right?

"You look amazing, MaryAnn. I'm so happy you're here. Are you home for good?"

The dark-haired woman, who hadn't completely made eye contact with either of them, shook her head and looked around, uneasily.

"Not yet, but soon, according to the doctor. Right, honey?" her husband asked, putting his arm around his wife's shoulders. "The kids are really missing their mommy."

MaryAnn's smile slipped and her eyes took on a haunted look. Liz handed David her wineglass and went to the couple, putting her arms around them both. She said something to them, too softly for David to hear, but he saw them both react with pleasure.

After the couple moved away, Liz explained their situation. "MaryAnn's breakdown caught us all by surprise.

That doesn't say much for a people that puts so much stock in family, does it?" she asked, shaking her head.

"People get busy with their own lives." That had been his excuse for neglecting Kay and the children.

"True, but my mother says things happen for a reason. What we learned from MaryAnn's crisis was that we all need to pay more attention to those around us. Alex has been a big help with Gregor and MaryAnn's kids. Luca, the oldest, has really had a rough time of it."

"I'm sorry to hear that. Kids are always caught in the middle when their parents' lives blow up."

She cocked her head as if hearing something revealing in his comment. He knew she was going to ask him to elaborate, but before she could speak, someone with a loud, commanding voice hollered, "Liz, you're needed in the house."

She looked at him and rolled her eyes with obvious resignation. "Yes, Grace," she called out. To David, she said, "I'll be back as soon as I can. Family is supposed to sit in the front couple of rows. If you get tired of standing, I draped my wrap across two chairs. It's a lacy silver thing, remember? I'm really sorry to abandon you, but I have a feeling they want to take some pictures."

"I'll be fine. I'm going to check out the landscaping. Professional curiosity," he added, keeping his tone light.

He watched her walk away—struggling with her spike heels in the thick lawn. Before she was halfway there, she stopped, kicked off the shoes then picked them up and completed the trek barefoot. David chuckled as he polished off his wine.

She was far more beautiful than she knew, although he suspected outer beauty wasn't high on her list of priorities. He was certain she'd put more stock in a person's integrity than looks. And she obviously didn't worry about social or financial status. Why else would she kiss a gardener? A man who drove a run-down truck and apparently couldn't afford a phone.

"Hi, there. We haven't met. I'm Rob. The groom."

David switched his glass to his left hand so he could shake the hand of the man who'd just walked up. "Nice to meet you. Congratulations. I'm with Liz."

"Yes. I know. The sisters have been buzzing about you for days. The mystery gardener, I believe they're calling you."

David chuckled. "Not so mysterious. Name's David."

"Glad you could come. Liz is a terrific person. She was so supportive of my mom during a recent medical scare. She helped Mom find the right doctor. Plus, her teas are amazing. If you're ever sick or hurt, give Liz a call before you go to the pharmacy."

David had experienced her healing hands and herbal teas and couldn't agree more, but all he said was "I'll do that."

Rob, who seemed like a genuinely decent fellow—the kind of person David would have liked as a friend if they'd met in his former life, introduced David to some of the other guests. An accountant with twins. Two more male Radonovic cousins and their kids. A young guy who had the upper torso of a bodybuilder but was holding a tiny baby dressed in pink frills.

"Hey, do you play poker?" Rob asked when the group of friends had moved on.

"I don't gamble much." A person who's lost everything doesn't need to risk any more, right?

"I don't mean for high stakes. Just a guy's-night-out kind of thing. A few friends—those guys and a couple of others. We call ourselves the Dad's Group, but it's not like I have a kid…well, I'll have Maya after the wedding, but you know what I mean. You'd be welcome to join us. No kids required."

But he had kids. Three of them. And he missed them so much that at times he felt like someone had taken a dull shovel to his stomach and tried to mine for gold. Which is why he did his best not to think about Ariel and the twins. And why he couldn't join a "dad's group"—even if he weren't leaving town.

Tomorrow. He'd already laid the groundwork with his landlady. "I'm heading into the desert to collect some new stock," he'd told her a few minutes before Liz had arrived to pick him up.

She hadn't appeared surprised. Probably since he'd been making regular forays into the desert for the past couple of years. He'd also taken a number of desert-survival courses and had participated in two cactus-rescue projects with a volunteer conservation group.

In the morning, he'd drive north to Beatty then cut over to Death Valley. He planned to abandon his truck in the most remote place he could find. The last thing he wanted was anyone to conduct a "missing hiker" search. Eventually, he'd work his way into California, winding up in L.A., where he had a new identity waiting.

"Thanks, but I'm not a joiner. And I'm planning on doing some cactus hunting in Mexico pretty soon." That was the story he planned to tell Liz to explain his upcoming disappearance.

Rob took something from the inside pocket of his handsome tux. "No problem. But if you change your mind or have time when you get back, give me a call. That card has my cell number on it, too."

David held it up to read: Robert J. Brighten, Attorney-at-Law. He smiled and made a point of tucking the card in the pocket of the new shirt he'd bought that morning. Twenty-five bucks on sale at Mervyns. His big splurge.

Money that should have been squirreled away into his emergency-travel stash.

"I'll do that."

As he watched Rob move into the crowd, David reflected on his past two days. He'd cashed the check for his plants and paid his rent for the coming month. He'd cleared up his small bills by sending money orders for his utilities and car insurance. The rest of the time—when he wasn't at his landscaping job—had been devoted to planning his next move. Free Internet at the library had helped.

Was he overreacting? A part of his mind said yes. The person nosing around his truck on Canto Lane could have been innocent—somebody looking for a business card, perhaps. He hadn't noticed any strange cars in the area. Nobody had contacted his landlady asking questions. The trip wires he'd set up around the greenhouse were still intact. Nothing seemed to indicate that he was in trouble—except for a feeling that someone was watching.

But he didn't feel that now, in the midst of a Gypsy wedding. He felt…snug. And accepted. And surprisingly safe. Which, he knew, was an illusion.

"HE'D BE GORGEOUS if it weren't for that mustache. What's with that?"

Liz looked at her baby sister and rolled her eyes. "I thought so, too, the first time we met, but I haven't gotten up the nerve to ask. I guess he likes it."

"He really doesn't look like a gardener," Alex said. "A college professor maybe. History? Geology? Biology? Yes, definitely one of the earth sciences."

Alex, Grace and Liz were gathered in the second-floor master suite of what would soon be Kate's new home. Kate was pacing—and adding the finishing touches to her makeup. "I can't wait to meet him. Liz's mystery man. He sounds so you, sis."

Alex and Grace chuckled in obvious agreement. Liz didn't bother arguing the fact. In a way, they were right. David was a hermit, nearly as prickly as the plants he cultivated. Liz had been accused of being a changeling herself—distinctly antisocial for a Rom.

A minute later, a vision in white lace emerged from the adjoining bathroom. "Ta-daa. What do you think? If I look silly, blame Grace. She bought the dress, even though I told her white was for first-time brides, not the recycled variety."

"Oh, Katie, you look like royalty."

"It's a gorgeous dress, but on you, it glows."

"I told you it was perfect. Absolutely exquisite."

The last was from Grace, who looked so proud she could have popped a button on her chest, except her simple sapphire sheath was a halter style and didn't have buttons.

"And I don't think your handsome groom cares about your first marriage. He's so head over heels in love he's down there pacing—just like you. Isn't that cute?"

Liz walked to the tall window where Grace was standing and looked down at the crowd below. She wobbled just a bit on her three-inch heels. Grace was the one who loved sexy shoes, but tonight all four sisters were in pumps. Walking on the grass was a nightmare—she'd be lucky if she didn't hyperflex her Achilles tendon, but she had liked the way she'd accidentally fallen against David. They'd fit together perfectly thanks to the extra height from the shoes. She couldn't wait to slow dance with him.

Kate joined them, dropping an arm across both sisters' shoulders. "I love the dress, Grace, really I do. You have amazing taste—and the tents are so festive. Thank you for everything." She kissed her on the cheek then looked at Liz.

"You've been a big help, too, Liz. You must have blown up twelve zillion balloons today."

"Photo op," Alex called from behind them.

"My camera, too," Liz said, pointing to the little digital on the dresser.

As soon as Alex lowered the camera, Liz switched places with her. "I know Rob's hired·a professional photographer who is going to burst through that door any second, but I want a couple of shots of my own." She planned to send a group photo to Prisha so the little girl would recognize her aunts when Liz brought her home. "Let me grab somebody to take one of the four of us."

"Not Rob," Kate hollered after her. "I want to watch his jaw drop when I walk up the aisle."

Liz poked her head into the hallway—and spotted a tall man in neatly pressed black slacks and a dark blue shirt. She couldn't believe her luck. Her date was standing at the end of the hall, peering over the railing at the crowd on the first floor. "Psst," she called. "David. Come here a minute."

He turned around at the sound of his name and walked toward her. His long legs cleared the distance in seconds, but watching him move gave Liz the same thrill she'd experienced when she'd picked him up that evening. His shirt was made of fine cotton and looked brand new. The burnished gold tie was simple, but of good quality. Except for the mustache, he almost looked like a different person.

"Could you take a photo for me?" she asked.

"I can try."

She held the door open and followed him in, keeping the introductions short. "You've met Grace and Alex. This is Kate, the bride."

"Obviously," Grace added with a snort.

Liz ignored her. "Let's put Kate in the middle. How 'bout over by the balcony?"

Since the bedroom faced east, the last rays of the setting sun had turned the hillsides in the distance tangerine and ruby. A perfect foil for Alex's purple, Grace's blue, Kate's white, and her own wine-colored dresses.

David looked through the viewfinder a moment then lowered the camera and said, "Wow, you ladies are gorgeous. You don't even have to smile and this will be a great shot, but go ahead and show me what's in your hearts."

Liz felt pride and pleasure warm her midsection, until Grace, who was standing at Liz's side, whispered, "Ooh, I like him. Too bad he's not who he says he is."

Liz glanced at her sister. "Huh?"

"Look at me, Liz," David called.

"He's…not real."

"Smile."

Liz wanted to strangle her youngest sister, but she plastered a not-real smile on her face. Everyone trusted Grace's ability to see beyond the obvious. And her recent experiences had added to Grace's confidence in her gift—something Liz couldn't claim. In Bosnia, Liz had failed to give heed to the warning voice that told her not to return to the hospital that night for a second shift. And when she was taking care of her father, Liz had pushed him harder than she should have, ignoring the voice in her head that said he was only going through the motions to give his family time to prepare themselves for the inevitable. Liz hadn't listened either time, and both outcomes had broken her heart. She desperately needed to hear what Grace saw that she, herself, had missed where David was concerned.

But first David insisted on taking a dozen more shots,

then included Yetta in a few when she showed up to tell Kate it was time to start the ceremony. By the time he handed the camera back to Liz, her sisters were laughing and hamming it up like they were on a photo shoot for a magazine.

"Ahem."

The pointed cough from the doorway made everyone freeze.

"Hi, honey," Grace called. "Wait till you see these shots. David's a genius. Have you two met?"

She dragged David across the room to where her fiancé, Nick Lightner, was standing. The two men, who were nearly equal in height—although Nick had a good twenty pounds of muscle on David, exchanged a quick, perfunctory greeting. "The music is swelling," Nick said, taking Grace's hand. "If we don't get down there now, they'll be playing 'Here Comes the Bride' for us."

Grace kissed him playfully. "Think of all the money we'll save. Bye, all. See you when we change for the dance."

Argh. Liz wanted to ask Grace to explain her earlier comment about David, but now she'd have to wait until after the ceremony.

"Shall we join them?" David asked, suddenly appearing at her side.

He's not real. Well, hell, who was? "Sure," she said, offering him her arm. "I had no idea I'd invited the Annie Leibovitz of gardeners to the party. Where'd you learn photography?"

"I always take a disposable camera with me when I go into the desert after new stock. Believe me, if you can get a cactus to smile, working with four beautiful women is a breeze."

Liz laughed, letting go of her worries. He was handsome, multitalented and fun. And her instincts were telling her to relax and enjoy the moment, so that was what she planned to do.

He seemed comfortable letting her link her arm through his as they descended the grand, curving staircase. "You've got an interesting family," he said.

"Loud."

"Boisterous."

She smiled. "You're too kind. Wait till the food and drink arrives. And the storytelling starts. Thank goodness we don't have a fire. Give my uncle Claude a bottle of brandy and a fire pit and you'd be here all night."

"Sounds romantic—in the sense of tall tales being passed on through generations."

She chuckled softly. "Sometimes, yes. Depends on who's telling. My father used to make up fairy tales about each of his princesses. We were always doing valiant things like rescuing villages and taming unicorns. Unicorns are actually quite difficult to catch and the tips of their horns are poisonous to the mean of spirit. I bet you didn't know that, did you?"

Her tone was a mix of tenderness and something else. Regret? Remorse? David couldn't tell, but he was curious. When they reached the foot of the stairs, he impulsively pulled her to one side to let the rest of the latecomers file past.

"How long ago did your father pass away?"

She didn't have a chance to answer because two servers in black pants, white shirts and wine-colored aprons rushed past, trays clanging with empty wineglasses.

"We need to sit down."

He could tell she was intentionally avoiding his question. Why? he wondered.

They went out the side door and joined the last of the

guests slowly making their way down the center aisle. Liz's grip on his arm intensified.

"You miss him a lot, don't you?" he asked softly.

She nodded, moving closer. "He was an amazing man. Larger than life, as they say. You should have seen all the people at his funeral. The local paper ran a story called The Last Gypsy King. Losing Dad was…well, it rocked our world. None of us was prepared—even though we probably should have been. We had nearly a year between his first stroke and the one that took him."

If only it was that simple. "Is anyone ever really prepared to lose a parent? Mine died when I was twelve. In a car accident. My grandmother's friends tried to tell me that sudden was better, but I don't think that's true."

She looked at him while they paused to let an older woman with a walker get settled into her chair.

"Twelve?" The sympathy in her eyes was easy to read even in the waning light. "That must have been so scary. I can't imagine."

David very rarely talked about that time, which was why he couldn't figure out why he was bringing it up now. Maybe the empathy in her eyes encouraged him to admit, "It was tough. I was an only child and we'd always done everything as a family. That was the first trip they'd ever taken without me. A second honeymoon, they'd called it."

You stay with your grandmother, honey boy, and we'll be back before you know it. Have fun, sweetheart. Fun? Fun was the last thing his grandmother ever thought about—especially after she learned that she was expected to take over raising her dead daughter's child.

David stepped forward to help the older woman fold her walker. He tucked it to one side of the aisle then returned to escort his date to their seats. The sweet trill of a harp filled the air along with the low murmur of the fifty or so guests. An empty chair on each side of them created an island effect, which might have accounted for the reason David confessed, "I never really forgave them for not taking me with them."

She gripped his hand in hers and said softly, "It took me six months in an ashram in India to stop blaming myself for my father's death. Finally, one morning I woke up and a voice in my head said, 'You're a physical therapist, not God.'"

She shivered. He reached behind them for her loosely woven silk shawl and draped it across her shoulders. He decided they both needed a change of topic. "Tell me about Rob, your new brother-in-law. Seems like a good guy."

She lifted her chin and looked toward the altar where Rob Brighten stood to the left of a short, plump woman dressed in a black robe topped with a colorful stole. "He's a sweetheart. He and Kate are so madly in love it's almost painful to watch, but I'm really happy for them both. Kate pushes herself too hard, and Rob's a bit more laid-back, so I think they'll be good for each other."

"Why is it painful to watch?"

Her skin tone turned dusky. "I didn't mean that exactly, but when everything is going well for someone else and your life is in chaos, it's tough not to be a little envious. Unless you're a saint, and I'm definitely not that."

He wasn't so sure about that, but he didn't argue. Partly because the music changed to the wedding march. Heads started to turn. David pivoted in his chair. His knee brushed against Liz's thigh. Warmth seeped into his bones. How long had it been since he'd made love with a woman? Too damn long. She wasn't a saint and he wasn't a monk, but did that mean they belonged in bed together? A guy could dream, couldn't he?

Chapter Ten

Liz decided the only way to get through this dance was to let her mind play. She wouldn't worry about whether or not she was any good. She'd try to recapture the joy she remembered from when she and her sisters had danced for their father.

She could almost picture him in the front row, his thick wavy black hair gleaming from the greasy tonic he used to keep it in place. His wide grin always beamed with pride when he watched his girls, his princesses. He'd named them each after strong women who knew their worth and made a lasting impression on the world around them.

A lot to live up to, perhaps, but when he was healthy, he'd always made Liz believe she could do anything she set her mind to. She needed to remember that, now, when inhibition told her she was going to make a fool of herself.

"Ready, ladies?" Alex asked.

"Absolutely," Grace said, rising up on her bare toes to stretch her calves. "We are going to rock."

Or sink like a rock.

Liz adjusted the snug bodice of her costume, being careful not to snag any of the hand-sewn sequins that made it shimmer in the stage lights. She'd been pleasantly surprised to find that the outfit fit as well as it did. Her body had changed some over the past few years, but she still exercised. Not the vigorous, athleticism of dance, but they were only doing three numbers. She was pretty sure she could keep up.

"Well, here goes nothing…." Alex said, nodding to the DJ who pushed a button on his console.

The distinctive sound of a flamenco guitar filled the tent. Drums and castanets blossomed. A beautiful but foreign voice seemed to float on the desert breeze that teased the colorful scarves Grace had tacked about.

Alex and Grace moved into the spotlight, to a swell of applause.

Liz gave an encouraging nod to her niece, who positively glowed in her miniature belly dancer costume. White, like her mother's gown, Maya's sheer pantaloons and sleeves were trimmed in gold. Her hair was loose and wild, a flowing mane of deep chocolate curls, like Kate's.

On cue, Liz wiggled the finger cymbals she'd played since she was Maya's age and lifted her arms. She and her niece danced onto the platform that been hauled out of storage for this performance. The squeaky sound of bare feet against the shiny flooring sounded loud in Liz's ears, but she knew the crowd would hear only the music, which seemed to course through her veins like a drug.

They finished the first number with a flourish and a low bow. Liz glanced up see David clapping and cheering— surprise and pleasure in his eyes. He was glad for her, proud of her. Oddly, his presence made what was coming next less intimidating.

Their second routine gave each sister a few minutes in the spotlight to a song by Dulce Pontes, a Portuguese singer whose *fado*, or poetry set to music, appealed to Liz's love of the exotic. The raw passion of the music touched something deep inside her soul, but putting that emotion on display for public consumption was never easy for Liz.

But this time, she wasn't dancing for everyone. She was sharing a personal, private gift with David, the man whose sad childhood had touched her deeply. As the haunting chords of the singer's voice swelled, Liz twirled, giving herself over to the love story she heard in the words of a language she'd never studied. She unconsciously searched the audience for her father. Tears worked their way into her eyes. Intellectually, she knew he was gone, but…then she saw him. At the back of the audience. Right where he always stood. Smiling. Clapping and nodding. Enjoying the spectacle as any proud father would.

Her spirit soared with a lightness she couldn't explain. A healing had taken place. She stumbled slightly as she exited the stage to give Alex her time in the spotlight.

"Wow, where'd that come from?" Grace asked, embracing her. "That was gifted."

A gift. Yes. That was what she felt. She had her father's blessing. His forgiveness.

She was too overcome with emotion to speak, so she hugged Grace back, then turned to clap to the music. Alex looked ethereal—as graceful as any ballerina. Her long, slender arms swaying with undeniable loveliness—and sorrow, Liz realized.

Suddenly, the music changed and Grace and Maya traded places with Alex, who returned breathless to Liz's side. Smile in place, Alex appeared happy and content with her performance—and her life.

Liz made a mental note to have a serious talk with her big sister in the near future. Now wasn't the time. Now was about celebrating—love, hope and gifts too precious to question.

"Wow. I've never seen anything like that before."

David had had to fight his way through the crowd to find Liz after the Sisters of the Silver Dollar performance. The entire audience seemed energized by the dazzling efforts of the Radonovic sisters and their adorable niece.

Laughing, Liz took a drink from a water bottle someone had handed her. "Thanks. We didn't suck, huh?"

She was still in costume, and he had to make a conscious effort not to stare—and drool. Her skin seemed to glow against the garish spangles and beads sewn to the shimmering material that hugged her curvaceous body. A girdle of amethyst jewels and gold coins rode low on her hips over a skirt of silken material that was both modest and revealing.

"You were amazing. And you look gorgeous."

Her brown eyes seemed alight with joy—and some residual passion he'd felt during her solo. He'd never been much of theatergoer and could only name one or two live performances that he'd attended in his life, but her dance had touched him in a way he hadn't expected. He'd felt almost as though she'd been dancing for him.

She licked her lips and smiled. "I think we pulled it off. A couple of little mistakes, but not bad, huh?"

"Mistakes? I didn't see any. That last song—where you and your niece were telling a story—was amazing. Even though I couldn't understand the words, I felt the tragedy and the happiness."

She dipped her head modestly. "Thank you. I'd never danced that part before. Alex used to handle the lead, but she's had some health issues the past couple of years and her stamina isn't what it used to be, so, since Grace and Maya danced the Dulce Pontes song together, Alex thought Maya and I should do the one about the mother and her little girl."

"No one could have danced it more convincingly. When

your sisters pulled the child from your arms, I heard the women around me gasp and cry out. I think several wept."

"Really?"

He nodded. "It was very moving."

"It's supposed to symbolize a daughter getting married and leaving her mother's house, but having a child dance Kate's role changed the tone, I guess. I couldn't help thinking about what it would feel like to lose a child. To know that I wouldn't get to watch her grow up. Never dance at her wedding." She blinked rapidly and looked away.

He stepped closer, needing to comfort and reassure, but knowing anything he said would be a lie. The pain she'd imagined was the worst thing he'd ever known. Powerless to stop himself, he put his arms around her and pulled her tight.

She sighed then melted against him.

He wasn't sure how long they stood like that, but finally it crossed his mind that music was playing and they weren't dancing. He cleared his throat. "Tell me about this music," he said softly, drawing her hand to his chest.

She put her other hand on his shoulder and moved in step with him. "My cousin Gregor—you met him, right?" David nodded. "He arranged for the DJ. Joaquin something. A distant relative, I think. He teaches at the college and has traveled all around the world collecting and recording indigenous music. I guess because the Romani have lived in so many diverse lands over the course of history, our taste in music leans toward the exotic."

"What's playing now?"

She tilted her head. "I don't know, but I brought him a CD from India. He promised to play my favorite later. It's slow and romantic. Maybe I should change first."

His fingers splayed wide across the middle of her back, touching both silk and bare skin. "Are you cold?"

She tossed her head and laughed. "Are you kidding? Between the adrenaline and the exercise, I can't feel a thing."

"Not even this?" he asked, softly strumming a spot in the hollow of her low back with his thumb.

She stilled in his arms, even though everyone around them was laughing and dancing to the Calypso beat. Their gazes met, and he read the look in her eyes all too easily. She was falling for him. Maybe even telling herself that no matter how busy her life was or how unmotivated he might be—career-wise—they might be good together.

And if things were different—if he were a different man—she might have been right. He desired her. A part of him felt a pull toward her unlike anything he'd ever felt before. But the masquerade would end, sooner or later, and David had no intention of making Liz pay for his mistakes.

He knew what he had to do.

One more dance. Then, I'll call a cab and get out of here. No harm. No foul. Just one more dance.

Liz stepped away, shivering. She sensed something changing between them, as if a vein had been opened and the blood that raced in anticipation of the hot sex to come was slowly seeping away.

"Breeze," she said, rubbing her bare arms. "Night on the desert. Gets you eventually, doesn't it? I'd better get dressed."

David cocked his head, obviously surprised by the sudden change of plans. Close, sexy dancing one second, partner on the run the next. But he graciously escorted her to the sidewalk, where she left him with a stupid little twitter.

What is wrong with me? she silently asked herself as she dashed into the first-floor guest room where she and her sisters had changed into their costumes. Why do I always pick guys who are emotionally unavailable?

Three glittering outfits were hung up, draped over a chair and tossed on the floor, respectively. One hanger and empty plastic dry-cleaning bag waited beside her party dress and high-heel shoes.

She changed quickly. No use putting off the inevitable. She couldn't explain exactly how she knew that David was planning on telling her that they didn't have a future together, but she did. She would do her best to enjoy what was left of the evening then she'd take her guest home. No hot and sweaty sex in his tiny house. No detour to her place.

Disappointing? More regret than one date and a couple of conversations together should warrant, she told herself, but the pain was very real. She liked him. A lot. And strange as it sounded, something had happened during one of her dance numbers that told her her father would have liked David, too.

She hung up Maya's and Grace's dresses then turned to leave, but a sudden sadness stopped her. Tears welled up in her eyes. Her knees wobbled. Feeling unsteady and a bit overwhelmed, she sat on the end of the bed.

The door opened and her mother walked in. "There you are. I knew I'd find you here."

Liz discreetly wiped her tears. "Those Gypsy mind-reader correspondence courses are finally paying off, huh?"

Yetta laughed lightly and sat down. "That sounds like something Grace would say. You're supposed to ask me what's wrong."

"Is something wrong?"

"No, but that's what you usually do—try to fix whatever is bothering someone else."

Liz didn't bother to disagree. "I guess I'm having some

kind of personality meltdown tonight. I didn't even dance like myself."

"I agree. You are usually more like me—self-conscious. Tonight, you were inspired. I'm sure your father was grinning from ear-to-ear."

Liz hiccupped. "I saw him, Mom. For a moment. In the back. He was clapping, the way he always did."

Yetta put her arm across Liz's shoulders and hugged her. "I know you miss him, dear. We all do, but it's probably different for you since you tried so hard to stop the inevitable."

"I tried to save him. Like my prophecy said. But I failed."

Liz felt her mother go still. "Your prophecy?"

Liz nodded. "Daddy was in a dark place after his stroke. I tried to bring him back into the light, but I couldn't." She decided it was time to share her secret. "But, the good news is, I have a handle on the other part of my prophecy. I found the child of light."

"You did?"

"Her name is Prisha. She lives in the orphanage in India where I worked after Daddy died. I can save her, Mom. I plan to adopt her and bring her here."

She looked into her mother's eyes and saw such pain her throat closed up and she couldn't swallow. "What?"

Yetta put her forehead against Liz's. "Oh, my dear girl, what have I done?"

"Mom, what are you talking about? Have you seen something? Is it Prisha? Is she okay? She was sick last week, but she's better now. Mom, what is it? You're scaring me."

"Darling, take a deep breath. I have no information about the child. I sensed that you had some secret that you weren't sharing with us, but I didn't want to pry. I knew you'd tell me when the time was right. I'm sure the child is fine."

"But something is wrong. I can feel it."

Yetta folded her hands in her lap and looked at them. "I hadn't realized that you blamed yourself for Ernst's passing. You left here to mourn him, and I was glad for that. I was too incapacitated to be much help to you. But, Elizabeth," her mother looked Liz straight in the eye and said, "your father is not the man in your prophecy."

Liz's heart made a funny, painful twitter. "Sure he is. It fits. Think about it. He was the light of our world and after his stroke everything changed."

Yetta slowly shook her head.

"But, Mom, if Dad wasn't the one then…"

The door to the room suddenly flew open. Alex rushed inside and looked around. "Liz, thank God, come with me. We have to find your date."

"Why?"

"Zeke just got a call. Apparently, David's house is on fire."

Liz looked at her mother. *A man of darkness. A child of light. You'll only be able to save one.*

"Oh, God, no. Not David."

Her mother nodded, almost imperceptibly, but the truth suddenly seemed so obvious.

What did she know about David? Practically nothing. He was an intriguing puzzle, a wounded soul who had appealed to that part of her that was always on the lookout for someone to fix.

She'd played right into fate's hand, hadn't she? She'd let herself believe that she was safe from her potentially tragic either-or prophecy. That she finally had a chance at the whole enchilada—a decent man who really mattered to her and a child who needed her. But no. Life was never that simple, was it?

"Liz, snap out of it. David is going to need your help."

Liz looked at her mother. It was on the tip of her tongue

to say, "No way. Help him yourself." But she suddenly knew the gesture would be futile. She'd welcomed the man of shadows into her life. There was no turning back.

"Your sister is right," Yetta said, standing up. "You need to do the right thing by him. You brought him to Katherine's wedding and that makes his concerns our concerns. We aren't the kind of people who turn away from someone in need."

Liz started to protest—one date didn't mean they were bound for life, but her mother turned to look at Alex. "Alexandra, I want you to go with them. I need to stay for the rest of the festivities. This is my place, but Elizabeth needs your help. Make sure she brings David back to the Compound. If the fire is bad, he'll need a place to stay."

"No. Mom. No. That's not a good idea," Liz protested.

Her mother gave Alex a look both sisters knew meant they'd better do as she said…or else.

Alex took Liz's hand and led her toward the exterior door. "Come on. Let's get this over with. I don't know why I have to be the one to go with you, but, at least, my date left early so I don't have to worry about abandoning him."

Liz didn't have time to ask about the story there. She'd spotted David talking with Zeke and knew that he'd already heard the news. This wasn't about her or her prophecy anymore. This was about a man with very little to lose finding out he'd just lost everything.

Chapter Eleven

The fire was pretty much out by the time she, Alex and David arrived on the scene. The smoke in the air was strong enough to bring tears to her eyes. Or maybe the tears were from the loss that she saw everywhere. Most of the roof of the house had fallen in. The blackened timbers that remained were still smoldering.

David had rushed off to check on his landlady, an old woman with frizzy red hair who was clinging to his arm as if he was the last person on earth. Liz was standing alone near the eight-foot-tall hedge waiting for Alex, who'd returned to the car to call Yetta with an update. She'd lost track of Zeke, who had followed them in his own car.

She wasn't sure what to do or how to help, and was startled when a voice said, "Liz? Hey, it is you. This is a shock. What are you doing here?"

Liz wiped her eyes and turned to look at the man addressing her. His regulation turnout jacket was open to reveal street clothes. His voice was familiar but it still took a few seconds to place him. "Mark," she exclaimed. "I didn't recognize you. When did you become a fireman?"

"Arson investigator. I sort have one foot in both camps."

Mark Gaylord. Alex's ex-fiancé. The man who broke

her sister's heart by marrying another woman. His partner. Who'd been pregnant with his child.

No way. The chances of Mark Gaylord working a fire where she and her sister were both present...in a city the size of Las Vegas...on the same night their sister got married. She let out a low groan. *Mother.*

"Seriously, Liz. What are you doing here?"

Liz didn't know where to begin. Instead of trying, she asked, "You suspect this was arson?"

"The neighbor who called it in—actually, I guess she owns this place, too—said she saw a man running away just minutes before the explosion."

"What explosion?"

"Gas water heater is my guess. My team is going to be sifting through the rubble trying to figure out if there was a faulty switch or something."

Or something?

She looked to where David was standing—near the burned-out shell of his pickup truck. Outwardly, she couldn't tell what was going on in his head. He hadn't seemed panicked when she and Alex approached him and Zeke. In fact, he'd insisted on going with Zeke alone. "Both of you should stay. This is a special night. I don't want to ruin the occasion."

Alex, in her usual take-charge attitude, had overridden his concerns by producing Liz's purse and keys, which Yetta must have handed to her, and hustling them all to the street. Cars were everywhere, but Liz's little SUV was conveniently parked and ready to go.

Alex had even volunteered to drive, as if sensing that Liz's usual rock-solid grace-under-pressure was missing. Stoic and calm. Usually, those were her strong points. But not tonight. Not after the revelation her mother had dropped in Liz's lap.

Finding out that her comfortable belief about her father being her "man of darkness" was a lie had been like being told the bomb in her purse was live after all. And could go off at any second.

"You still haven't told me what you're doing here," Mark said, pulling her attention back to the present. "How do you know this guy?"

"He's a landscaper who did some work in my subdivision and he was my date to the wedding."

"A wedding, huh? Who got married?"

Although the question carried no real inflection of emotion, Liz sensed that Mark's curiosity was more than professional. "Kate. She married a lawyer. Grace is next up in the spring. She's marrying a cop. Strange twist of fate, huh?"

They both knew how much Ernst had lobbied against his eldest daughter dating Mark, who had been a rookie police officer at the time. Liz hadn't been around during the tumultuous period of Mark's defection, although she'd heard all the devastating details after the fact. Mark was a jerk, in her family's opinion, but at this moment, he was just a guy doing his job. And the sooner he left to do that job, the better for all concerned.

She looked around him toward the street, hoping Alex was still on the phone. The last thing her sister needed was to bump into her ex. Alex had moved on. Mark had married his partner. They had a kid together. End of story.

Or was it?

"A gardener, huh? What else do you know about him? How long has he been in town? Does he gamble? Any known enemies? Any reason someone would want to kill him?"

She suddenly wrapped her arms around her middle to ward off the chill. "Kill?"

His right shoulder lifted and fell. "Small place. Water heater's right next to his bedroom. If he'd been sleeping, he'd be dead."

The words seemed to echo in the night. She didn't want David dead—just out of her life so that she wouldn't have to choose. *A man of shadows. A child of light. You can only save one.*

"He grows cactus," she said, mostly to herself. Looking across the open space that just two days earlier had seemed so peaceful, she couldn't locate David at first, but a second later he and Zeke walked out from behind a large pumper that blocked her view of the greenhouse. Someone had told her the larger building had sustained some water damage, but thanks to its metal roof had escaped complete destruction.

Both men looked serious, and appeared to be arguing. Forgetting about Mark, she started toward them.

"Whoa, stay here, Liz," he said, grabbing her arm. "It's easy to trip over a hose or get run over during a mop-up. Your boyfriend will be here in a minute."

"He's just a friend. An acquaintance," she stressed, wishing the word could make it true. "Do you have any idea what it's like to show up at a Rom wedding without a date?"

His scowl told her the question had hit home.

"No, of course, he doesn't," another voice answered. "The only Rom wedding he was invited to was called off, remember? After he found out he'd gotten another woman, someone other than his fiancée, pregnant."

Mark blanched visibly and turned to look at Alex, who was standing a foot away, arms crossed like an Amazon warrior who was about to crucify her enemy. Liz was sure she heard a very soft groan coming from Mark, but before either could speak, Zeke joined them, David at his side.

"Liz," Zeke said. "Your mother said to bring this guy back to her place. I'm not wild about the idea."

"You're taking him to the Compound?" Mark asked. "Why?"

"That's none of your business," Alex answered.

Liz could tell Mark thought David's presence in the Radonovic family was a mistake, and she had to agree. Even if the fire had been an accident, it was becoming increasingly obvious that David had secrets, and everyone knew that secrets flourished in the shadows. *A man of shadows.* She couldn't afford to become involved in his life, his problems. She had to stay focused on her goal. Her main goal. Her only goal. Prisha needed her. If she could only save one…

"Zeke's right," David said. "I'll be just fine in a motel."

Zeke looked at Mark. The two appeared to know each other, which didn't surprise Liz. Mark had also been a cop. She wondered whether her mother told Zeke about her eldest daughter's near-miss at matrimony—and the anguish that resulted from Mark's defection. Probably, but Liz couldn't tell from their body language. Nor did she care. This wasn't about Mark and Alex. It was about David—the topic of a low, intense conversation between the two law enforcement officers.

"My gut says this was set."

"I agree. The question is why and who profits?"

"Exactly. But this guy is a renter. His landlady doesn't even know if the place is insured. And the only loss is some secondhand furniture and a rattletrap truck."

"Hey," Liz protested without thinking. "That's a man's life and livelihood you're disparaging."

Zeke looked at her. "Tell that to your pal, who seems to be suffering from amnesia about everything that happened before he arrived in Vegas."

Liz looked at David whose stubborn frown was easy to read, even in the harsh shadows cast by the fire equipment. She realized they'd reached an impasse. Looking to her sister for help, she said, "Mom wants us to bring David back to the house, right? Fine. Let's do that. He doesn't have to stay if he doesn't want to. And Zeke, you can use the time to decide whether or not you want to arrest him, okay? I promise he won't go anywhere until you make up your mind."

"I don't like it," Mark said. "If someone wants him dead, his presence in the Compound puts your whole family in danger."

"Yeah, well, that's our problem. You're not a part of this family, remember?" Alex said. Even in the dim light, her regal dismissal was clear.

Zeke stepped between Alex and Mark. "Don't worry. Nick, the guy Grace is going to marry, is a cop. He and I are both going to be on the premises tonight." *Zeke is staying at Mom's?* Liz and Alex looked at each other in surprise. "Plus, I'll get a couple of patrols to add the Compound to their rounds."

Liz sensed that a decision had been made and each of the five was giving in—for different reasons. Personally, the noise, the smoke, the stress reminded her too much of a war zone. She couldn't wait to get away from it.

As she trudged to the car—David and Alex following a few steps behind, she made a new plan. First, she'd drop David off at her mother's, then she'd go home to bed. Alone. Not the way she'd first pictured the evening ending, but…

On the drive back, Alex, who was sitting in the rear this time, asked David about Zeke's attitude. He was scrunched low in the passenger seat, his gaze pinned to the side mirror. "Surely he doesn't suspect you of setting the fire? You were at the wedding the whole time."

"No. He doesn't think that."

"Then why was he so hostile?"

"Because I'm an enigma. Cops don't like things they can't label or check off in a box. White male, check. DOB—ten, twelve, whatever, check. SSN—a number that matches the name and date of birth he already has. That sort of thing."

"And some of your boxes don't match." It wasn't a question.

His soft sigh told her he was tired of pretending. "None of them match."

A part of Liz's mind acknowledged that receiving information like that could get a person killed in some circles, but she wasn't afraid of this man—even if his boxes didn't jibe.

He sat upright and reached over to place a hand on Liz's arm. "I think for your own safety, you should stop the car and let me out."

Liz glanced around. They were near the Stratosphere. The freeway wasn't far. The always-busy downtown area—a popular tourist attraction—was within walking distance. But at this time of night, the streets weren't safe for a man alone. "Not on your life."

He leaned closer. "What about on your mother's? Or your sister's?" She sensed him looking behind her to address Alex. "Zeke said Grace and her fiancé are staying at your mom's. Your niece will be around, too, I presume. Are you certain you want to put them all in jeopardy?"

Liz looked in the rearview mirror. She could almost hear her sister's change of heart. "Those are valid points, but I'm too tired to fight about this. Mother wants you there. What you do after we drop you off is your business."

David gave up arguing. She was right. He was free to

slip away once he'd had his little talk with Zeke—a talk David knew there was no way to avoid. He just wished he'd handled things differently. Regret and self-recrimination made him want to hit something. He'd blown it big-time. He'd waited too long, and, now, this strong and generous woman and her family were in danger.

He hadn't seen any sign of a tail. Maybe the bomber thought David was dead. Maybe he wouldn't know otherwise until he read about the fire in the morning news. Maybe.

But David was pretty sure Ray was involved. Ray, who paid attention to every little detail would have stuck around to watch the coroner haul David's dead body away.

That scenario meant Liz and her family were at risk. And that wasn't okay. Because David cared about her. In another life, he probably would have fallen deeply, irrevocably in love with her. Which might explain why he wanted to tell her the truth before he left. To clear the air between them before he took off for good.

"So, who was that fireman you were arguing with?" he asked. "He seemed to know a lot about your family."

Liz gave a nervous chuckle and glanced in the mirror at her sister in the backseat. "He should. He dated Alex for almost two years, right?"

"We were engaged. Until he got another woman pregnant," Alex said.

"Oh. Sorry."

"Yeah, me, too."

"But Mark did tell me your landlady saw somebody running away before the explosion." She suddenly stomped on the brakes, throwing David and Alex forward.

"What?" Alex cried.

"I just remembered about David's cat. We should turn around and go look for him."

Her concern touched him deeply. His throat muscles seemed unusually tense when he told her, "I asked the firemen. There wasn't any sign of him. Dead or alive. Mrs. Simms, my landlady, is going to keep an eye out for him."

Liz let out a sigh. "Thank goodness."

"Scar's a street cat. He probably saw the guy messing with the water heater and figured it was a good time to make himself scarce."

"Scar?"

"He's seen his share of battles."

Nobody spoke again until they reached the cul-de-sac where Liz stopped to let Alex out. In the glow from the headlights, David could see a chain-link fence and a purple-and-pink sign that read The Dancing Hippo. The two sisters exchanged words in a low murmur David couldn't interpret.

A moment later, Liz parked in front of a ranch house a few doors down. "Apparently, Mom isn't back yet. Come on. Let's go in and figure out what's going on."

David followed her inside, only because she didn't leave him any choice. Most of his options—certainly his carefully laid plans—had burned up in the fire, but he wasn't helpless. He had a few bucks in his pocket, but maybe a cup of coffee to clear his head…

The first thing Liz did upon entering her mother's kitchen was fill an electric kettle with water. Next, she called her mother on the phone. The wedding, he gathered, was dwindling down.

"Mom and Grace and Nick will be here shortly," she said.

"Where's your niece staying? Surely, she's not going on the honeymoon."

She took a large, cloth bag filled with some kind of tea, he surmised, and placed it in a squatty ceramic teapot. "No," she said, not looking at him. "Maya's spending the next few days with Jo. Rob's mother. Jo has a dog that Maya's quite attached to. This should be a good bonding experience for all three of them."

Rather than waste what private time they had in small talk, David decided to tell Liz the truth. "My name wasn't always David Baines. It used to be Paul McAffee."

Liz turned around so swiftly she accidentally bumped into the counter. He reached out and took her hand and led her to the table. She started to sit down, but returned quickly to where she'd been standing and reached for the teapot. "Just a sec. This needs to brew."

The minute she was sitting down, David said, "I used to live and work on the East Coast in a highly competitive industry where there was a lot of money to be made if you didn't mind sidestepping a few government safeguards. My boss was that kind of man. When I decided my conscience wouldn't let me risk poisoning a million unsuspecting consumers, I took my proof to the Justice Department. My life changed overnight. And my boss, the man who should have paid for this travesty, lawyered up. He bought just enough time to disappear—after making it clear that he planned to kill me for turning him in."

"You're a whistle-blower?"

"So they say."

"And you think what happened tonight is tied to your past?"

He nodded.

Neither spoke for a minute or so, then Liz asked softly, "Can you talk about your other life? Or is it… like…classified?"

He had no idea where he stood with the government. He hadn't talked to anyone about what had happened to him since the day he'd parted ways with WITSEC. Soon, he'd be another person. This could easily be his only chance to leave behind a record that Paul McAffee had existed.

Once he started talking, he couldn't seem to stop. He told her about his ex-wife and her children. About feeling blue the day he'd yelled at Liz over the cactus because of his little girl's birthday. About the good he'd hoped to accomplish in his career and how those dreams had been destroyed by a bastard who only thought of money. His dreams had gone up in smoke when his laboratory burned—and the irony wasn't lost on him that the new life he'd created from scratch had met a similar fate.

In the process of opening up to Liz, he managed to drink a couple of cups of her tea. He'd never taken his tea with honey and milk but discovered he liked it that way, despite the brew's unusual aroma. When her family returned from the wedding, she kept them at a distance with just a nod of her head. She listened to his story and added only a question or two for clarity. And when he ran out of words, she reached across the table and said, "You need to stay here tonight."

He didn't have the energy to argue. His confession had left him feeling drained. Yes, a couple of hours of sleep would be good, he thought. *I'll set my watch alarm for three, then slip away in the night.*

But when he looked at his wrist, his watch was gone. That was when he remembered taking it off and placing it on this bedside table because it had looked too cheap to wear with his new shirt.

Oh, well, he thought, I'm a light sleeper. I'll wake up on my own. No use putting these kind folks in danger for any longer than absolutely necessary.

LIZ PUT DAVID in Kate's old room and closed the door. He'd declined the use of a pair of her father's pajamas, but had smiled his thanks when she'd pointed out the extra toothbrushes her mother kept in a drawer in the main bath.

He wouldn't be there when she returned in the morning. She was certain of that, but, at least, he'd get a few hours of deep, dreamless sleep. The tea she'd brewed contained jatamamsi, brahmi, cardamom and rose petals, to which she'd added milk and honey to mitigate the strong taste of the herbs.

She'd created the special sleep formula for her mother who several months earlier had complained of disturbing dreams and too many sleepless nights. She closed the door and started toward the front of the house, intending to head home, but paused when she heard voices coming from the patio. Her mother and Zeke were sitting side by side in the glider. Several candles in hurricane lanterns gave the area a romantic glow.

Liz was happy that her mother had found a man who interested her. Whether or not the relationship would lead anywhere, she couldn't guess. The two came from such different worlds. The odds were against them, but at least Zeke didn't have a madman on his back lusting for revenge.

Nope, leave it to me to fall for a guy whose shadowy past includes a killer who likes to play with matches.

Liz started away, but stopped when she heard her name. "Elizabeth."

She popped her head out the sliding glass door. "Just leaving, Mom. David's asleep."

"Come here, dear. Just for a minute. I know you're tired, but Zeke and I were discussing your prophecy."

"Mother, I really wish you wouldn't. That's personal."

Yetta made a negating motion with her hand. "But hardly a secret. You and your sisters used to make up wild stories about the men who would someday come into your lives. Yours was always by far the most tragic and dramatic. Do you remember?"

Vaguely. Although there had been one story that had haunted her dreams for weeks. In it, she'd married her very own Mr. Rochester, only instead of a wife in the attic, he'd had a child. A son, who his father claimed wasn't right in the head. When the mansion they'd been living in caught on fire, she'd had to choose between rescuing the man or the boy. She never seemed to make the right choice. If she saved the man, he'd slowly go crazy with grief and guilt. If she saved the boy, he would grow up hating her for not saving his father.

"Sorta."

"David and I are going to have a long talk in the morning," Zeke said.

I wouldn't bet on it, Liz thought, but didn't say aloud.

"I'm going home."

"I'd rather you stayed here, dear. You can have Maya's room since she's spending the weekend with her new grandmother."

"I'll sleep better in my own bed."

"Please, darling. If you leave, Ezekiel will feel compelled to follow you home, and he and the others were up much too late last night at Rob's bachelor party. That's why he's staying next door tonight. Since Jurek wasn't feeling up to making the trip with Nikolai and Grace, we have an extra bed."

Liz was certain her mother was describing the sleeping arrangements to allay any fears her daughter might have about another man taking her father's place. Liz cared, but at the moment she was too tired and emotionally depleted to worry about such things.

"Plus, your mother tells me your roommates are out of town for the week," Zeke said. "Do you really think it's a good idea to be alone tonight?"

That gave Liz pause. So much had happened, she'd almost forgotten about Lydia and Reezira. Thanks to the Internet, the two had connected with family members of Reezira's who lived in Phoenix. Although the girls had been invited to the wedding and regretted not having more time to spend with Grace, they'd gleefully boarded the bus early yesterday morning—excited about a chance to see more of America.

Zeke had a point. Suddenly the idea of an empty house didn't sound too attractive. "Okay. Can I borrow a nightgown?"

"Of course."

Zeke followed them inside. While her mother went to her room, Liz used the opportunity to ask him, "What did David tell you about his past?"

"Not enough. How 'bout you?"

"Too much," she said, shaking her head. *Was this his way of telling me goodbye?* She feared so.

"He should have stayed in the Witness Protection Program. Turning down the government's help…" He shook his head. "Alone, you're a sitting duck."

Well, she wasn't the government. She couldn't protect a man who didn't want help, but even if she could, she had Prisha to worry about. A vulnerable child whose future was in jeopardy. Liz had to get her out of the orphanage. Her choice was obvious, wasn't it?

Chapter Twelve

David opened his eyes to light. He sat up in bed and looked around. Pale peach walls. A woman's room. He knew instantly that his plan to wake up in the middle of the night and sneak out had failed. Today was Sunday. The day after the wedding—and the fire.

He exhaled loudly and sank back down to the pillow. He was still dressed in the same clothes he'd worn to the wedding. The only clothes he presently owned. His carefully packed backpack filled with all the stuff he needed to survive in the desert had been hidden behind the seat of his truck. Gone. Just like his house.

Fortunately, he still had his buried waterproof stashes of money waiting to be picked up. Unfortunately, without his truck and tools, he'd look rather suspicious if he started digging around plants with his bare hands, especially dressed as he was.

Pushing up, he put his feet on the floor and looked around for his shoes. He rested his elbows on his knees and tried to jumpstart his brain. "What the hell is wrong with me?"

"You probably need caffeine to offset the effects of Elizabeth's tea," a voice said.

He looked over his shoulder and found Yetta standing

in the doorway with a tray. It even included a white rose in a cobalt-blue vase. He quickly stood up. "Oh, please, no bother. Not for me. I shouldn't even be here."

"You're my guest. We'll talk while you eat and then you can decide where you're in such a hurry to be off to."

She placed the tray on the bed and motioned for him to sit down beside it. His mouth watered at the delicious smells of bacon and maple syrup. He was starved and couldn't resist tasting the thick, golden brown French toast. The hint of cinnamon enticed him to take a second bite. And a third.

"What do you want to know?" he asked. "I told your daughter everything about my past last night."

"That's good. There shouldn't be such big secrets between people who love each other."

"L-love?" he sputtered, nearly choking on the bite he'd just swallowed. "She…we…no, I think you're mistaken."

She smiled serenely. In the bright light streaming through the east-facing window, he could see lines on her face that he hadn't noticed before. But in her Middle Eastern–print caftan, with her long, wavy silver hair hugging her shoulders, she looked exotic and youthful.

"Perhaps. It wouldn't be the first time, but Elizabeth and I have always shared a special bond. I knew the moment a brutal pain entered her life—even though she's only recently revealed what happened. And I felt a renewed lightness about her after she met you. If not love, then something very similar to it exists between you. Deep fondness, perhaps."

Deep fondness. Did lust qualify under that header? Probably not. "Your daughter is a remarkable person. I am…*fond* of her and I wouldn't want to see her get hurt, which is why I'm leaving. Right after breakfast. This is delicious, by the way."

"I'm glad you're enjoying it. I miss being able to watch a man dig into a hearty breakfast. The girls' father was a big eater. He gobbled up life and seemed to radiate the energy that he got from the food like a small sun. It's not surprising she misread her prophecy."

Her tone held a reflective quality, as if the thought just now made sense to her. He didn't want to talk about Liz's future, since he was pretty sure he wasn't going to be a part of it. He shook his head and picked up the coffee mug on the tray. "This isn't drugged, is it?"

Yetta threw back her head and laughed. "Of course not. And neither was your tea last night. Elizabeth told me she used the tea bags she'd made for me when I was having trouble sleeping. The herbs encourage relaxation, and because the fire was so traumatic, she was afraid you'd spend the whole night fretting."

He took a gulp of the strong black brew. "Where is Liz? Did she get home safely?"

"She slept right next door to you. In Maya's room. Now she's out back talking to Ezekiel. She and Grace just got done trying to outswim each other. I've somehow managed to raise a very competitive bunch of girls."

Shaking her head, she picked up the tray and started to leave, but paused to say, "I left a fresh razor on the bathroom counter and one of Ernst's old shirts on a hanger behind the door. It's clean and pressed. I'm afraid his pants won't fit. You're much taller and thinner." She smiled. "But I don't think he would have held that against you. In fact, I think my husband would have liked you."

How is that possible? David asked himself. *I don't even know who am I—or who I'm going to be next.* True, he'd set up one possibility, but, with Ray on his heels, David wasn't sure he trusted that identity, either. As soon as he left this house, he planned to disappear. How could her late husband possibly have approved of that?

"HE STOOD UP for what he believed in. How can that be wrong?"

"Liz is right, Zeke. You're making David sound like some kind of criminal. He got out of a bad situation without selling poison to the innocent masses. Tell me why we shouldn't be carrying him around on our shoulders?"

Liz looked at Grace with such a burst of love she almost hugged her, but since they were both resting their forearms against the block-wall fence between their mother's and uncle's backyards, she didn't. As they had every morning since Grace returned, the two had met for a sunrise swim.

"I didn't say he was evil. I said he ditched the identity the government set up. That makes him suspect."

"Or really smart," Liz returned.

Grace nodded with a wink. To Zeke, she said, "So what are you suggesting? We keep him here until the bad guy shows up and tries to kill him? Sounds a bit...problematic...as Alex would say."

Zeke didn't answer.

"Oh, my God, that's your plan, isn't it?"

He had dark glasses on so she couldn't see his eyes, but the crinkles on either side of the shades deepened so she knew he was squinting in thought. "His greenhouse wasn't ruined. He could stay there with protection. From what I've been able to find out, this guy who's after him is a real hothead. People like that are usually fairly easy to catch."

"Before or after they kill their target?" Grace quipped.

Liz held up her hand for a high five.

"He wouldn't be at any greater risk here than he would on the run. Paranoid people make mistakes."

"Tell that to Paul McAffee," a deep voice said.

Liz and Grace both turned to look at the man standing behind them. "Who's Paul McAffee?" Grace asked.

"The person I used to be," David said, stepping closer.

Liz could see that he'd shaved the sides of his face and chin. He'd also changed into a short-sleeve shirt that seemed familiar. He looked like an ordinary guy who couldn't possibly be the person they'd just been talking about—a research scientist who once worked for a madman out to poison the world.

"I'm leaving," he said, looking at Zeke, not her. "There's no reason to put these good people at risk."

Grace stepped close and put her arm across Liz's shoulder. They'd both wrapped beach towels around themselves after exiting the pool. The morning breeze, although warming up, left a trail of gooseflesh across Liz's shoulders. The display of nerves matched the uneasiness racing through her insides.

She wanted him to leave. Leaving was good, right? Then why did hearing him say the words make her want to cry?

"It's your call, but I've always believed facing your enemy makes it a helluva lot easier to sleep at night," Zeke said.

"Our father used to say, 'Hold your friends close and your enemies closer,'" Grace added. "Remember, Liz?"

Maybe. But surely that didn't apply to a stranger who accidentally showed up in their midst bringing the threat of fire and destruction?

Grace jostled Liz slightly and added under her breath, "And Mother always says there's no such thing as an accidental meeting. People come into our lives for a reason."

Liz pulled back and snarled, "I really hate it when you do that."

"Do what?" Grace blinked with a smile too innocent to be real. Nobody really believed in Grace's ability to read minds, but she was extremely astute at guessing what her sisters were thinking. And she'd nailed Liz's thoughts this time.

Was David here for a reason? Was he the man from her prophecy? The possibility confounded her, frightened her. "I have to go," she said. "The cats are all alone and probably need food. Plus, I have some tea orders to fill."

"And you're swinging by my office later, right?" Zeke asked, his tone more of an order than a question. They'd discussed his request before Grace had shown up to swim. He wanted Liz to let him put a global positioning system responder on her car…just in case.

For a private person like Liz, that was asking a lot, but she was really too worn down at the moment to argue. She'd spent a miserable night torn between dreams of losing Prisha and chasing after a man who wove through the shadows like a ghost. "Yeah, sure. Whatever." To Grace, she said, "I'll be back around two to take you and Nick to the airport, okay?"

"We'll be ready. Nikolai suggested we take a taxi, but once I made it clear I wasn't driving, he was happy. He said he hadn't gotten to spend enough time with you, so this will be nice."

Liz started away but stopped. She couldn't leave things totally in the air between her and David. "Mom has my number. I know you'll be busy sorting out stuff with Zeke and at your place, but if you get a chance, we should probably talk."

His too-black mustache wiggled slightly giving the hint of a smile. "Sure thing. And, uh, thanks for the tea last night."

His tone was so intimate she almost blushed. She knew what he meant. She'd more or less drugged him. For his own good. She dashed off, tiptoeing around puddles left on the concrete by the automatic sprinklers. Today was going to be rough, and negotiating the safest path through obstacles seemed to be her fate.

FOUR HOURS LATER, David was grimy and disgusted. He'd let Zeke Martini talk him into sticking around—at least temporarily. Was that smart? Hell, no. But his plan to leave had been severely compromised, and the guy was right about one thing: running away without a plan in place was utter foolishness.

But so was hanging out with Liz and her family. He had no intention of doing that. Mimi, his landlady, had coughed up a World War II–era cot and some bedding that David set up in the potting shed, the one building left completely untouched by the fire and water. Yetta had donated an over-size cooler filled with ice, water, juices and snacks, which Zeke had delivered an hour earlier. And, an even bigger surprise, a couple of stores that he frequented in the neigh-borhood, had donated food, beer and money to help him get back on his feet.

The only thing he lacked at the moment was transpor-tation and a shower. And a phone. He'd told Liz he'd keep her informed about his situation. He could flag down one of the undercover units staking out his place, but that was probably tacky, he decided.

He went to the cooler and took out a beer. He tossed back the bottle and chugged a long, refreshing drink—and almost fumbled the bottle when he felt something touch his ankles.

A rasping purr filled the small space. "Meow."

"Well, what do you know," he exclaimed. David hadn't

seen Scar at all. He'd halfway decided the cat was gone for good. "Glad to see you made it, buddy."

He sat down on his makeshift bed and bent over to pet the animal. No evidence of singed fur, he was pleased to note. "I hate to tell you this, but your cat food got burnt up, bud. There's a little bit of kibble left in that bowl on the workbench, but that's it."

"Meow."

The cat sprang to the mattress and rubbed up against David's side. He'd never known the animal to be so affectionate. Had the fire scared him? Maybe the poor guy was tired of being alone and had thought he'd lost his only friend in the world. The thought made David's throat close up.

They sat there like that until the crunching sound of car tires on gravel made the cat hop to the ground and disappear under the bed. David stood up, his nerves humming. He didn't expect Ray to drive up, guns blazing, but you never knew.

Not Ray. Liz. *Next worst thing,* he murmured under his breath. He couldn't pretend that a part of him wasn't overjoyed to see her, but the realist inside him wanted to shut the door and pretend to be gone.

She got out of the car and waved. *Too late.*

"Hey, I just left Zeke. He said you'd decided to stick around a few days. Good. I'm glad."

He shrugged. "My truck isn't going anywhere. Fast."

They both looked at the burned-out shell.

"That's why I'm here. Zeke said you'd probably appreciate a shower and a decent meal. So come on. Let's go."

"That's not a good idea."

She stopped in her tracks and turned to face him. "Why not? I'm taking you to my house, not Mom's. I have a high-tech alarm on the doors and windows. Zeke's planted some kind of bug in my car. I know self-defense." She dropped into an exaggerated pose that made him chuckle. "I'm not the chef my sister is, but I promise not to drug or poison you."

He hesitated. The idea of crawling into his miserable little cot without a shower wasn't too appealing. And they could probably stop at a store on the way back for some decent cat food for Scar.

"Oh, that reminds me," she exclaimed. "I brought your cat a couple of cans of food from home. I hope he's not too picky."

She dashed to the car and returned with a selection of beef, chicken and fish-flavored meals.

"How'd you know he was back?"

She paused. "I didn't. He is, though, right?"

David nodded.

"Good. Then, shall we feed him and leave? I have short ribs in the Crock-Pot, but I still need to make a salad."

He took a deep breath. The smell of burned wood was etched into his nostrils and he nearly gagged. He needed a break—if only to breathe fresh air. And she was offering food to boot. His stomach made a sound very similar to Scar's plaintive mewl. She wanted to feed him, and damned if he could say no.

Chapter Thirteen

Dinner was a simple affair. Beef, lots of it. Succulent and tender, seasoned with a soy barbecue sauce of Kate's. Salad topped with Romantique's house dressing and fresh bread she'd picked up when she'd stopped for the cat food. She'd lied about taking cans from her roommates' stash. She hadn't wanted David to think she'd gone to a lot of effort. After all, she hadn't been sure he'd accept her invitation.

But he'd come.

He'd made use of her shower and changed into clothes provided by Kate—or, rather, Rob. The newlyweds had spent the first night of their honeymoon in their new home and were presently winging their way to Tahiti—a wedding gift from Rob's father and his wife. Before leaving for the airport, Kate had called to tell Liz that Rob, who was similar in height and build to David, had left a bag of clothes on the porch.

Liz had been touched that the couple had taken the time and effort to help out a relative stranger. Not that she was surprised. Roms were by nature a generous lot, and it didn't take much to make a person "family." Just knowing your sister cared for a guy could mean he was one of them, apparently.

"More wine?" she asked.

They were dining at a wrought-iron café table in her backyard. Twilight had descended and she'd lit two fat candles on a nearby hand-me-down baker's rack that she'd spray-painted brick-red. Her collection of plants was nothing compared to David's, but the spider plant on the top shelf was lush, with tiny white flowers and oodles of babies.

He held out his glass. "This is good. What is it?"

She showed him the label. Chianti that she'd stocked up on when the liquor store near her mom's had held a going-out-of-business sale.

"Everything is delicious. I haven't had a meal like this since…well, last night," he said with a grin.

Liz laughed. The food at the wedding had been phenomenal, she had to agree. "My sister is an amazing chef. I'm surprised you've never eaten at Romantique before."

"I never met anyone I wanted to take to dinner," he said, simply. "Until you."

His wistful tone grabbed her by the imagination and wouldn't let go. She'd been picturing their could-have-beens all day. They could have been lovers. They could have laughed and teased and played together. They could have gardened, replanted her yard and really driven up the value of her house to impress those darn appraisers.

She still hadn't heard back from the bank about her loan. Her gut said it was hopeless. Even if she got the money to initiate the home study and start the paperwork necessary for a foreign adoption, there was still the cost of getting Prisha to the United States, once the adoption was approved.

"Where are your roommates?" David asked, bringing her back to the present.

"Visiting Reezira's family in Arizona. Her aunt sent both girls bus tickets. They were so excited. These past months they've been in a kind of legal limbo, not knowing if they're coming or going. Canada doesn't want them back. Romania doesn't give a damn about them. And the U.S. immigration is dithering because of 9/11."

He nodded. "I understand completely. I had to deal with a lot of conflicting information when I first contacted the Justice Department. With the advent of Homeland Security, the communication between government agencies has gotten more complicated. Doing business with any branch can be very frustrating."

"Do you regret it?"

"Selling out my boss? No. Giving up my life? Hell, yes."

"What would you be doing right now if you were Paul McAffee, instead of David Baines?"

His hand seemed to flinch when she used his real name, but his voice remained impassive when he said, "Working in my lab."

"On a Sunday evening?"

He nodded. "I was the guy who gave workaholics a bad name."

No wonder your wife divorced you, she almost said.

"My values changed for a while right after I got married. Having kids around was a real treat, and I made an effort to get home in time for dinner at least four days a week."

Her look must have been obvious because he laughed and said, "I know. Pathetic, right? At the time, it felt like a huge concession. No wonder my wife got involved with the guy next door."

She winced. "Nobody deserves that. I mean, if she wanted a change, she could have suggested counseling or something."

He smiled and took another sip of wine. "She did. I was too busy. By then, I had a pretty good idea that the wonder drug my boss was pushing through clinical trials was a disaster waiting to happen."

"You had to deal with your wife's defection, a divorce and your life's work disintegrating all at the same time? Wow. How'd you keep it together?"

He snickered softly. "Who said I did?"

Neither spoke for a minute or two, then David said, "I guess the drama in the lab had me so shook up it sort of lessened the blow of Kay's leaving me. She'd only been gone about six months when it became obvious that what was happening at Norcross, the company I worked for, was going to end badly. At that point, I became completely preoccupied with getting out alive."

Impulsively, she reached out and covered the hand resting on the table. "I was in a situation like that once. The mind is an amazingly adaptive organ. Your focus shifts and tightens when self-preservation is on the line."

He turned his hand palm up and squeezed her fingers gently. "Can you talk about what happened?"

"You already know the gist of it. I was attacked by two men. They seemed to materialize out of the shadows. I walked the same path every day and had never been threatened. I honestly felt sure the red cross on my jacket made me invincible." She laughed at her naiveté.

"I've never understood bullies—even though I worked for one. He was a corporate shark, dressed in designer suits and Italian shoes. He paid lip service to community and social issues and women's rights, but he drove a Hummer, he hated minorities—even though he's part Hispanic—and he only dated very young women with very large…bank accounts. Don't ask me what they saw in him."

"He sounds as if he was on a real power trip."

David nodded. "If the drug had lived up to its hype, he stood to make billions, worldwide."

"How much would you have made?"

The question seemed to surprise him. "A lot. Tens of millions, I suppose."

His honest answer touched her deeply. The fact that he'd given up a fortune to do the right thing made him so dear to her, she could barely swallow. This was a man she could love. Maybe she already did. Even though she knew he was leaving. Heck, she wanted him to go. But she also needed him to stay. Tonight, at least.

She stood up and waited for him to stand, too. "Sleep here tonight. With me. No strings. No commitments. Just two people who have seen the dark side and need a little comfort."

"No. It's too dangerous."

She threw back her head and laughed. "I promise to go easy on you. Come on. We'll turn on the alarm and shut out the world for a few hours."

DAVID WATCHED HER push the code into the electronic box in the hallway. Deep down he knew that no home alarm could protect them from a man like his former boss, but the patrol car he'd seen cruise past an hour earlier might do the trick. Either way, he was prepared to turn off his mind and listen to his heart. If Ray had his way, David would be dead soon. This could very well be his last chance to live, to love.

And he knew he did love Liz. He liked her, respected her and, in a perfect world, would have courted her and told her what he felt for her. But his world was far from perfect. So, he wouldn't burden her with his feelings, but he would take what she was offering.

The moment she was done setting the alarm, he caught her hand and pulled her against him. She smelled like teriyaki and candle wax, fresh air and Liz. He buried his nose in her hair and nuzzled her ear.

She didn't hesitate. She pressed against him, making him to step back. The wall stopped their momentum.

Blood pumped through his veins with a force that made his ears ring. Too long without. His needs were great. His body craved fast and furious, but David wanted this to be good for Liz, too. He tried to slow things down. "Which of these doors leads to your room?"

She looked at him and smiled. "You're afraid I'm going to break, or be traumatized by this, aren't you? Because of what happened to me."

He nodded.

"Don't worry. You're not the first since the rape. I met a man in New Zealand. A friend. He helped me enjoy sex again."

Her frankness—and purposefulness—was refreshing. There would be no game-playing with Liz. He took her hand. "Then lead on before I ravish you in the hallway."

She laughed and took his hand. "I think we can do better than the hall. It's a bit claustrophobic, and I'm not a fan of small, dark places."

"Me, either." For months after his funeral David had had nightmares about waking up in the empty box under his headstone.

She took him to the last door on the right. The decent-sized room seemed smaller because of the desk, bookshelf and filing cabinet in the corner. "My office-slash-bedroom. Terrible feng shui, I know, but—"

He didn't have time to talk decorating. He needed her. Now. He pulled her against him and waltzed her backward to the bed. Her twitter told him she was game and ready to play.

"Let me set the mood."

"You already have."

"Candles…music…"

"Later."

Maybe the urgency he felt came through in his tone because she stopped talking and started unbuttoning the shirt her new brother-in-law had given him. A nice shirt made of some silky material that popped free of the buttonholes as if they were coated in Teflon.

She pushed it over his shoulders and nuzzled the triangle of light gold hair on his chest. She murmured something that sounded like "I knew it."

He didn't know what she meant, but he honestly didn't care. All he could think about was seeing her naked. Touching her. He worked his hands under her stretchy black top, but discovered a band of elastic around her middle. "What's this?"

"Built-in bra," she said. "Here. I'll do it."

She gathered the material by the hem and yanked upward. The top went flying and his first glimpse of her bare torso nearly robbed him of breath. Her breasts were perfect. Not too big. Not too small. The dark reddish brown nipples were large and engorged.

Like a teen catching his first peek at his high school sweetheart, he reached out to touch. Her soft moan nearly did him in. He rubbed the nipples between his fingertips until she squirmed beneath him, groaning with pleasure.

"You're beautiful."

"I'm turned on. My nipples have always been one of my most sensitive erogenous zones. Want a quick tour of the rest?"

He filled his hands with her soft but firm flesh and nodded. Her teasing tone was also husky and sexy as hell.

She quickly unzipped her shorts and stepped out of them. Her underpants were simple white low-cut briefs. No lace, no frills. He wasn't surprised. But hugging her flat belly and prominent hip bones, they were the sexiest things he'd ever seen.

She offered her arm and pointed to the inside crook of her elbow. "Here."

He leaned over and kissed the tender flesh, licking and sucking until she gave an all-over shiver. "Oh, nice," she said, eyelids half-closed.

"Where else?"

She moved his hand to her belly. "Here," she said, rubbing the back of his hand against the inside curve of her pelvis.

He dropped to his knees and dipped his tongue into the hollow between the fabric and her skin. She shivered. "Oh."

"Are there more?" he asked, looking up.

Her lips were ruddy from being crimped under her teeth. She licked them and nodded.

"Here," she said, turning around and pointing to the spot at the base of her spine where her beautiful buttocks began to curve outward.

She looked over her shoulder, a scampish twinkle in her eyes. He rose up on his knees, wrapping his arms around her upper thighs. His bare chest rubbed against her lower back as he slowly sank down, his tongue trailing a path down her spine.

"Your mustache tickles," she said. "In a good way. Who knew?"

She leaned over slightly and he took her breasts in his hands and squeezed. Her hips undulated as they had when she danced. Sensual and erotic.

He made her turn around, then he removed her panties. Her nest of dark curls invited his touch. He covered her with his hand and let his fingers explore as she writhed and moved against his hand.

"Oh, David, I like that. Very much. But more…"

He understood what she was asking. He needed more, too. More flesh. More heat.

He scooped her up in his arms and placed her on the bed, reclining against the pillows, then he quickly shed the rest of his clothes. He stood for a moment savoring how beautiful she was—her pale skin against the deep rust velveteen cover. "You look like a harem slave. Brought to pleasure your master."

She made a languid motion with her hand, feathering back and forth through the air until it settled on her breast, then down her belly and even farther. "It's actually the other way around, slave. I am master. You are here to pleasure me."

Then she rolled toward him on her side and reached out to touch him. Her fingers were cool and smooth. Her nails stimulating as she pushed and pulled in a way that nearly ruined him. "I…can't…take…much—"

She moved like a cat, so fast he didn't have time to prepare. One minute she was toying with him, the next her mouth was on his fully engorged penis. He let out a yelp and made two fists to maintain control. The pain, the pleasure, the—he couldn't think. He was so damn close to losing it he had to push her away.

She looked up and wiped her mouth with the back of her hand. "I think you're ready now, slave. Pleasure me."

She didn't have to ask twice. Which was a good thing, Liz thought. She'd nearly come when he licked the inside of her pelvis. His touch did things to her like no man she'd ever been with. She'd never felt sexier or more liberated. Maybe knowing this was for one night only gave her permission to act out her fantasies. Take risks. Play.

He eased her into a prone position and spread her legs. He wasn't violent, just firm and intent. She could see the intensity in his eyes and felt the same way. She needed him inside her. Now.

He paused a second as if savoring the moment, then entered her wet, waiting body. The fit, the friction, the synchronized movement culminated in a fast, intense act. She closed her eyes and gripped the fabric of her bedspread. He held her knees and thrust. Again and again. The sensation in her core didn't have to build up, it simply hit her. So fast, so powerful, she screamed in shock…and pleasure. His low, loud groan rocked her a second later.

"Holy…smoke," he said dropping on top of her.

Little aftershocks in her loins made her wrap her legs around his hips. She moved her hips in circles, savoring every sensation. She'd never experienced an orgasm like that in her life. It made tears form in her eyes and a laugh bubble up from the bottom of her diaphragm. "That was amazing. I love you," she said, before she could stop herself.

David tensed, just for a second, then he rolled to the side, taking her with him. "I know what you mean," he said. "That was incredible."

I know what you mean. No, he didn't. He thought she'd said the words in the heat of passion. Grateful for good sex. But he was wrong. She loved *him*. The man she knew him to be, the man she'd never met but had shaped the man she'd first met—the grower of cacti on the run for his life.

But she couldn't save him. She didn't even know how or where to begin. She'd made her choice and mapped her course—and it led straight to India. So, she'd let him think he understood what she'd meant by the passionate declaration. That was the only way they could possibly say goodbye to each other when the time came.

Fortunately, that time wasn't yet.

They still had tonight. And who knew? If the results of Mark Gaylord's investigation came back negative, maybe they could all breathe easy. Maybe David would be David for as long as he chose to be. Gardener extraordinaire.

And Liz could live with that because she knew who he really was—a decent man who made her whole being hum with excitement and possibility.

Chapter Fourteen

Two days. A honeymoon, of sorts, Liz thought as she folded one of David's new shirts that she'd bought him. He hadn't carried comprehensive insurance on his car or renter's insurance for his property, but he'd managed to salvage a few things: some tools, his cat and an old motorcycle that had belonged to his landlady's husband. She'd given him the thing, which to everyone's surprise had current tags. The poor woman hadn't even realized she'd been paying to license it all these years.

He couldn't work as a gardener any longer, but the mobility had allowed him to collect funds from the last of his accounts due. He disappeared every morning, leaving Liz wondering if she'd ever see him again, but, so far, he'd returned each evening.

She didn't ask about his plans. She did share with him the very good news that the bank had approved her home equity loan. Once they cut her a check, she would send the money to the international company that would start the adoption process.

"I'm so happy for you, Liz. Show me her picture again. I want to be able to imagine the two of you together," David said.

They were in her bedroom, fully dressed for a change. She'd filled half a dozen tea orders early in the morning and had just finished printing the invoices that would accompany each delivery. She slid back on her desk chair to allow him to pull the folding chair he was sitting on closer to the computer.

A few key strokes and they were at the ashram's home page. "Normally, Prisha wouldn't have been allowed to stay here because of her disability but I pleaded her case and convinced the ashram to keep her until I could make other arrangements."

"What's the story? Did her mother give her away because of her feet?"

"I was told that the mother was young, upset and emotionally immature. The family was afraid she might commit suicide. No doubt Prisha's in-turned feet played a factor, but Prisha is such a sweet and loving child, I'm just happy the family brought her to a safe place like the ashram."

"Will Prisha remember you when she sees you?"

Liz shook her head. "No. Probably not. She was just a tiny baby when I first met her and I had to come home to start the adoption process. I would have stayed if I could have, but it's important that we start treatment soon. The orthopedic surgeon I consulted said she would probably need a series of operations."

He looped his arm across her shoulders. The weight was solid and comforting. She'd gotten used to having him in her space. Lydia and Reezira were due back in the morning. Liz didn't know how they'd handle his presence.

"How'd it go today?" she asked. He'd been helping his landlady clean up the rubble.

"Good. Mimi heard from her insurance agent. She had some kind of rider on her policy that guaranteed replacement of the building. He said at today's property values, she could probably move in a three-bedroom modular."

"Wow."

"I know. I think that's why she's being so nice to me—the fire did her favor. I'm the only one who really got burned. No pun intended."

His green eyes—that weren't artificially green anymore since his colored contact lenses had been lost in the fire—twinkled with humor. She liked his eyes. And his body. She liked everything about him, except his mustache.

She put her finger to his lips and started to bring up the subject, but the sound of the doorbell stopped her. She got up, leaving the page open on the screen. "I wonder who that could be?"

David followed her, nearly tripping over Reezira's fluffy gray cat. "Check before you open it," he warned.

She smiled at the concern in his voice. "Yes, Daddy."

"Oh," she said a moment later after peeking through the side window. "It's my neighbor. And her…um, son."

"Hello, Crissy. What's going on?"

"Eli has something to say to you. It's part of his court-ordered reparations. Do it, Eli."

Liz was surprised by the woman's stern tone. She looked different, too. Older, more focused.

The young man at her side took a deep breath, his broad shoulders lifting. He wasn't wearing a cap so she could see his eyes more clearly. He seemed far younger than his appearance suggested. And his stance was far less aggressive than she remembered. "I'm sorry I hassled you. It was a stupid thing to do. I don't really think I'm better than you—or the ladies who live here. What I did really sucks. And me 'n'…um, Mr. Baines, are gonna fix things."

Mr. Baines? She looked at David, who cleared his throat in a meaningful way.

Eli blushed and dropped his chin to his chest. "I mean, I'm gonna do the work and he's gonna supervise to make sure I do it right."

"What work?"

Crissy pointed to a wheelbarrow parked beside the gate leading to Liz's backyard. It was filled with plants from David's greenhouse. She recognized the little mark on the side of the boxes. "We used my SUV to haul all these over here. After," she stressed, "we proved to your police friend that my son had nothing to do with setting that fire. You believe that, don't you?"

The question was directed at David.

He nodded. "Yes, I do. Eli and I had a long talk and I know that he's not stupid. He knows that violence and aggressive behavior will land him in jail. Taking his frustration out on a patch of ground is a lot smarter bet."

Liz was touched. And truly impressed that David had gone out of his way to make this happen. "Well, I think this is great. I can't pay for the plants right now, though."

Crissy waved off her words. "Eli and his father worked this out. Buying some nursery stock was a lot cheaper than hiring a lawyer to keep Eli our of jail. Believe me, Eli's getting off easy and he knows it, right, son?"

The boy winced at the word *son*, but he nodded.

"I…I really don't know what to say. This is so unexpected. Are you sure…?" She looked from David to Crissy and back.

Crissy took a step closer. When she looked into Liz's eyes, Liz could read her plea. This was important. Her neighbor needed to prove something, and she needed Liz's help—endorsement—to make the plan work.

"Well, let's go see where everything is gonna go."

BY SUNSET, DAVID was pleased with how the backyard looked, but the new landscaping paled in comparison to the improved relations between neighbors. Crissy had started out detached and tense. Eli, like every other sixteen-year-old kid David knew, was snarly and tense. Liz had been just plain tense. But three hours of dirt, sweat, loud music, water fights and a tangible finished product had changed the dynamics.

Digging in dirt was a great equalizer, he'd learned. *Nothing like a few cactus stickers in your fingers to bond people together.* Plus, it helped that Liz was gracious and kind and genuinely wanted to make peace with Eli—and his stepmom.

The two women were presently out front, discussing Liz's idea about building a skate park in the neighborhood. David had a few empty pots to pick up and he'd be done for the night. Dusk had fallen. They'd started late to avoid the worst heat of the day and Liz had fed them tofu dogs and chips and her refreshing iced tea.

He'd put off leaving town until he could do this favor to repay Liz for all her kindnesses. Plus, he'd wanted to make sure his plants went to a good home. Scar was going to stay with Mimi for the time being, but she'd promised to call Liz if that arrangement changed for any reason.

In the early, early morning, he'd hop on his ancient motorcycle and head off on Plan B. He hadn't been able to replace all his survival gear, but he'd picked up a few essentials.

A sound from the far side of the yard made him straighten up. Had they left the gate open? He could have sworn they'd closed it after they finished moving the large agave from the shaded spot up front. He twisted a tie around the top of the garage bag he was holding, and then started that way. He'd double-check to make sure Eli had tapped the padlock tight.

He'd only taken two steps when the beam from a flashlight hit him squarely in the eyes. "Eli, cut it out," he barked, momentarily confused. Hadn't the boy gone home before Crissy?

"If you mean the kid, you got the wrong person."

David froze, his blood stalling about midway to his heart. He didn't recognize the voice, but he knew who the person on the other end of the flashlight was. Someone sent by Ray to kill him.

He'd stayed too long. Let down his guard. Convinced himself the fire was an accident—the result of a malfunctioning water heater. He'd been a fool and now Liz was in harm's way.

Liz. He had to warn her. He hurled the garbage bag in his hand, like his namesake taking on a giant. But his aim wasn't as good. Just as he let go, a sharp prick exploded in his shoulder. He sank to his knees as the quick-acting tranquilizer pumped through his system. "Take me. Just me."

He didn't know if the words made it out or not.

LIZ WANTED to leave. She needed to check on David. No, that was a lie. She wanted to grab David by the hand and pull him into her bed so she could thank him properly. What an amazing man he'd turned out to be. Thoughtful, kind, creative and genuinely interested in others. Not many men would have done what he'd done—helped her make peace with her neighbor.

"I think this might be the start of something good, don't you?" Crissy said, her tone tired, but slightly wistful.

Liz hadn't been listening too closely so she was afraid to act too enthusiastic. She was pretty sure Crissy wasn't still talking about the skate park idea Liz had brought up. "Pardon?"

"Elijah never made it easy for me and Eli to like each other. Understandable, I suppose, given the fact that they don't see each other on a regular basis. Every time Eli showed up, our lives would turn upside down. That isn't right, either. But with this new arrangement, I think Eli and I will be able to build a relationship that's not adversarial."

"From what I could see, he's a normal kid dealing with normal kid things, plus trying to fit in with two families. Be patient."

Crissy gave Liz a quick hug. "You're really such a nice person. I blame myself for making Eli think you were different. Not intentionally, but when he was talking to the counselor about why he said those things to you, I could almost hear my voice in the background."

"What do you mean?"

Crissy's face turned crimson. "Stupid stuff. Unfeeling. I remember saying something like 'People without kids don't have a clue about the real world.' I know that's not true, but your life does change when you have children."

Liz couldn't argue with that. She didn't even have her daughter yet, but her life had changed dramatically.

"And I assumed that your roommates were paying rent. I didn't know you were helping them out by giving them a place to stay. I remember grousing about you not wanting to do the beautification project. I probably called you cheap. I'm sorry. God, I was an ass."

Liz was surprised by Crissy's honesty, but since she'd held her own preconceived idea about Crissy and her life, she really couldn't point fingers. "Wars have been fought over less," she said, with a shrug. "At least we've cleared the air. Now, I'm dirty and pooped. Time to call it a night."

"Okeydokey," Crissy said with a corny giggle. "I'll let you go. Tell David I really can't thank him enough. 'Night."

Oh, I'll thank him all right, Liz thought as she started toward the backyard. She had several methods in mind. She'd just stepped inside the rear gate when she stopped short and looked around. Her Gypsy sense told her something wasn't right, even though her newly landscaped backyard looked great. Only a white trash bag, lying cockeyed against the fence, seemed out of place. It was squishing one of her new hedgehog cacti, the same kind she'd run over with her car the day she met David.

"That's odd," she murmured under her breath.

The immediate stillness seemed ominous, despite the familiar sounds of the city around her. Bells and whistles went off in her head. Bells and whistles she'd ignored once before. This time she listened.

She turned and started running as fast as she could along the sidewalk between her garage and Crissy's fence. She didn't look back. She didn't know what or even if someone was chasing her. She made it to Crissy's porch and had her hand on the clapper when a voice said, "I wouldn't do that if I were you."

She didn't know the voice, but she knew the tone. Cold. Hostile. Deadly. She'd heard it before—in Bosnia. The sound of a man who had nothing to lose.

Chapter Fifteen

"I was going to kill only him, you know," said the man behind the wheel of Liz's car. David's former boss, she'd discerned from watching him give orders to the thug who'd been standing over David's prone body when Liz entered her garage at gunpoint. "The fire should have done that. I watched it burn, expecting to see him run out of the building, screaming in pain with his clothes on fire. Like in the movies. Only it didn't happen. That old bag next door called the cops too soon, and Paul wasn't in there anyway."

Liz found it disconcerting when the man called David Paul, but she made herself focus. If they were going to survive this, she'd need to play it smart. And listen.

They'd been driving for what felt like hours. A cloth of some kind was bound tightly around her eyes. A thread, dangling above her upper lip, had been driving her nuts until she finally managed to catch it with her teeth and snip it off.

Stupid thing to be distracted by, she thought. *I'm tied up and stuck in the backseat of my own car with my lover.* She could hear David's shallow breathing and recognize his familiar smell, but other than that, she knew nothing. Was he injured? Bleeding? Dying?

Her life should have been passing before her eyes, and she was distracted by a ticklish string. "Stupid," she muttered softly.

"Eh? What's that, Gypsy Girl?"

That's what the nutcase who'd kidnapped her called her. David was Paul, and she was Gypsy Girl.

"My name is Elizabeth."

"Oh, I know your name. I know everything there is to know about you." His low laugh gave her the creeps. "Well, not everything, but I always left the nitty-gritty intense research to Paul."

"His name is David."

The voice laughed again, only this time it was colder, less indulgent. "No, Gypsy, the man beside you is Paul Andrew McAffee. A poor, unloved orphan who came to me right out of college, filled with ambition, brains and not much else. I paid for his graduate school courses, his travels, his research. I molded and shaped him into a man who was poised to introduce to the world a drug so novel and revolutionary people would kill to own the patent."

People would have been killed if you'd had your way, she thought but didn't say out loud.

"Where are you taking us?"

She tried to wiggle her fingers. Her hands were bound behind her back, which made sitting upright a challenge. The digits were starting to fall asleep, the blood flow compromised by the thin strip of plastic holding them tight. She was sure the chafed flesh at her wrists was bleeding, but inching sideways toward the door had taken a little pressure off her arms.

She couldn't move far though because David, who was unconscious—well, unmoving—beside her, had fallen sideways. His head had rested against her shoulder until the driver took a sharp corner. Then his body had plopped forward, facedown on her knees. She'd spread her knees as much as possible so as not to block his access to air but, given the similar plastic band around her ankles, she could only pray that he didn't suffocate.

Her abductor ignored her question and resumed talking about his first attempt to kill David. "As I was saying, after the fire was out and the cops were standing around, I figured maybe they just hadn't found the body. Nicely barbecued. A crispy critter," he said with a morbid chuckle. "But then you showed up, driving this little car. Four-wheel drive. Perfect for taking off-road, right?"

Liz didn't answer. She hadn't had time to go camping or playing in the desert since she'd moved back from India. Her cousin Enzo had salvaged the Honda after an accident and rebuilt it with her in mind. The price had been right.

"I saw Paul get out of your car. When he was dressed in the old man's getup—that tan jumpsuit, I wasn't sure it was him, but the night of the fire, he had on a tie. He looked like a science professor, and that's when I knew I'd found the right guy—and he definitely hadn't been asleep in his bed."

"You set the fire without knowing for sure that David was the man you were looking for?"

Her scandalized tone apparently amused him. He let out a loud roar that coincided with the car leaving the pavement. Liz was jostled from side to side. The pain in her wrists was excruciating. David's head bounced up and crashed back to her knees. She thought she detected a low groan from him, but the noise of the tires crossing dirt and rock made it impossible to be sure.

"Here's what you need to know about me, Gypsy. I don't suffer liars, cheats or betrayers. And when I set my mind on something I never stop until it's accomplished."

Liz knew better than to argue with a maniac. Plus, the off-road path they'd entered was deeply rutted, making conversation difficult. She was thankful for the seat belt that his accomplice had clicked in place despite her twisting protests. His comment had been "Don't want to attract police attention, do we?" But poor David wasn't as lucky.

His groans were getting louder with each bump, she thought. She had no idea how long they'd been on the road, but maybe whatever drug the crazy guy and his henchman had used to stun David was wearing off.

Liz's first thought when she'd seen David facedown on the floor of her garage—arms and legs trussed up—was that he was dead, and she was going to be next. She'd turned to look at the man holding the gun. David's nemesis didn't look anything like she'd pictured.

Bald, with pale skin that obviously hadn't seen the sun in ages, he had the sickly appearance of an invalid. But what struck her most was the taut skin around his eyes. He'd had some kind of cosmetic surgery. She'd have staked her life on it.

"Why are you doing this? Why me?" she'd asked, her brain frantically searching for a way to get loose and call for help.

"Because Paul has the hots for you," he'd said, apparently enjoying the moment. "And that's when it occurred to me that simple death was too easy for Paul. No, the real payback comes when I see the look on his face as he realizes that the woman he loves is going to die because of him. Is that not sweet revenge?"

"You're sick."

His laugh seemed pleased, as if the word were praise.

"Gypsy Girl, Paul here is my last loose end. For four

years I've endured painful surgeries the likes of which make reality TV come off as kid's stuff. I've spent my recuperative hours searching for some sign that the man I'd grown to love as a son was still alive."

"So you could kill him?" Liz cried.

"So I could hear him beg for his life."

"That will never happen."

"Maybe not. But I betcha anything he'll beg for yours."

The driver was now humming some country-and-western tune Liz couldn't quite place. She pushed the memory of his gleeful comment out of her mind. Things had turned ugly fast after that. The other man—a larger, bodybuilder type—had overpowered her and tied her wrists and ankles then placed her in her car. This was the one thing that gave her hope. After all, Zeke had installed some kind of tracking device in the Honda. Surely the madman and his accomplice hadn't thought to look for one. Why would they?

Because they're paranoid psychos who have been outrunning the law for four years, a part of her mind had answered.

But no one had mentioned finding the bug, she comforted herself.

What good the device would do, she had no clue. She hadn't asked Zeke how the darn thing worked or if it was even turned on. "Damn, damn, damn," she muttered under her breath.

At least, she knew part of the bad guys' plan because she'd overheard them talking outside the car right before they parted company and both drove away, the boss behind the wheel of her Honda.

"Follow me to the junction then wait. Once I drop them off, I'll meet you and we can dump this wreck at McCarran. Even if someone finds it, they'll waste time trying to see if Paul and the girl took off somewhere. Too bad I don't have time to arrange a fake wedding. That would really throw the cops off."

A fake wedding. Just a few days earlier she and David— she really couldn't think of him as Paul McAffee—had been dancing at Kate's wedding. She'd invited him into her life and look what had happened. If she didn't get free and find her way back to safety, all would be lost. Prisha would never get the help she needed. The little girl would become another statistic. The sparkle in her beautiful eyes would dim and eventually disappear.

Stay focused, she silently ordered. She'd taken a survival course before her assignment overseas. The instructor had discussed hostage situations. The first rule was not to panic. "People who panic, die. Your brain is a tool. Use it. Stay alert. Be prepared to take advantage of any opportunity that comes your way, no matter how small."

She slouched down until her fingers touched the seat cushion. Her normally pristine car had been seriously neglected the past few weeks. Every time she took her roommates somewhere, they had to stop for some kind of fast food. Happy Meals were a favorite. And Arby's sandwiches. Some of the Arby's wrappers were shiny. Shiny things could be used as a signal, right?

But finding one proved impossible. She couldn't reach anything on the floor. And she had to assume her captor would check her waistband to see what was making the material of her pants so lumpy. But she did find one small treasure—a metal nail file that Lydia had complained about losing weeks ago. Liz used her thumbs to slip it down her pants. Would it be sharp enough to cut through their bindings? Who knew, but she'd take what she could find. A couple of soft, rubbery objects she guessed might be old French fries went in her pants, too. And a screw top lid from a water bottle.

The driver hit the brakes and David's body was suddenly launched forward. He gave a loud groan when he landed on the floor, his face near her feet.

"Oops. Big rock. Don't want to blow a tire. We're not far enough in, yet. Can't have some miraculous rescue by a couple of day hikers, now can we? You just stay down, Paul, my boy. If you think you can play the hero twice in one lifetime, you're sadly mistaken."

Paul—David—moaned, but didn't move.

"We'll be there soon. You just relax and enjoy the sights." His laugh was so eerie, Liz shivered. Tears squeezed past her eyelids, soaking into the fabric of the blindfold. Panic rose and she had to fight back a scream.

Silently, intently, she focused her thoughts on reaching the man at her feet. *David. David, stay with me. Keep breathing. I need you. Don't leave me. Please. I love you. I need you.* She kept up the silent litany, praying it might reach him.

THE URGE TO VOMIT was so powerful it woke David up like a slap. He fought to keep his roiling stomach under control, but motion sickness and whatever had been in the tranquilizer was a potent combination. His mouth flooded with spit. His head felt as if it might explode. He opened his eyes and could see nothing but black. His vertigo intensified.

He tried to move and realized his arms and legs were bound. Lifting his chest up gave him some sense of where he was—on the floor of a vehicle that was bouncing over a rough road. The abuse had taken a toll on his hip bones and ribs. Every inch of his chest and abdomen hurt, but the pain was good. It meant he was alive.

He turned his head to listen for any sounds beyond the motor, drivetrain and road noise. Within seconds, he realized he wasn't alone. A coldness grabbed his insides and twisted. Liz. The bastard had Liz, too.

He rolled over, ignoring the shaft of pain that shot up his arms. Parts of his body were asleep from lack of circulation. But he had to find out if she was alive. He had to touch her.

His head bumped bone and denim. He rubbed his chin up and down. A low gasp gave him hope. She wasn't dead, but she was undoubtedly trussed up just like he was.

What Ray had in mind was anybody's guess, but David was pretty sure it didn't involve bloodshed. Ray wasn't above ordering someone to kill, but David had never seen his former boss handle a gun.

Of course things might have changed in four years. Ray's looks certainly had. David had only caught a distorted glimpse of his ex-boss's face when Ray helped his hired goon drag David's body into the garage, but he'd been shocked at the changes. Even Ray's voice had been altered.

He moved again trying to find a position that inflicted less pain. If Ray left them alive in the desert, they still had a chance. Not much of one, granted, with no water, but four years of hunting cacti had taught David a few things about desert survival. He'd take his chances with Mother Nature any day over dealing with a madman.

And though he wanted to touch Liz, to comfort her and reassure her that everything would be okay, he wasn't a hypocrite. He was the reason she was here. He was the reason she might die. If they made it through this, he vowed to do the right thing. He'd leave and never come back. She deserved a whole hell of a lot more than he had to offer—starting with the assurance that she could work in her backyard without being kidnapped at gunpoint.

Despite the rough road and frequent bottoming out that tortured his joints and added new bruises on top of old ones, David dozed off and on—probably from the residual drug in his system. He didn't fight it. He'd need every ounce of strength to protect Liz once they stopped.

Which, finally, they did.

David woke up fully when Ray killed the engine. He couldn't see anything, but he listened hard, trying to follow every movement Ray made. Now he could hear the low tuneless humming that always indicated Ray was focusing on a problem. Ray was thinking. Nothing good ever came of that, David thought.

The driver's side door opened and closed. A moment later, the door near David's feet opened. "Ah, the boy fell down," Ray said in a childish, singsong tone. "Too bad."

A second later, rough hands grabbed David around the shoulders and forced him to sit upright. Ray yanked off David's blindfold, taking a painful clump of hair with it.

Blinking, David saw that night had fallen with a vengeance. The only light came from the car's headlamps. The overhead dome light wasn't turned on even though the door was open.

Still, David craned about to see Liz. She was sitting, her chest pushed out, her hands behind her back.

"Let her go," he pleaded. "She doesn't have anything to do with our business. I only met her a couple of weeks ago."

"Braggart," Ray said. He took hold of the plastic zip tie that bound David's legs and tugged brutally. There wasn't room for David's hips to fit through the opening straight on, but twisting on his side meant slamming his ear against the raised drivetrain shaft. Even the car's carpeting couldn't ease the pain that shot through his head. He tried not to moan, but couldn't stifle the sound completely.

"David? Are you okay? What's happening?"

"I'm fine, Liz," he said, even as his knees crumpled beneath him. Lack of movement had rendered his feet numb. He fell on his shoulder and rolled on the rocky ground, hoping he wouldn't smack into some unseen boulder.

He had no idea where they were, but they appeared to have reached a dry wash of some kind. The glow of the car's high beams illuminated a rock formation as high as Liz's SUV. No wonder Ray had stopped, he thought.

The door slammed and Ray disappeared around the rear of the car. "Okay, Gypsy Girl, time for you to join Lover Boy."

Ray was a big man—nearly as tall as David and at one time had weighed fifty pounds more. No longer. He was thin, but obviously not lacking in strength. David sat up and tried to move to his knees, but the pins and needles in his legs made him want to scream. "Liz? Are you okay?"

There was a soft grunt and a sob, but she didn't answer. Fury filled every inch of David's body and he fought to a kneeling position.

"Oh, relax, hero. She's fine. Just heavier than she looks."

Ray half dragged Liz's body around the car and dumped her in front of David. She curled up in a fetal position, as much as her restricted movement would allow.

David cursed. "You rotten son of a bitch. Why God let you live is beyond me!"

"God?" Ray hooted. "He and I parted ways years ago. Guess He couldn't take the competition. And if it hadn't been for you, I'd have been richer than God, and worshipped by more people. I was going to give them youth. Till you, Judas, sold me out."

The truth struck David harder than the back of Ray's hand, which knocked him sideways, so he landed closer to Liz. His former boss was totally crazy. He'd read about a condition called narcissistic personality disorder. He'd even heard the term mentioned in regards to Ray, but at the time, he'd told himself the truly gifted, the movers and shakers of the world were entitled to an inflated ego. But few of those types believed they could replace God.

Ray squatted a few feet away. "Here's how this going to go down, my boy. I'm going to take Gypsy Girl's blindfold off. The two of you can huddle together for the rest of the night. Exchange sweet nothings. Weep and moan together. If no hungry coyotes wander by, you'll probably be okay until say…two or three tomorrow afternoon. By then, you'll be roasted and toasted and dehydrated." He made a bridge with his hands and cracked his knuckles.

"I've heard that death from exposure is a really nasty way to go. Your tongue swells up and your lips crack and your eyeballs sorta pop out of your head. If there is a God, He'll make sure she dies first. Not because I give a damn about her suffering, but because I want you to watch her agony and know that you're responsible. Too bad I won't be here to watch, but knowing that you'll be tormented with guilt until you take your last breath is almost a fair trade for all the billions you cost me. So long, Judas."

Choking on Ray's dust as he backed up the SUV and pulled away was the final indignation. But all too soon, the darkness closed in on them and Liz and David were alone. In the desert. With only the clothes on their backs and their wits to save them.

Chapter Sixteen

Survival.

Liz knew they didn't stand a chance unless they could get free of their bindings. She wasn't going down without a fight, but in the silence after her car drove off, she had a tough time getting hold of her emotions. One hiccup of a cry turned to a sob. Tears followed.

"No, Liz," David shouted, his voice panicky. "No tears. Tears are moisture. Your body's going to need every ounce to survive. Don't cry."

"Go to hell. I'll cry if I want. I hurt all over and I've been left to die in the desert. This is when people cry."

She kicked at him with her feet. Thankfully the bastard who left them here had removed her blindfold before he drove off. So David could see her eyes bug out before he took his last breath, the disgusting creep had said.

"Your ex-boss is a certifiable whack job. How could you possibly have worked for a man like that?" Liz heard the hysteria in her voice.

"He's changed," David said. "They say genius and dementia are closely related."

"They could be blood kin for all I care. If we make it out of this predicament alive, I vow to do everything in my power to see that psycho monster brought to justice. If we survive."

"We're not going to die," he said passionately.

The only light came from the stars, which though plentiful, had little impact over such a vast openness. She could make out shapes, though, and David's body was the most obvious, since he was inching back and forth to get turned around.

"Ha," she snarled, her tears drying up as anger became her predominant emotion. "We're gonna be bugs under a magnifying glass once the sun comes up."

The word reminded her of the bug Zeke had planted in her car. Would someone in Zeke's office notice that her car, which was normally parked in her garage, was driving all over the place tonight? Would they call Zeke?

"Not if we get these damn handcuffs off and build a shelter."

"And how do we do that?"

"Scoot around until you find a sharp rock. It won't be easy, but we have all night. We're not going anywhere, right?"

"Very funny. What if a coyote or javelina or an army of scorpions decides to visit us?"

"We probably have a better chance of seeing a UFO. Quit talking and save your energy for getting free."

She made a face at him. She knew he was right. The instructor at her survival-training course had stressed how important focus and a will to live were to a person in a trying situation. She struggled to block out the pervasive fear that threatened to strangle her and brought to mind an image of Prisha. Her sweet little girl's smile. That smile would dim and fade if Liz didn't make it out of here. She had to stay calm.

"I have something in my pants that might cut through these ties."

David didn't say anything for a few seconds then he started to laugh. "And what might that something be?"

She fought to keep from grinning. "A nail file. Lydia lost it last week. I found it between the seat cushions. I can't reach it, now, though. It was stuck in my waistband, but when your sick friend dragged me over here, it went lower."

David's rocking motion brought him closer. It took another few adjustments to scoot around so his face was next to her butt. His nose poked and prodded until he said, "I feel it. But how in the hell are we going to get it out of there?"

"Do you think you can undo my pants with your teeth?"

She rolled onto her back. The position of her hands thrust her pelvis upward. David labored to his knees and bent over her. His stubbly jaw chafed against her skin and the downward pressure hurt her hands but she lifted up as much as possible to help.

"This isn't as easy I thought it would be," he mumbled.

Her shirt had come up and his mustache tickled her bare belly. She breathed deeply the way her yoga instructor had taught her. At last, the button gave, but she still needed to get the zipper down if she was going to reach the file.

His teeth made a horrible clicking sound on the metal tab, but he persevered. His breath was hot and damp on the tender flesh. She'd worn frilly underwear instead of her usual functional white briefs. She didn't know if bright red bikinis had helped or hindered the file on its downward trek.

"There. Is that far enough?" he asked, rearing back.

The cold night air, which she'd been too preoccupied to notice earlier touched her bare skin and she immediately started shivering. "Y-yes, I think so."

She rolled over, trying to find a spot that didn't have nine thousand little rocks poking her.

"What are you going to do?"

"Yoga," Liz said through clenched teeth. "Stay close and take the file if I get it, okay? My fingers are kinda numb."

She took a deep diaphragmatic breath, letting it lift her upper torso. At the same time, she raised her feet and pushed her hands into the gap in her jeans. She blocked out the sensations from the sharp stones and gravel and reached deeper with each exhale until her fingertips touched something metal.

The pain in her lower back was excruciating. Her shoulders felt as if they might break apart, but another inch gave her control of the little tool. Lying flat, face turned to the side in the dust, she said, "I got it."

Seconds later, his humming mumbles told her he had the file in his mouth and needed her help. More mumbled instructions and she managed to transfer the file from his mouth to his hand. "Now what?"

"This feels pretty sharp. I'll try to saw through the tie around my ankles, first. You rest. Can you lean up against that big rock without too much pain?"

"Why can't I lie on the ground?"

"The chill will seep into your bones and your body will start to shiver. Once my feet are free I might be able to kick together some kind of bed from dried reeds or whatever's around. In the meantime, rest."

That little exercise—and stress of the kidnapping—had exhausted her, and the pain in her shoulders and ankles was wearing her down, so Liz did as he suggested. Her knees hurt from trying to walk on them—each step yielding just an inch or so of forward progress—but eventually she reached the large rock formation that had caused Ray to stop driving.

She tried not to think about the worst that could happen. She tried to think about Prisha. But within seconds she wasn't thinking about anything. She was asleep.

David felt a trickle of blood run down his shin. The back-and-forth sawing motion was torturing his shoulders, but he pressed through the pain. He had to do this. If he and Liz couldn't free themselves, they had no hope. Even with the use of their limbs, they wouldn't have long. David knew that the survival rule of thumb was one gallon of water per day per person. That meant they were starting out two gallons short.

He knew where to find water, if there was water to be found. At certain times of the year, the outside edge of a dry creek bed retained small caches of groundwater. Experience told him this spot had potential. Ray had been stopped by large boulders, which had probably been pushed downstream by flash floods over the years.

Unfortunately, this was summer and most of the potable water was deep underground. They'd dig. With luck they'd find enough to keep them alive through the day, but then they would have to walk for who knew how many miles to find help.

The durable little strip that bound his ankles gave a fraction of an inch, then a few strokes later broke apart.

"Yes," David cried softly, not wanting to disturb Liz. He'd sensed her collapse and was glad she could rest for a few minutes. Although tempted to free her feet next, he went to work on his wrists instead.

He was almost ready to give up when the blasted strip finally let loose. He looked toward the heavens and murmured a little prayer before getting up. "I don't care what happens to me, but please keep Liz safe and let her get home."

Walking was tough at first, but he took his time. He surveyed the immediate area and located a decent spot out of the wind to spend the rest of the night. There was an abundance of dried brush that he collected and assembled in layers.

Although there was fuel for a fire, he had no matches or time to devote to using the bow-and-drill method. His first priority was making Liz more comfortable.

Once he was satisfied with the arrangement, he returned to where Liz was resting. He jostled her shoulder gently and said, "Liz, my love, I'm going to saw these ties off now."

Her soft moan nearly broke his heart. What courage she'd shown—and continued to show. She didn't flinch or cry out, even when he accidentally poked her with the file. She used her body strength to keep the plastic taut, which helped a lot. Sooner than he would have predicted, both pieces were cut.

"Oh, thank God," she cried, sitting back to massage her wrists. He took her feet in his lap and chafed her ankles to get the blood flowing. "Damn. That really hurts."

"I've built us a shelter. It's not much, but it's out of the wind and I think we should try to rest a few hours. As soon as it gets light, I'll look for water."

"I don't know if—" She stopped and shook her head. "Never mind. We'll talk in the morning. I'm so sore and tired I think I could sleep for a week."

He took her hand and slowly helped her through the maze of rocks, praying he could find the slight depression he'd discovered earlier. "Through here, I think," he said, giving her hand a little tug. "Be careful and duck your head."

She followed him into the nook where the ever-present wind didn't reach. "Oh, it's warmer. I didn't even realize I was cold."

"Shock. Adrenaline. Your mind's way of keeping your body out of the loop," he said. "We're not dressed for these temps, but we'll be okay for one night."

He hadn't meant to make that last sound so ominous, but he felt her shudder and could have kicked himself. "You lie down first, facing the rock and I'll spoon you, okay?"

She dropped to her knees then settled on her side. Turning slightly, she said, "No fooling around, mister. This is serious business."

He joined her, wrapping one arm and one leg over her as a sort of makeshift cover. "A boy can dream, right?"

She didn't say anything for a minute, then she asked, "What did you dream of when you were a boy? Did you always plan to be a scientist?"

He nuzzled her hair. "No. I wanted to be a farmer. My grandfather on my mother's side was a farmer. We only visited him once when I was little. He passed away shortly after that from a heart attack. Grandmother sold the farm and moved to town."

He let out a sigh. All through high school, he'd nurtured the dream of buying the land, refurbishing the old house, raising his children in the pastoral setting he remembered so fondly. "When I came home from college one year at spring break, I took a detour to visit the old place. The house was gone. Agribusiness is not the same as the old family farm."

"I'm sorry," she said drowsily.

"I'm not. Odd as it may sound given the circumstances, I'm glad. Farming was a boy's dream. One I hung on to after my parents died because I remembered us all being happy there. But in hindsight, I credit my grandfather with sparking my interest in science. He taught me things a city kid had no idea about."

"How old were you?"

"I don't know. Seven, maybe? Eight?"

"I bet you were adorable." Her words were starting to slur with fatigue.

A few seconds later, she added, "I hope I get Prisha home before she's seven. The light in their eyes goes out if children don't feel loved, you know."

The light goes out. How well he knew it. His grandmother had never shown him love. She'd let him know that she considered him a burden.

Liz would make a fabulous mother. He had to do everything in his power to make sure she got that chance.

THE NIGHT PROVED cold but tolerable. Liz actually managed to sleep, off and on. She hadn't been able to tell whether David was sleeping, too, or faking it for her sake. They'd survived for twelve hours after their abduction, but the next twelve would prove even more challenging, she was certain.

"Too bad neither of us has a watch," she said, returning her focus to David, who was using his shoe to dig at the edge of the dry creek bed not far from where they'd slept.

"Or a cell phone."

His comment put hers in perspective and she chuckled. "Yeah, why wish for a bicycle when you could wish for a car? Duh."

He looked up. "I wasn't being critical. A watch would actually come in handy for a lot of things, including using the glass as a signal, but since mine went up in smoke in the fire and you don't wear one, we're out of luck."

Luck. She'd been born into a family of gamblers, but she very rarely placed a bet. Everyone thought she was…thrifty. And practical. In truth, she just didn't trust in outside forces of any kind. Nor did she blame fate when something bad happened to her. She and David were in a fix, but they were smart and determined. They'd survive on their wits. Or not. The unwelcome thought echoed in her mind.

She moved from the patch of shade she was sitting in to another patch closer to David. He'd advised her to stay out of the sun as much as possible. "What should I be doing? And please don't say, 'Nothing.' I need to do something useful."

"Bird-watch."

"Pardon?"

"Track the flight of birds. They'll lead us to water or to plants that could provide sustenance. The screwbean mesquite blooms from May to August. Its fruit isn't as sweet as other varieties of mesquite, but the pods are fairly nutritious. Coyotes thrive on them."

She shook her head. "I thought coyotes were carnivores."

"They're opportunists. Animals that learn to adapt to their environment live longer. That's what we're going to do, too."

She put her hand to her forehead to shade her eyes and scanned the area for birds. "Food sounds good—even screwball mesquite pods."

His muffled laugh warmed her. They were in a perilous position, but David wasn't giving up, and neither was she.

But the mention of food had sent her hunger urges over the top. She even checked to see if what she'd thought were stale French fries were still edible. The lumps turned out to be wadded up twists of tissue—a product of Reezira's nervous habit.

"Aren't there other plants we can eat?" she asked. "Dad used to say certain cacti could keep a man from dehydration."

He nodded but didn't look up from his work. "If this hole doesn't pan out, we'll go foraging. But look, the soil is damp and I'm only six inches down."

She scooted closer for a look. Sure enough the walls of the hole were turning a darker shade of pewter, but that was a long way from something to drink. Just thinking of the word, made her mouth crave moisture.

"What else should I do? I haven't even seen a lizard, yet."

"Because I'm making too much of a ruckus. Um… what color underwear do you have on?"

She nearly fell off her perch. "Red panties. White bra."

"Take them off. You don't need the layers during the day and even a small patch of red might help a search plane spot us."

Somehow she doubted her bikini briefs would be much help, but she quickly complied. The relative coolness of the morning felt good on her skin. She had a feeling she was going to be hating her jeans before long, but according to David, keeping your skin protected was imperative.

He looked up when she held the two pieces of lingerie out to him. "Good. Maybe you can use the bra as a hat."

Liz started to laugh. "I'm afraid you have me mixed up with my sister Alex. She's the bosomy one. Well, she used to be—until she got sick. But even underweight she's still got me beat."

He wiped his hands on his pants and walked to her side. "It's vital to protect your head from the sun. As we become stressed for water, you'll also need to breathe through your nose and keep your mouth closed. And not talk. Or laugh."

He leaned over and kissed her. "Our last, until we're rescued."

"Do you think that will happen? I mean, maybe we need to think about walking out."

"We'll start walking this evening, just after sunset, if no search planes show up. To walk in the heat of the day would be suicide."

He took the bra from her and cleverly fashioned an odd-shaped, lumpy hat of sorts that he perched atop her head. "Now, find a long stick to attach our new flag to, but move slowly and deliberately. No wasted motions. And keep looking for signs of trails. Javelinas and burros know where to find water. They can lead us to it, if we're observant."

David watched her move off toward the grouping of rocks near where they'd been dropped off. He'd climbed to the top of the outcropping before she woke up to get a sense of where they were. In the middle of freaking nowhere, he'd decided. He'd marked the position of the sun as it peeked over the horizon in the far distance to get his bearings.

They would follow Ray's tracks for as long as they had light, but without water, they wouldn't make it far, regardless of the time of day. So he picked up his donated tennis shoe again—a lucky break that Liz's new brother-in-law bought durable, expensive footwear and wore the same size as David did.

He turned the shoe length-wise and resumed digging. The padded insole helped protect his fingers from the course soil. He'd never have broken through the rock-hard topsoil if he'd been digging anywhere but the riverbed. Once he cracked the outer crust, he'd found the going easier.

He focused on his task the same way he'd focused on the miracles he'd witnessed under his microscope. Worlds shifted, collided, bonded and metamorphosed while he watched. He'd missed that part of his life, he realized.

A noise of some sort made him look up some time later. He blinked to get his bearings. And when he saw Liz, his heart did a funny little lift and fall. She was sitting cross-legged a few feet away, eyes closed in a meditative pose. Her misshapen bra hat tilted rakishly on her head. Directly behind her, on the highest part of the embankment, a small red flag atop what appeared to be a creosote branch fluttered in the breeze.

His feelings for her were so powerful he was afraid his heart might explode. He respected her, admired her and, above all, loved her. And he damn well would keep her alive.

He cleared his throat, which was dry and coated in dust.

Swallowing was getting harder. The back of his neck felt blistered and his arms were probably bright red under the layer of dirt he'd accumulated. "Liz," he croaked.

She opened her eyes and smiled.

"I need your hat…um, bra."

She pulled if off her head and leaned over to hand it to him. "What for? I've grown rather fond of it. Could be the new rage, you know?"

He inverted it, doubling the cups to make one. "Perfect," he said. Then he dipped the soft, slightly padded saucer into the well of off-gray water that had accumulated in the hole he'd dug. "Ambrosia, my dear."

Liz scrambled closer and didn't hesitate. After checking the supply, she slurped down a few ounces. "Yuck," she exclaimed, choking slightly. "That's really bad."

"But your body needs it. Don't spit."

She made a face and stuck out her tongue, like a cat choking back a hairball, but eventually she stopped gagging. "Are you sure it's safe?"

"Not really. But it's better than dehydration. We could try filtering it. Maybe through my sock."

He sat back and started to pull of his other shoe, until Liz's laugh stopped him. "Don't take this the wrong way, but I think I'll stick with the plain, unfiltered kind. Sweaty-sock water just doesn't have the same appeal, you know?"

He chuckled and took the bra/cup from her. He choked down two gulps, and had to agree. It was bad. Wet, but alkaline-tasting and gritty. "Nice job on the flag," he said. "Did you see any more creosote around? It burns nice and smoky if can get a fire going."

"We don't have any matches."

He slowly stood up. "Matches? We don't need no stinking matches."

Her brow arched wryly. "Pathetic, but I give you credit for trying. You need me to gather wood, I take it."

"Anything flammable. Reeds. Thistles. Little plastic thingees. We'll stoke this before we start walking, and the glow, if it's big enough might help us chart a course so we don't wander around in circles. Hopefully, we'll be able to follow the tracks your car tires made, but it won't be easy in the dark."

"Did I tell you that Zeke put a GPS tracking device in my car?"

David stopped abruptly. "No, you didn't. Why'd he do that?"

"Precautionary, I guess. Just in case your bad guy came looking. Smart, huh? I should have mentioned it earlier, but since he hasn't shown up…" He got her point. "I don't know how GPS works, do you?"

"In theory, but I've never used one." He sighed. "But even with GPS, this is a big damn desert. If Zeke's looking for us, we need to send up a sign. So look for wood."

It took longer than he'd anticipated to construct the bow and drill. He'd practiced this skill off and on ever since he arrived in Vegas—just for such a circumstance. He found a little depression in the rock and mounded some bits and pieces of dried foliage in a pile beside him. The sound of the friction as wood and rock created heat was pretty much drowned out by the wind, which had continued to rise all afternoon. He sheltered his work with his body, only paying attention to his task.

"Oh, my God, smoke," Liz exclaimed. "You really are a Boy Scout."

Not really. His grandmother hadn't wanted to take him to regular weekly meetings. He hadn't argued or pleaded. So instead of interacting with a group, he'd become a nerd who liked science. A loner. When Ray visited colleges looking for bright young chemistry students, his first criterion had been social outcasts with a limited social life. People like Paul.

Liz suddenly materialized at his side. She carefully fed the flame and blew on it. Within seconds they had a small fire going.

"Wow. I'm impressed."

David felt good about his accomplishment, too. He waited until he had a bed of coals then popped one plastic strip on the pile. The black smoke twirled upward, but was quickly dispersed by the breeze.

Oh, well, he thought. *We have several more hours of daylight. We can try again.*

He did…until all four pieces were gone.

Hope was disappearing, too, but he didn't tell Liz that. Their tiny sips of grayish water weren't going to do much to rehydrate their bodies. They needed help. Soon. Or Ray would win, and David couldn't let that happen.

Ray was an abomination, a clever manipulator who survived through sheer perseverance. If even a fraction of the tales he'd shared about his youth were true, his mere survival was a bit of a miracle. He'd grown up so poor, he'd scrounged for food from local restaurants in Tijuana while his prostitute mother worked the streets. He'd never known his father. His mother disappeared when Ray was ten. David once thought that their histories—both being orphans—made them closer and more alike, but he'd been wrong.

As an idealistic chemist, David had wanted to make the world a better place; Ray wanted to make the world pay for his misfortunes.

Chapter Seventeen

Their rescue, when it happened just before dusk, was a surreal combination of miracle and anticlimax, Liz thought. She and David had rested in the shade of a makeshift lean-to he'd constructed against the rock where they'd slept the night before. The heat had at times felt like a mean child tormenting them with the occasional stinging wisp of wind-driven sand. Liz had done her best to remain still, conserve energy and nurse her dwindling supply of hope. She'd even concentrated very hard on sending her mother a directional signal of sorts.

No helicopters or spotter planes gave them any warning. Just the low roar of two unmarked black SUVs with tinted windows. FBI, she later learned.

"Your smoke signal really helped," Zeke, who was the first to exit from one of the cars, said. "Smart move."

David took the praise with a bare nod of acknowledgment, greedily guzzling from the bottle of water one of the three agents who were with Zeke had handed him. Liz had choked down two or three swallows before her mind even registered the relief.

"Thank God you stayed put," Zeke said. "We didn't know what the hell we were going to do if you'd left these coordinates."

Neither Liz nor David could talk right away, but, fortunately, Zeke had plenty to say once he helped them into the backseat of one of the vehicles.

In response to David's barely croaked "How…?" Zeke answered, "Liz's mother called me about midnight and said you two were in trouble. I didn't ask how she knew—she's Yetta, right?"

Liz nodded.

"First, I checked to see if there was any action on your car. Sure enough, it was moving slowly in an odd meandering motion way the hell out in the middle of nowhere. Not your typical driving pattern."

He was facing them from the front seat, as the driver, a sober-looking fellow with reflective sunglasses and a black ball cap, drove.

"He was going to leave my car," Liz said in a hoarse whisper, "at the airport so you'd think we'd run off together."

David gave her a funny look and Liz realized he'd been unconscious during that part of his ex-boss's conversation.

"Yeah, well, that didn't happen," Zeke said.

He and the driver exchanged a look. Liz's intuition told her something bad was coming. She reached out and took David's hand in hers.

"Let me back up," Zeke said. "Yesterday, the arson team made a breakthrough in their investigation. Mark Gaylord called me and said they'd found part of the trigger device and when they entered it into the computer, the match rang all kinds of bells higher up."

He looked at David and said, "Apparently, your ex-boss had made a hobby out of lighting fires. Might have been where he made his money starting out. After you blew the whistle on him, he went underground, had some cosmetic surgery done, then he started exacting revenge. His first incendiary device destroyed the federal courthouse in Virginia where he'd been brought up on charges. Two agents and a judge died. That's why the Bureau is here."

"So, you caught him?" Liz asked.

Zeke hesitated. "Two units intercepted him when he reached the feeder road. There was another car waiting for him. Several helicopters and some county boys got in on the chase. We had no way of knowing whether Cross was behind the wheel of Liz's car or the other one."

"What happened?"

"We threw tire spikes in his path. He swerved to miss them and crashed over an embankment. He died at the scene."

"Ray's dead?" David asked.

Zeke let out a sigh and nodded.

David appeared too stunned to react. Liz was relieved to the point of tears, but the reservoirs of her tear ducts must not have filled up, yet. The madman was dead. David was free to start his life over. Together, they'd beaten the odds and made it out of the desert.

She looked at Zeke, who was staring at her as if gauging her emotional stability. There was something he wasn't telling her.

She took a deep breath. "What else?"

Zeke turned away, facing front. "Nothing. Your mother's at your house. Your roommates are back. We're going there, first. Baines, I need you to come with me to Metro, if you're up for it. We want to get a statement. And Cross's accomplice is still at large."

Liz looked at David. His brow was crinkled, but she could tell by the set of his jaw he was prepared to do whatever was necessary to tie up all the loose ends. He nodded. "Will you be okay?"

No. She knew she would be, but delayed shock was setting in. A shiver passed through her body and her teeth started to chatter.

"I think Liz should be checked out by a doctor," David said, in a tone that made both men in the front seat look back at them.

Zeke shrugged. "Good idea. Maybe you both should."

Liz didn't have the energy to argue. She was suddenly exhausted. She pulled the jacket someone had handed her up around her neck and snuggled down as far as the safety belt would allow her. David leaned inward to offer his shoulder and in seconds she was asleep.

"How does it feel to be a free man?" the younger of the FBI agents asked.

How does it feel? David thought a moment, but no glib answer came to mind. He was alive—thanks to Liz and Zeke. The threat that had been hanging over his head for four years was gone. Truly and completely. Ray had no children to avenge their father's death, no friends or partners who gave a damn about him. Instead of finding comfort in the thought, though, David had to fight back a wince. *How is my life any different?*

"I'm still trying to get used to the idea," he responded, to be friendly. He'd spent too long on the fringe—both as a scientist holed up in his lab and as a fugitive. Did he have the social skills he needed to fit into society again? He wasn't sure.

"Are we done here?" he asked. Exhaustion was lurking just under his consciousness. Sleeping for a week sounded like a great idea, but he knew that wasn't going to happen. He had less than a thousand dollars to his name, no car, no house and a few straggly cacti that he needed to find homes for.

Zeke, who'd left the room to take a call, returned. He spoke to the agents before motioning for David to follow him. David stood up. Someone at the E.R. had handed him a pair of green scrubs to put on after he'd taken a much-needed shower. And paper slippers to replace his ruined tennis shoes. The tile floor was cold but life-affirming.

He nodded his thanks to the three agents who'd been involved in the rescue then shuffled after Zeke. What he needed more than anything was to see Liz. Alex had been waiting at the hospital when they'd arrived. The two sisters had embraced with tears and hugs of joy. After a quick once-over by the attending physician, Liz had been free to leave. She and David really hadn't had a chance to talk.

"I know you're ready to close the book on this," Zeke said, leading David to his office at the end of the hallway, "but there's one more thing we need to talk about—Liz."

A hint of foreboding in Zeke's tone made David wary. He ignored the hustle and bustle around him. "Is she okay?"

She'd seemed fine at the hospital. Exhausted and disheveled, but still on top of things, refusing the IV the doctor had recommended. "I'll pick up a couple of bottles of Gatorade to replace my electrolytes," she'd told the man. "A shower and nap are my number-one priorities at the moment."

"What's going on? Is something wrong?" David asked as he sat down across from the silver-haired detective.

Zeke's nod was ambivalent at best. "Yetta just called. She was at Liz's place while we were looking for you two. I guess having Liz's things around helped her pick up her daughter's Rom ESP frequency or something."

His tone was dry but not denigrating. David had a feeling Zeke put more stock in those ESP messages than he wanted people to know. "And…"

"Some lady from India called while Yetta was there. Do you know anything about a baby Liz wanted to adopt?"

David nodded. "Her name is Prisha. She's an orphan living at the ashram where Liz volunteered. She's been sick recently. Liz was worried about her. Oh, God, no…"

"Whoa, son, slow down. You're jumping to the wrong conclusion," Zeke said. "I don't know the whole story, but apparently when the mother found out that Liz wanted to adopt the baby, she changed her mind and came rushing back into the picture. I don't know exactly what that means to Liz's plans, but Yetta is going to break the news to Liz as soon as she wakes up. She thinks maybe you should be there."

David closed his eyes. Poor Liz. "Are we done here?"

Zeke nodded. "I'll give you a ride. I told Yetta I'd pick her up and run her home, but I thought you should know what's going on."

"Thanks."

Before exiting the office, Zeke paused. He looked at David and said, his tone severe, "This family has been through hell the past couple of years. I don't know what you have planned, but if you're heading back East, then do the right thing and make a clean break now. Stringing Liz along while you figure out whether you're David Baines or Paul McAffee isn't going to do her any favors."

A clean break. The words stuck with David during the drive to Henderson. He honestly had no idea what to do, where to go, how to start again. Staying alive and living in the shadows had been his main focus for four years. Now he was free to go anywhere, reclaim his past, his credentials, his life. But rebuilding his career in the research field would take an incredible amount of effort. Years, months, weeks of 24/7 focus. The kind of dedication that already had cost him one family. Would the same thing happen if he asked Liz to join him back East?

Maybe I should stay here, he thought. *And do what? Rebuild my gardening business?*

The truth was obvious. What did he have to offer Liz? Not a damn thing.

LIZ AWOKE with a momentary sense of confusion. She thought for a few seconds that she was back in Bosnia in the farmhouse where she'd stayed immediately after her release from the hospital. She ached all over. Her feet, her ribs, she could barely turn her neck.

Groaning, she sat up and as she became fully awake, images from the past twenty-four hours filled her consciousness. The desert. David. The rescue.

She let out a long, heartfelt sigh. Alex had picked her up at the hospital and brought her straight home. Her mother had prepared a hot bath with scented oils that had helped her relax. A soothing cup of herbal tea and she'd been off to la-la land.

She glanced at her bedside clock. Three hours. Not long enough, but something had woken her up. She wasn't sure what, but she couldn't go back to sleep. An uneasiness seemed to hum in her veins. Post-traumatic stress again? she wondered.

Her lightweight robe was lying across the foot of her bed. She pulled it over her Chicks Rule T-shirt and cotton boxers. The house was quiet, but she could feel the presence of her roommates down the hall. *Maybe Alex and Mom are still here, too,* she thought, but Liz knew she wasn't ready to face them. She needed a minute alone, with Prisha.

She got out of bed and, barefoot, walked to the make-shift desk in the corner of the room. She sat down in the chair stiffly, like an old woman. Her mailbox had fourteen new messages. Most were jokes from Grace.

She quickly scrolled down until she spotted a familiar name. Jyoti.

Her finger shook as she double-clicked on the message.

My dear good friend,
What I am about to write is going to come as a great shock and even greater disappointment, I fear, but there is no way to avoid the pain this news is going to inflict. Formal word of your intention to adopt Prisha arrived last week. As is our legal obligation, we notified Prisha's mother of your wish.

Liz braced herself for what she sensed was coming.

The young woman came to visit her child and after much weeping and prayer announced to all that she couldn't bear to give up Prisha to be raised in a foreign land.

Liz had read of this kind of thing happening. Online adoption sites contained horror stories of people who'd adopted only to have the child they'd come to love ripped from their arms.

I tried to explain that Prisha needed the medical care that you were arranging in the United States. The woman vowed to find medical help nearby. As you know, the government goes to great lengths to keep families together when possible. Representatives con- tacted me personally to say that a doctor in Delhi has volunteered to do the surgery on Prisha.

Liz reread the passage twice, trying to make sense of the words. "Why now?" she muttered. "Where were these people when I couldn't even get a pediatrician to examine her?"

Her question was answered a few lines down.

It seems that after Prisha's birth, her mother tried to take her own life and needed to be hospitalized. While undergoing treatment for depression, she met a doctor who took pity on her and has agreed to perform the surgery free of charge.

"Free of charge?" Liz croaked. How could she compete with free?

Forgive me for saying so, but it's quite possible he plans to run for political office soon. Maybe he feels Prisha's story would be good news. But none of that really matters. Prisha will get the help she needs, and I truly am happy that this darling child will be taken care of.

Despite her pain, Liz understood. And agreed.

I'm providing a link to the doctor's new Web site that is already up and running. He's going to do the surgery as soon as possible, and people will be able to follow Prisha's progress and contribute money to her recovery. I hope you can take comfort in knowing that you were the catalyst that united mother and daughter.

Liz moved the cursor over the highlighted blue letters but couldn't bring herself to touch the button. Her heart felt bruised and bleeding. To see her precious face and know that she hadn't even been able to say goodbye was too much to take in.

Prisha, the courageous baby girl—a fighter, just like Liz—would never make the trip from India to live in this house that Liz had bought purposely to provide a home for her. She'd never do any of the things Liz had imagined them doing together.

Liz pushed her laptop out of the way and dropped her head on the desk. "No," she softly cried. "This just can't be."

The sobs that rolled up and out of her mouth seemed to start in the bottom of her soul. Questions careened through her mind. What if this doctor lost interest after the election? What if the mother's depression returned or she couldn't care for Prisha?

A sense of helplessness—hopelessness—engulfed her. Even the voice that said this was a good thing—Prisha would know her mother's love and have a nice life in India—was drowned out by the sad truth that Liz had lost her baby.

A light tap at her door made her look up. "Not now."

The door opened anyway. The head that popped in wasn't her mother's. "David," she cried, stumbling to her feet. Unsteady as a drunk, she crashed into his open arms.

She wept freely, knowing he understood what it meant to lose a child that you loved. Blubbering, she tried to explain. "P-Prisha is gone. H-her real mother came back."

"I know, sweetheart."

Liz shook her head. "No. How?"

He put his hand in her hair and drew her head against his chest. "Someone from India called to see how you were taking the news. They were worried about you."

Her mother had known when Liz arrived home. That explained the profound sadness she'd read in Yetta's eyes. Liz had been too exhausted to give anything around her much thought, but she'd picked up on the fact that something was amiss.

"The woman who called wasn't able to talk for long because of the cost. Yetta was under the impression you hadn't discussed this with your sisters and she wasn't sure what to say or why you'd chosen to keep this to yourself. Is it because of what happened to you in Bosnia?"

Liz had kept Prisha a secret partly because she was afraid something might go wrong in the adoption process. She'd been warned time and again about how unpredictable foreign adoptions could be. She hadn't wanted to disappoint her family—again. She'd already failed them where her father was concerned.

"I should have told them, but I knew they'd want to help. Grace would have given me the money from her trust fund in a heartbeat, but then I would have felt that Prisha was partly hers. I was selfish. I wanted her all to myself. And now, I'm paying for that."

He rocked her back and forth as a father might a little child. "Liz, this isn't your fault. It's mine."

She pushed back to face him. "What do you mean?"

"Think about your prophecy. A man of darkness. Me. If you hadn't rescued me, Prisha might still be at the ashram, waiting for you to adopt her."

Liz wanted to deny the validity of his words, but she couldn't. She'd thought the same thing just before he walked in. If she hadn't invited him to the wedding…no, she refused to believe that her life would have been better if David had died in the fire that consumed his home.

"I don't know why I'm surprised," he said, standing up. "Everything I've touched in my life, I've ruined. My grandmother used to call me a hard-luck kid. We've only known each other a few weeks and I've managed to upset your whole life. You narrowly escaped death in the desert. Your car is totaled and now the child you love is gone. I'm bad news for those who mean the most to me." He looked at her. "That's why I'm leaving."

She wasn't surprised by his statement. She'd known that once he was free of the threat Ray Cross posed, David would want to reclaim his old life. Who wouldn't choose being a respected chemist over peddling cacti? "When?"

"Soon. Your mother suggested I call your cousin—the one who's a long-haul trucker and see if I could catch a ride on one of his transports. He's got one leaving at midnight for Tennessee. That's close enough for me."

"You're going home."

"I have no idea where that is. Hell, I'm not even sure I know what that word means. But I can't stay here."

She knew she should try to stop him. He meant more to her than any man she'd ever known. He'd brought joy and beauty into her life, too, but what if he was right? What if in saving David, she'd made a fatal choice that she would have to live with for the rest of her life? What if Prisha's surgery turned out to be nothing more than a publicity stunt? If Prisha died, Liz knew she'd never be able to forgive herself—or David.

Chapter Eighteen

Two weeks had passed since David had hitched a ride on an eastbound 18-wheeler. Liz's tears had long since dried. Was she happy about the situation? No. But life did go on. Routines reappeared.

Like the weekly roundtable of sisters.

Liz, who hadn't slept a full eight hours since her desert escapade, usually arrived at her mother's early to talk to Yetta for a few minutes before Kate and Alex joined them.

"Katherine told me your teas have become a hot item at several local markets," her mother said once they were both seated at the table.

The kitchen smelled familiar and reassuring. Liz stirred the liquid in her cup. "I know, it's really weird how this sorta took off. I set up a display in this trendy little market near Romantique the day after David left and I've had to restock it every other day. I can barely keep up production, which is why I'm looking for a place to rent. I've outgrown my garage. Especially if Reezira and Lydia are going to work for me."

Work had been her salvation. She'd lost so much so fast, she probably would have lost her mind, too, if her roommates and her sister hadn't conspired to keep her busy. Jo,

Kate's partner, had been the first to call, needing more tea. Then the market had placed a triple order. And Crissy had appeared with a request for several herbal teas she suddenly couldn't live without.

Instead of running away from her pain—as she always had in the past—Liz was working through it. But one thing was still bothering her.

"Mom, it hit me last night that my prophecy was wrong."

Yetta looked up from the newspaper Liz had brought in with her. "What do you mean?"

"Well, I saved David, the man of shadows, and lost Prisha, the child of light, but now I don't have either one of them in my life. Is that how it was supposed to work?"

Yetta rocked back in her chair and sighed. "That's a very good question. But are you sure you saved David? It seems to me that you both saved each other. That's what people who love each other do. Your father rescued me from becoming a dried-up old maid—you'd be surprised how many boys were put off by my ability to see beyond their smart suits and nice manners. And I kept Ernst grounded. If not for me, he'd have drifted around like…well, like his brother."

"I never would have been in that danger if not for David."

"And the bad man wouldn't have known where to find David if not for you."

Liz's mouth dropped open. She'd forgotten about that. "Does that matter? I mean, we saved each other on the desert, but I still lost Prisha." And David.

Yetta leaned over and took Liz's hand. "Prisha came into your life at a time when you desperately needed hope. She gave you that. When you came back from India, I remember thinking that I'd never seen you so focused and driven. And happy."

"But if I was never meant to save her then—"

"Darling girl, you did save her. You reunited her with her family. You gave her mother time to deal with whatever was keeping her from embracing her daughter wholeheartedly. And because of your interest in adopting Prisha, you motivated her family to take action. Isn't that something to celebrate?"

Liz had actually come to the same conclusion herself, but hearing her mother say so out loud drove home the point. She was happy for Prisha. According to Jyoti, Prisha's mother appeared to be trying to make up for the time she'd missed in her daughter's life.

The sound of a car in the driveway caught Liz's attention. She stood up and walked to the window. Alex, who was strolling up the driveway, paused to embrace Kate, who had returned from her honeymoon a few days ago, but had been so busy with Maya, Jo and Romantique that Liz had barely seen her.

And she looked absolutely glowing.

I know how that feels, she thought with just the tiniest pang of envy. She'd felt the same all-encompassing joy with David, and she wanted it back. But how could she reclaim that feeling when she didn't know where—or who— he was.

She turned to look at her mother, who was grinning. "If you need our help, all you have do is ask," Yetta said. "Your sisters are a tremendous resource. Especially Grace."

"She's in Detroit. What can she do?"

"She's engaged to a *gaujo* cop. And if Nikolai can't help us, I'm sure Ezekiel will."

"Speaking of Zeke, I haven't seen him around here lately. Did you two break up?"

"One has to be going steady to break up, doesn't one?" She didn't wait for an answer. "His daughter just gave birth to her first child. I encouraged him to go to California to be with her and try to make peace with the past. As Katherine will attest, moving forward is a lot easier if you're not struggling with bonds of guilt and remorse that keep pulling you backward."

Liz opened the door for her sisters and hugged them both. They looked a bit surprised by her display of affection, but neither said anything. After giving Kate a chance to relate the highlights of her honeymoon in Tahiti, Liz got down to business.

"Okay, here's what I need. First, I'm—"

Kate interrupted. "Wait. Stop. Did I miss something? You're not the sister who asks for help."

Alex waved the question away. "That was before she nearly died on the desert after the madman totaled her car and tried to kill her boyfriend."

Kate's eyes went wide and she looked at Yetta. "Mom, tell Alex to quit teasing. What really happened while I was gone?"

Yetta looked at all three girls then, with a low chuckle, sat down. "You see, this madman intent on revenge kidnapped your sister and…"

Liz tuned out the story. She had more important things on her mind than yesterday's news—like how to find David and convince him that he had a life waiting for him here in Las Vegas. A life with her.

ALTHOUGH IT HAD BEEN two weeks since David left Nevada, he'd put off contacting his ex-wife. He'd passed by Kay's house, which was right next door to the home he'd owned when they were married, a dozen times, but had yet to figure out a way to gracefully return from the dead.

He'd finally decided to use an intermediary—Kay's

husband, Brent. Once he'd cleared up the matter of his official death certificate, he faxed a copy to Brent at his office. Brent had called back almost immediately.

Shock and disbelief were Brent's first response, followed by concern for his wife. "Kay is pregnant," the man blurted out after David reassured him this wasn't some kind of sick joke.

"I drove past the house yesterday. She was putting a baby in the back of an SUV. She didn't look pregnant."

The admission that David had been in the old neighborhood apparently gave Brent pause, but he quickly added, "Just barely. A total surprise. We had to have help conceiving B.J., um, Brent, Junior. He just turned nine months. The older kids adore him. We haven't even told them about the new baby. Just in case…well, you know the first trimester can be tricky." His voice trailed off as if realizing that his assumption that David knew anything about pregnancies might be flawed.

"Then it's a good thing I notified you, instead of just knocking on Kay's door one day, right?"

"Yes," said the man who'd been David's neighbor for nearly eight years. For six of those years, Brent had been married to a woman who'd also worked in government. One day, the wife drove off never to return. Brent had kept the house; she'd remarried a few months after the divorce was final.

"Look, I don't want to cause problems, Brent. I'm just trying to get my bearings. I know I left Kay holding the bag after the fire at the lab, and I want to apologize. A very wise woman told me that moving forward is a lot easier if you're not carrying the full weight of your mistakes with you."

"Do you think apologizing is going to make up for the hell she went through after the explosion?"

David didn't know what to say.

"She was devastated at first. Then, later, after the funeral, she read something that made her change her mind."

David snickered. "She decided it was better that I'd died?"

"No, she told me she didn't think you were dead."

"Why did she think that?"

"You can ask her when you see her." Brent sounded resigned. "I'll call her and set up a meeting. Probably without the kids, if you don't mind. The twins took quite a while to warm up to me, and they're at an age that…well, we'll see. Maybe Kay will disagree. I know you cared for them when you two were together."

NINETY MINUTES LATER, David was standing on the porch next door to the home he'd once owned. Both places looked exactly the same, although someone had painted the front door of David's home a dark purple.

He pushed the bell.

Kay answered the door almost immediately. Brent stood behind her, his expression far less welcoming—less jubilant than his wife's.

"Paul," she cried, wrapping him in her arms and pulling him close. She seemed shorter and rounder than he remembered, but she smelled the same—Youth Dew and cookies. She'd always loved to bake.

"Paul," she said again, her voice wobbling with emotion. Tears rolled down her cheeks when she pulled back to look at him. "You're too thin. You're not eating, are you? And, oh dear, what a hideous mustache. Is it fake?"

For the first time since leaving Las Vegas, he threw back his head and laughed. "Why don't you tell me what you really think, Kay?"

She put her hand on his arm and coaxed him inside.

"You know me, speak first, think about propriety second. But it really isn't you."

He chose to ignore her observation. "Thanks for seeing me. Brent, you must have really made good time to get here."

"I have a different job now. With a private contractor. Closer to home."

Kay insisted on serving them coffee, along with a plate of homemade cookies. The smell was intoxicating and brought back memories he'd thought long gone. "Brent probably filled you in on what happened, right?" he asked Kay.

She nodded. "You did the right thing, Paul. I always had misgivings about Ray's miracle fountain of youth. I knew you were too honorable to poison the public just to make a buck."

"A couple of billion bucks," he said, surprised by how good her praise felt.

He finished his cookie then sat forward, elbows on his knees. "I came to apologize, Kay. I should have figured out a way to tell you the truth. To warn you. But the U.S. marshals convinced me that any deviation from the plan would put you and the children in danger."

Before she could say anything, a high thin wail sounded from the counter behind him. David jumped slightly and turned to see a small speaker of some kind.

"I'll get him. Probably needs a change," Brent said, standing up.

"You can give him some juice—half juice, half water, remember." To David, she said, "I'm trying to wean him. We just found out…" Her smile was so bright it almost hurt to look at her. "Did Brent tell you?"

David nodded. "Yes, congratulations."

"I know five children isn't politically correct, but we can afford them and, damn it, I'm a really good mother. It's all

I ever wanted to do. Be the best wife and mother I could be." Her red-apple cheeks glowed a little brighter. "Which is why I felt so guilty about Brent. You were my hero, Paul. You rescued me from purgatory. But I never should have married you."

"Kay, you and the kids filled a huge void in my life. But I was so caught up in my work—and my ego—I didn't appreciate what you brought to me."

She smiled sadly. "We both made mistakes, but I'm not making excuses for myself. Brent is a good man. Neither of us meant for the affair to happen. But I was lonely."

He knew she didn't intend to sound as if she was making an accusation, but he wouldn't have protested if she had.

"I never believed you were dead, Paul."

She'd been using his old name since he'd shown up and he hadn't corrected her. "That's what Brent said. How come? I saw a video of the funeral. You seemed pretty choked up."

She frowned. "You're right. I was convinced at first, but a few days after the funeral, I read a newspaper report that said you'd perished trying to save your animals. I remembered you mentioning months earlier that the research portion of the lab had been shut down."

"Wow. That's pretty clever deductive reasoning. If they'd asked me first, I would have told them to delete that part of the story. And they should have known better. My instructor always said that too many details will bring everything down like a house of cards."

Brent still hadn't returned. Maybe he'd wanted to give them a few moments alone. David appreciated the gesture, but his feelings for Kay had coalesced into friendship—the kind that existed between distant relatives or pals who went through hell together in college but somehow survived.

"Kay, I'm moving to Vegas. I've met someone. We left things kinda up in the air, so I'm not sure what I'll find when I get there, but I have to give this a try. I think it's best where your kids are concerned, too. I don't know if my showing up again would cause problems between the boys and Brent, but why take chances? They probably don't even remember me."

She shook her head. "That's not true. Come with me."

He followed her through the neat, but well-lived-in house to a large oak-paneled room off the kitchen. The family room, he assumed. One wall was made up entirely of shelves and an oversize projection-type TV. Scattered amongst the books and knickknacks were dozens of framed photos.

He picked up one that had once rested on the dresser in his bedroom. His parents and him. Taken just a few weeks before their accident, this photo was one of the few his grandmother had saved. She'd claimed that looking at pictures of her daughter was too painful.

"You've remained a part of our family, Paul. Ariel loves this photograph. She calls you her angel. The twins used to talk about you a lot. Mostly to upset Brent, I think. They blamed him for our divorce."

"Which is wrong. I'm to blame for that."

When he started to put the photo back on the shelf, she shook her head and pressed it into his hands. "No. Like you said, we both made mistakes. Maybe neither of us was honest about why we got married in the first place, but that doesn't matter now. I'm just so happy that you're alive."

He gave the framed picture a little shake and asked, "This reminds me. Did you keep any of my old stuff? I'd certainly understand if you didn't, but—"

Her laugh made him stop midsentence. She looked past

him and said, "Paul wants to know if we kept any of his stuff."

David looked over his shoulder. Brent was standing there, a curious, towheaded toddler in his arms. Brent smiled for the first time. "Oh, yeah, have we got stuff. Half a garage full. My car will worship you if you take it off our hands."

David shook his head. "You kept my crap? Why?"

"I ask her the same thing every spring and fall. She says, 'Because I can't get rid of it. I just can't.'"

David looked at his ex-wife. "Why?"

A mischievous grin made her eyes twinkle. "Same reason I sold the house next door, used what I needed to to settle your affairs, then gave the rest to my brilliant, utterly anal husband to invest. Because I knew you'd be back for it."

Brent joined them. "Anal?" he said peevishly to Kay. He handed the little boy to David then walked to a built-in desk with a computer on it. After sitting down to type in something, he said, "I'll have you know every penny of the royalties from your patents went into a separate account. I only risked the interest in the stock market. And I did pretty damn well, if I do say so myself."

David juggled the child who eyeballed him suspiciously but didn't cry. "What patents?"

"Ray or someone in the company must have filed patents on your new formulas on your behalf. I know how focused you were on the discovery end, but someone knew there was money to be made over the long haul," Brent said. "I think you'll be pleasantly surprised."

"What if I'd never come back?"

Kay smiled and brushed a hand over her son's downy hair. "We have four-going-on-five children. We'd have found a use, but the bulk I'd intended to set up as science scholarships in your name."

The baby let out a loud sound and threw his little body sideways, nearly causing David to stumble. The boy wanted his mother and wasn't afraid to say so. "How much are we talking?"

Kay took the child from his arms. "Show him, Brent."

Brent got up and gave David the chair. Even at first glance, he could tell there were a lot of zeroes. "This is mine?"

"Brent's devoted as much time and planning to your portfolio as he has ours," Kay said.

David stood up and walked to the couple. "I don't know what to say. I wasn't expecting anything from you. All I was hoping for was your forgiveness." He shook Brent's hand. "Thank you so much."

Kay made a sniffling sound and Brent put his arm around her shoulders. The baby tugged on his mother's blond hair and put a few strands in his mouth.

David left a short time later—before the older children returned from school. He might see them at some point in the future, once their parents felt the time was right. Until then, though, he had a lot of things to do, starting with picking a name. Was he David Baines or Paul McAffee? A thing like that was important when a man planned on asking the woman he loved to marry him.

Chapter Nineteen

Liz looked around the half-painted interior of her new workspace and smiled. Pristine walls, excellent ventilation and good lighting would help increase productivity once her eager workers started sealing tea bags in earnest.

The space had been provided by Mimi Simms, David's landlady. After some debate, the older woman had decided to pocket the insurance money rather then rebuild David's house, but she wasn't happy not having someone or something besides a cat to fuss about, so she and Liz worked out a rental arrangement. Liz used the money that had been refunded from her adoption application to enclose a third of what had been David's greenhouse. If he came back, he could still use the other two-thirds and the potting shed, which had escaped the fire, for his business.

If he never came back, Liz would eventually move into the rest of the space. She had a good feeling about her tea company, which thanks to word of mouth—and Romantique—was taking off.

"We are done?" Lydia asked.

Liz nodded. "Yep, Mom's picking you up for your ESL class. I bet you can talk her into stopping at some fast-food restaurant on the way."

The girls gave each other a high five and laughed as they stripped off their rubber gloves. They'd returned from their trip to Arizona with a renewed determination to stay in the country. A family friend had volunteered to handle their case and had already made progress. Just this morning, the postman had delivered two temporary work permits, which Lydia and Reezira showed to anyone who came near.

Liz was happy for them. In fact, she was happy. More or less. She still missed Prisha, but had finally broken down and visited the Web site that provided updates on her progress. A video had documented her first surgery. Liz's throat had been knotted the whole time, but seeing the child smile up at her mother after the anesthesia wore off had been worth the agony.

Prisha was going to be all right. Liz knew it. The little girl was a fighter. One day she'd walk without crutches. Maybe one day, she'd visit America and come to see the woman who had loved her so dearly. Liz wasn't giving up hope. Using Jyoti as an interpreter, Liz had been able talk to Prisha's mother, who, to Liz's surprise, had thanked Prisha's "American angel" for helping to bring her daughter home.

The sound of car tires on the gravel outside made the young women squeal and race around, collecting their purses and backpacks. Liz, who planned to paint the trim until it was time to pick up her roommates at the community college, followed them outside.

"Hello, dear," her mother called. "How's the painting going?"

"We're all done except the trim. I should finish that tonight, then we can move in and set up operations."

Liz had spent a lot of time since David's departure thinking about what she wanted to accomplish. She was tired of physical therapy, although she'd been approached by a new holistic healer in town about handling a few clients. She liked the young man's approach and energy, and had agreed to try a test case. Maybe she'd find a balance between her new business and her former career.

"Wonderful. I had a lovely dream about you last night. I think you're going to be wildly successful."

Liz smiled. "Well. Coming from you, that's a good thing. You didn't happen to see a tall man with a shaggy mustache in that dream, did you?"

"No," her mother said, but she didn't seem very sad about dashing her daughter's hope that David would return.

"Oh."

"Ta-ta. We have to run," Yetta said as the rear doors of the older Lincoln slammed shut. "Oh, and Elizabeth, I'll pick up Lydia and Reezira after class today."

That was a surprise. "Why?"

"You'll see."

Then she drove off.

"'You'll see,'" Liz repeated. "My mother is getting stranger and stranger, Scar."

The cat was a constant presence whenever Liz was working in the greenhouse—almost as if the animal expected Liz to magically produce his former master. Liz would have liked nothing better, but she hadn't heard from David since he left. Not a note, e-mail, postcard or letter.

She was mad about that, and more than a little hurt. But she'd kept busy. She still dreamed about him every night. She still watered his cacti and fed his cat. She still missed him.

She returned to her new room. She'd just donned her rubber gloves and paint cap when she heard the sound of tires on gravel again. The girls must have left something behind, she figured. They weren't the most organized thinkers.

"What'd you forg—?" she asked, reversing course.

The compact, sand-colored car wasn't her mother's. She recognized its distinctive style—one of Honda's new hybrids. She'd drooled over the fuel-efficient model last week when she'd gone shopping for a new car. She was using a loaner from her cousin while she waited for her insurance company to cut her a check.

This beautiful vehicle still had the dealer plates in the window, but she quickly lost interest in the car when the door opened and the driver got out.

David.

Or someone who looked a lot like him.

PAUL WASN'T SURE what kind of reception to expect. He hadn't called, figuring what he needed to say had to be said in person, but…

He took a breath and walked toward her, hand extended as if meeting her for the first time. "Hi, Liz, my name is Paul David McAffee. I'm new in town, but I'm here to stay."

Her hand lifted, but the dazed look on her face didn't change until their fingers met. She looked down, then up, quickly, as if confirming the touch truly belonged to the clean-shaven man in the top-end suit. At his ex-wife's insistence, he'd visited a salon where his overdyed hair had been trimmed and styled and his shaggy mustache removed. He'd bought new clothes as soon as his identity had been cleared up and he was able to access his accounts.

He'd bought presents, too. An early Christmas for Kay's children. Gifts from a man who would probably always be that distant uncle-figure who lived far away but sent money on their birthdays. The things for Liz's family were in the back of the new car he'd purchased online—which had been waiting for him at the airport that morning.

"Paul David McAffee," she said softly, her gaze searching his face, as if looking for the man she'd last seen. Her free hand lightly skimmed the area above his upper lip. She smiled. "I like this. And your hair, too. You're not blond."

"This is closer to my real color," he told her, his heart thumping so loudly he was sure she had to hear the racket. "Although the lady who worked me over said to expect some gray as it grows out."

Her tentative smile turned into the beaming grin he knew so well and had missed so much. "Ah, well, that happens to the best of us."

He squeezed her hand and brought it up between them to kiss her knuckles. Only then did he realize she was wearing gloves. "What are you doing here?"

She pulled her hand free and tore the gloves off, letting them drop to the ground. "Later," she said, giving him a two-armed bear hug that made him let out a soft "Oomph." "Catch up. Soon. First. Kiss."

The words were probably imbedded in sentences, but all Paul heard was the part he'd been dying to hear. He didn't need to be asked twice. He pulled her even closer and kissed her, sharing all the emotion he'd been storing up. The separation had given his feelings time to gel. He knew who he was, what he wanted to do with his life, and how Liz fit into those plans.

The kiss might have gone on forever if not for the nail-grating screech that wound upward from their feet. Liz pulled back and laughed. "Scar," she explained. "He's been so unhappy without you."

Paul put enough distance between them to look down. Sure enough, the ugly tomcat was there, winding in and out between their legs, bellowing in his distinctive but hideous voice. Paul didn't want to let go of Liz, but felt compelled to greet his old friend. He bent over and picked up the cat.

"Hey, buddy, you've put on weight. Has Mimi been feeding you too much tuna?"

Liz gestured toward the greenhouse. Paul had noticed that the old foundation of his former house had been removed. The exterior and roof of the outbuildings had been repaired, and there appeared to be new, barn-type doors on the greenhouse.

"Actually, he spends most of his time here. I've been keeping food out for him, but the clever old beggar is probably hitting up our landlady, too."

"*Our* landlady?"

Her cheeks filled with color and she self-consciously swept the funky white painter's hat off her head. "Um, yeah, I'm in the process of moving my tea production into a third of the building. I decided if I was going to make a business out of this, I needed the right space."

Scar was purring so loudly the hum seemed to vibrate through the wall of Paul's chest and come out the other side. He almost missed what she said. Something about the future.

He bent over to set the cat down. "Sorry. I couldn't hear over the Mack truck engine. What was that?"

She took his hand and tugged on it for him to follow. "Let me show you."

Once inside the newly renovated space, he stopped dead in his tracks. "Wow. All this in a couple of weeks? How'd you managed that?"

She shrugged. "Mom calls it therapy. She says I'm the kind of person who has to work hard while trying to come to terms with tough breaks. Like after my dad died, I went to India to volunteer at the ashram."

The ashram. He'd talked to her friend there and had

some interesting news, but that could wait. First, they needed to discuss what the future held for the two of them.

"This will be where we make the teas. See the great ventilation system and energy-efficient skylights? And out here will be our distribution center. Teas and cactus can use the same space, if we coordinate properly."

He turned to look toward the opposite end of the building. Rows of pots were neatly lined up. All the plants looked healthy, cared for. The love he felt for this woman flooded every cell in his body. She'd done this on faith and belief in him. Belief that he'd come back.

"I love you, Liz."

Her arms dropped to her sides and she turned to face him. "I love you, too. That was never in question, but your past…everything you left behind…is that settled?"

"Where can we sit? It's a long story."

She appeared to think a moment, then she smiled and motioned for him to follow. She gently pushed Scar back into the tearoom and closed the door so he couldn't amble after them. "I left the potting shed pretty much the way it was. Our contractor fixed the roof and put in a little insulation so it's not quite such a sweatbox, but the rest…"

He saw what she meant. The cot he'd borrowed from Mimi was still in place, although now so neatly made it could have passed a marine sergeant's inspection.

Liz sat down and kicked off her paint-splattered mules. Paul took the other end, but kept his feet on the floor. What he wanted to do was pull her into his arms and make love with her, now, this instant, but that had to wait until they were clear about who he was.

"I've taken back my real name."

"I noticed. Calling you Paul might take practice."

He nodded. "I'm still getting used to answering to it, but

that was the name my parents chose for me. It was my great-grandfather's name. But I don't want to forget about my life as David. In a way, becoming David helped me find—or at least, redefine—myself."

She leaned forward, her attention fully on him and his story. He felt his nervousness ease. This was Liz. If anyone would understand, she would. "When I first got to Virginia, I was really confused. Lost. I had no idea where to begin, but after I contacted my ex-wife and her husband, the pieces started to fall together."

"You saw her? And the kids?"

He nodded. "She has a new son and she's pregnant. Her husband is over the moon. They seem like a normal, busy, functional family."

"How'd you feel after you saw them?"

"Relieved."

"Why?"

"Because I felt as if—at least in this instance—I'd done the right thing. Yes, my fake death was painful for them, but they were safe and now they've moved on. That was all good. Plus, Kay, my ex, insisted that she never really believed I was dead, which is why she kept such good track of my money."

Liz looked curious, but she didn't say anything, Paul filled her in on the extent of his unexpected windfall.

"You're rich?" she asked in obvious surprise.

"Not bad. A helluva lot better off than I was."

She made a funny face—sort of bemused and maybe a little worried. "Does that mean you don't plan on doing landscapes anymore?"

"Correct. No more digging in the dirt for neighborhood associations or demanding clients."

"Oh. Then you won't be needing the space in the greenhouse." She definitely sounded disappointed.

He shook his head. "Wrong. I came back for two reasons. The first, obviously, is you. The second has to do with those silly spiny plants that you've taken such good care of in my absence. As a scientist, I set out to improve the world through chemistry. Well, I didn't do such a hot job of that. For the past four years, I saw a side of the world you just don't get when you're trapped in a lab. I saw life, the beauty of adaptation and the sad state of our natural environment. We're losing desert species every day. As a scientist, and hopefully one day a father, I can't let that happen."

Liz couldn't stifle the little gasp that came when he said the word *father*. She'd followed his story with breathless attention, knowing deep down that he was here to stay.

She put out her hand and let it rest on his chest. Cat hair adorned the fine fabric of his suit. Outwardly, he looked very different. Dashing. Sophisticated. "You're sure about digging in the dirt and rescuing cactus? You look like a college professor."

He grinned. "An astute observation. I had a quick face-to-face with a couple of VIPs from the university on my way here. One was leaving for Europe this afternoon, so this was my only chance to discuss my funding of a dedicated chair in desert environmental studies and reclamation."

"Wow, you have been busy."

"I wanted all my hedgehog cacti in a row, so to speak," he said with a wink, "when I asked you to marry me."

Liz's heart did a little pirouette. "Really? Just like that. We nearly die, you leave, you come back, you ask me to marry you?"

His newly bare cheeks flooded with a ruddy color she absolutely adored on sight. "Did I miss something?"

"Uh, ye-ah," she said, using an intonation her niece employed all too often. "Where's the romance? The flowers? The ring?"

He jumped to his feet. "Wait right there."

She didn't, of course. She wasn't going to start an engagement by taking orders. Terrible precedent. She tiptoed after him and saw him dash to the new car and dig through some bags in the backseat. Her heart started thudding double time, when she saw him pocket what looked like a ring box.

Holy moly, he's serious about this, she thought, hurrying back to the cot. She was glad she'd spruced up this little room, but it still lacked a certain romantic ambience.

The thought disappeared when David…ah, Paul, returned, his arms filled with two dozen peach-colored roses, a beautifully wrapped dress box under his arm and a heart-shaped box from Ethel M chocolates in the other hand. "I wanted to make sure I covered all bases," he said hurrying to where she was sitting. "God, I hope the chocolates didn't melt. I forgot this was Vegas."

She pressed the candy to her chest and blinked back tears. No boy had ever given her chocolates. The gesture was sappy and sweet and it nearly broke her heart. "Thank you. I love chocolate—even slightly melted."

Next came the dress package. Big. The designer imprint subtly hidden in the bow and wrapping paper. "Dav—I mean Paul, you shouldn't have."

"I bought it online, but from a local store so you can exchange it if it doesn't fit. If it does fit, I thought you might wear it tonight. I have reservations at this great little restaurant I've never tried. It's called Romantique."

Her heart broke a little more, but in a way that felt good. He presented the flowers with a flourish, not giving her time to open the box. That was for later, she realized. After he'd done what he came here to do.

The fresh, heady smell from the flowers brought tears to her eyes. She buried her face in them, trying to keep from crying.

"Liz," he said, lowering to one knee in front of her, "I know this is asking a lot. In some ways, we're practically strangers, but in the ways that count, we're connected more deeply than even science could explain. I honestly believe you're the reason I moved to Vegas, although I knew nothing about you at the time. You shaped my life even before I met you. I realize I'm not the half of your prophecy you wanted, but—"

"No," Liz cried, unable to stop herself. "That's not true. Prisha saved *me* when I was lost in the shadows. She gave me a reason to let go of my demons and start living again, so I would return home…."

"To save me." He leaned forward and kissed her tenderly. "Are you sure you're not terribly disappointed that you've wound up with me and not Prisha?"

She slowly shook her head from side to side as she thought about his question. "I miss her, but I can't be sad about what's happening in her life. The surgery was a success, and she's reunited with her family. Her real mother."

"You're an amazing woman, Elizabeth Radonovic. I have a feeling our life together is going to be overflowing with kids—ones we have and ones we find. You are going to marry me, aren't you?"

She nodded. "Of course. And not to be crude, but is that a ring in your pocket or are you just glad to see me?"

He rocked back on his heels, laughing. "It's a ring. And I've never been gladder to see anyone in my life." The innuendo came through loud and clear, and Liz felt her body respond. The woman in her had come alive under his nurturing touch, and she couldn't wait to feel those juices flowing again.

He moved to the cot beside her and set her gifts on the floor at their feet. From his pocket, he pulled a small blue-velvet ring box. "I took some flack from my ex about buying this without any input from you, but I told her you were far too modest to pick out a ring worthy of your beauty."

Liz felt her cheeks heat up. "I honestly never felt beautiful until you came along. When you have three gorgeous sisters, it's less work to stay in the background."

He touched her hair, her cheek, her lips. "Not anymore. Not unless that's your choice. Because, as far as I'm concerned, you're the star of the show."

He opened the box.

Liz gasped. "Oh, my."

The pear-shaped diamond was the largest she'd ever seen up close. The setting was an inventive mix of yellow and white gold. Her fingers shook as she took it out of its satin niche. "This is for me? Really?"

He took the ring from her and slid it onto her third finger. "One of a kind. Just for you. Now kiss me before I turn into a pumpkin."

She laughed. "You really have your fairy tales mixed up, but that's okay. We have time to work on that before we have kids."

She threw her arms around his neck with such force, they fell sideways onto the cot. The narrow metal legs groaned, but Liz ignored the warning. She thought she heard Paul mumble something like "Not really," but she ignored that, too. She was in love. The man she loved had just proposed and given her the biggest diamond she'd ever seen. This was one part of her prophecy nobody could have foreseen, right?

Right.

She reared back and looked down at the besotted expression on Paul's face. "How did you know where to find me?"

He shook his head slightly. "I called your house, but when nobody answered, I called your mother."

"No wonder she volunteered to pick up Lydia and Reezira from school."

He gave her a curious look then asked, "Can we kiss again? I've been thinking about this way too often and in all the wrong places."

She wiggled her hips and grinned. "I can tell. You're ready to party, but…um, are we prepared for the consequences? I think not."

He let out a low growl, not unlike the sound his cat made when he was hungry and said, "Speak for yourself. My suitcase is in the car. It's well stocked for any emergency, but all kidding aside, the only thing that would make me happier than saying 'I do' to you, is finding out we're going to have a baby."

"Really?"

He nodded. "I love you, Liz. I want our life together to be filled with kids. In fact, I talked to a lady that your friend at the ashram put me in touch with and she knows a woman who is definitely planning to place her baby up for adoption. My ex-wife's husband still has connections in the State Department and he said he'd be happy to pull a few strings, any time you say the word."

She closed her eyes and let her kiss be her answer. She'd be ready soon, but first she needed to mourn Prisha a little longer. And celebrate her engagement. And get her new business on track. But soon. Soon she and this wonderful man would travel abroad to meet their new baby, a child of light and hope. And they'd bring their baby home to a diverse, complex community that bloomed on the desert much like the cactus—resilient, occasionally brilliant and elemental to the world at large.

Turn the page for a sneak peek at
THE QUIET CHILD, the final book in the
SISTERS OF THE SILVER DOLLAR *miniseries*
by Debra Salonen.
Coming in November 2006
from Harlequin American Romance

Mark had to be blunt. He was desperate. Only a truly desperate man would ask his ex-fiancée to care for the child who, for all practical purposes, was the reason they weren't married. If not for Braden, he and Alex would probably have a kid or two of their own by now.

Instead, Mark had spent nearly every minute since that fateful night when he gave into Tracey's no-strings-attached suggestion trying to make amends for his mistake. To his ex-wife, for not loving her enough to put up with her drinking and partying. To Braden, for not being able to pretend any longer that he loved the little boy's mother. To his conscience, which knew just how badly he'd hurt Alex.

"You want to bring your son to the Dancing Hippo?"

"Yes."

"Why? This is a preschool. Your son must be in what—second grade?"

"He's repeating first grade this year. He just turned seven. Tracey and I split up when he was three. She started him in kindergarten when he was four. His birthday is September twenty-third, so technically he was old enough, but I didn't think he was ready."

"It didn't work out?"

"He passed, but whenever I went to a parent-teacher conference, I could tell the teacher was concerned about Bray's socialization skills—or lack of them. He's very shy and has had a bit of a stuttering problem almost since he started speaking. At the time it wasn't debilitating, but his teacher thought he'd be better off repeating kindergarten. Tracey disagreed. She insisted that he'd catch up in first grade."

"Didn't happen?"

"Didn't have a chance to happen. About six weeks into the school year, his teacher called us both in for a conference. She said Braden needed speech therapy and should probably be placed in a special-needs class."

Alex winced. "I bet that didn't go over well with Tracey."

"She blew up. Accused the teacher of being lazy and showing favoritism. She called me the next day and said that since she wasn't working, there was no reason why she shouldn't home school him."

Mark looked away. In hindsight, the battle that ensued had been a waste of time and money, and had put his son right in the middle of his parents' war. "I hired a lawyer to try to make her take him to school. Odessa, Tracey's mother, got involved. I filed for sole custody. Then, in March, before we had anything settled, Tracey died."

Her mouth dropped open. "Tracey's dead?"

He nodded. "A fire. She and the man she might have been involved with at the time were killed." He didn't add the brutal details that the two had died in an explosion at a meth lab where Tracey had most likely gone to get drugs from her on-again, off-again pusher boyfriend.

"Oh, my word. Oh, poor Braden."

Mark hurried past her sympathy. "I put Braden back in regular school as soon as I could. Probably the wrong thing to do, in hindsight. He had a hard time adjusting. The other kids teased him." Mark could barely think about that time without breaking down. He'd felt like the worst father in the world.

"I know it's a cliché," Alex offered, "but kids can be cruel. Did the school test him?"

Mark nodded. "He's behind academically and, according to them, has problems with peer interaction. His cognitive functions…" He tried to smile. "See, I've learned a new language. His cognitive functions are within normal range, but his speech impediment has had a negative impact on his ability to make friends and communicate with his teachers. We have an ISP—Individual Student Program—designed to help him get back on track.

The concerned look on her face intensified. "Has he shown any improvement?"

"Not really. The school he's attending likes to mainstream its special-needs students. He's in a new first grade class and he works with a speech therapist a couple of times a week, but she's not having a lot of luck. Most of the time, he just doesn't talk."

Sympathy sparkled like tears in her gorgeous brown eyes. He'd always said he could see his forever in Alex's eyes. But he'd been wrong. He didn't want sympathy. He wanted…he *needed* help.

"I'm looking for after-school care. Your ad in the Yellow Pages says that's something you offer. I checked with his school and the bus would drop him off here, if you'll let him come."

She frowned. "I've had a few older kids—mostly siblings of a student in my preschool class—sign up for that program, but at the moment my cousin Gregor's son is my only after-school student. Your son would probably benefit from a more one-on-one type of program, and, frankly, I just don't have the staff for that."

She hadn't said no, exactly. "He needs a place where he can feel safe. He doesn't act out. The poor kid has missed out on a lot of things in his short life, including preschool. This might be really good for him."

"What are you doing for child care now?"

"I have a babysitter who comes to my house. She found a job that pays more and gave her notice. I advertised the position, but I've only had a couple of applicants, and Braden didn't seem to like them."

Thumbing through the Yellow Pages one evening, he'd spotted Alex's ad. A quick call to his friend Zeke Martini, whom Mark had learned was dating Alex's widowed mother, confirmed that Alex owned and operated the child-care center.

"How many days per week? What hours? If I remember correctly, a cop's hours are pretty sketchy."

Questions were good. Better than a flat out "no." Better than he deserved. "I'm an arson investigator with the Las Vegas Fire Department. I work eight-hour days with the third Monday off. Sometimes I might get called in off-duty if there's an emergency. There's a woman in my building who's a stay-at-home mom who helps out if that happens, but she doesn't want to take on another kid full time.

"So, you're just interested in after-school care, five days a week."

"From three to six-thirty, depending on traffic."

Her frown made him wonder what she was thinking. Was she remembering that day when their plans blew up into tiny shards of anger and disappointment? The day he told her that Tracey was pregnant, and he was the father?

"On rare occasions I might run late. I have to know

there's a safety net in place in case something comes up at work. If I don't work, I can't afford to pay for after-school care. It's a vicious circle."

She looked troubled. He knew how much she adored kids. But could she get past what had been between them for Braden's sake?

A little bell rang from inside the attractive ranch-style house that had—almost—been his. He could hear the muffled sounds of children's voices. Happy sounds. *God, he prayed, please let her take Bray. He deserves a second chance. I know I don't, but Braden does.*

"I really can't say for sure, Mark. Not until I've met him. Could you bring him by sometime next week? He might not like it here at all."

"He will."

Mark believed that, although he couldn't say for sure why. He'd tried everything to communicate with his son and still didn't have a clue what was going on inside that adorable blond head. Bray looked so much like his mother it was unnerving at times. Alex might have a problem with that—she *was* human, after all. But maybe she'd take pity on the poor kid and let the past stay where it was—buried beneath angry charges and a surfeit of tears.

"How 'bout Monday? That's my day off."

Her eyes widened as if regretting her offer. "I…I don't know if this is a good idea—given our history, but…okay. Bring him in. If he's not unhappy here, then we'll see."

We'll see. A small glimmer of hope, but more than he'd had in weeks. He'd take it.

The next book in
THE BRIDES OF BELLA LUCIA *series*
is out next month!
Don't miss THE REBEL PRINCE
by Raye Morgan
Here's an exclusive sneak preview of
Emma Valentine's story!

"OH, NO!"

The reaction slipped out before Emma Valentine could stop it, for there stood the very man she most wanted to avoid seeing again.

He didn't look any happier to see her.

"Well, come on, get on board," he said gruffly. "I won't bite." One eyebrow rose. "Though I might nibble a little," he added, mostly to amuse himself.

But she wasn't paying any attention to what he was saying. She was staring at him, taking in the royal-blue uniform he was wearing, with gold braid and glistening badges decorating the sleeves, epaulettes and an upright collar. Ribbons and medals covered the breast of the short, fitted jacket. A gold-encrusted sabre hung at his side. And suddenly it was clear to her who this man really was.

She gulped wordlessly. Reaching out, he took her elbow and pulled her aboard. The doors slid closed. And finally she found her tongue.

"You…you're the prince."

He nodded, barely glancing at her. "Yes. Of course."

She raised a hand and covered her mouth for a moment. "I should have known."

"Of course you should have. I don't know why you didn't." He punched the ground-floor button to get the elevator moving again, then turned to look down at her. "A relatively bright five-year-old child would have tumbled to the truth right away."

Her shock faded as her indignation at his tone asserted itself. He might be the prince, but he was still just as annoying as he had been earlier that day.

"A relatively bright five-year-old child without a bump on the head from a badly thrown water polo ball, maybe," she said defensively. She wasn't feeling woozy any longer and she wasn't about to let him bully her, no matter how royal he was. "I was unconscious half the time."

"And just clueless the other half, I guess," he said, looking bemused.

The arrogance of the man was really galling.

"I suppose you think your 'royalness' is so obvious it sort of shimmers around you for all to see?" she challenged. "Or better yet, oozes from your pores like…like sweat on a hot day?"

"Something like that," he acknowledged calmly. "Most people tumble to it pretty quickly. In fact, it's hard to hide even when I want to avoid dealing with it."

"Poor baby," she said, still resenting his manner. "I guess that works better with injured people who are half asleep." Looking at him, she felt a strange emotion she couldn't identify. It was as though she wanted to prove something to him, but she wasn't sure what. "And anyway, you know you did your best to fool me," she added.

His brows knit together as though he really didn't know what she was talking about. "I didn't do a thing."

"You told me your name was Monty."

"It is." He shrugged. "I have a lot of names. Some of

them are too rude to be spoken to my face, I'm sure." He glanced at her sideways, his hand on the hilt of his sabre. "Perhaps you're contemplating one of those right now."

You bet I am.

That was what she would like to say. But it suddenly occurred to her that she was supposed to be working for this man. If she wanted to keep the job of coronation chef, maybe she'd better keep her opinions to herself. So she clamped her mouth shut, took a deep breath and looked away, trying hard to calm down.

The elevator ground to a halt and the doors slid open laboriously. She moved to step forward, hoping to make her escape, but his hand shot out again and caught her elbow.

"Wait a minute. *You're* a woman," he said, as though that thought had just presented itself to him.

"That's a rare ability for insight you have there, Your Highness," she snapped before she could stop herself. And then she winced. She was going to have to do better than that if she was going to keep this relationship on an even keel.

But he was ignoring her dig. Nodding, he stared at her with a speculative gleam in his golden eyes. "I've been looking for a woman, but you'll do."

She blanched, stiffening. "I'll do for what?"

He made a head gesture in a direction she knew was opposite of where she was going and his grip tightened on her elbow.

"Come with me," he said abruptly, making it an order.

She dug in her heels, thinking fast. She didn't much like orders. "Wait! I can't. I have to get to the kitchen."

"Not yet. I need you."

"You what?" Her breathless gasp of surprise was soft, but she knew he'd heard it.

"I need you," he said firmly. "Oh, don't look so shocked.

I'm not planning to throw you into the hay and have my way with you. I need you for something a bit more mundane than that."

She felt color rushing into her cheeks and she silently begged it to stop. Here she was, formless and stodgy in her chef's whites. No makeup, no stiletto heels. Hardly the picture of the femmes fatales he was undoubtedly used to. The likelihood that he would have any carnal interest in her was remote at best. To have him think she was hysterically defending her virtue was humiliating.

"Well, what if I don't want to go with you?" she said in hopes of deflecting his attention from her blush.

"Too bad."

"What?"

Amusement sparkled in his eyes. He was certainly enjoying this. And that only made her more determined to resist him.

"I'm the prince, remember? And we're in the castle. My orders take precedence. It's that old pesky divine rights thing."

Her jaw jutted out. Despite her embarrassment, she couldn't let that pass.

"Over my free will? Never!"

Exasperation filled his face.

"Hey, call out the historians. Someone will write a book about you and your courageous principles." His eyes glittered sardonically. "But in the meantime, Emma Valentine, you're coming with me."

Silhouette® Desire®

**Introducing an exciting appearance
by legendary
New York Times bestselling author**

DIANA PALMER

HEARTBREAKER

He's the ultimate bachelor…
but he may have just met
the one woman to change his ways!

Join the drama in the story of a confirmed
bachelor, an amnesiac beauty and their
unexpected passionate romance.

"Diana Palmer is a mesmerizing storyteller
who captures the essence of what
a romance should be."—*Affaire de Coeur*

**Heartbreaker *is available from Silhouette Desire
in September 2006.***

SAVE UP TO $30! SIGN UP TODAY!

INSIDE *Romance*

**The complete guide to your favorite
Harlequin®, Silhouette® and Love Inspired® books.**

✓ Newsletter ABSOLUTELY FREE! No purchase necessary.

✓ Valuable coupons for future purchases of Harlequin,
Silhouette and Love Inspired books in every issue!

✓ Special excerpts & previews in each issue. Learn about all
the hottest titles before they arrive in stores.

✓ No hassle—mailed directly to your door!

✓ Comes complete with a handy shopping checklist
so you won't miss out on any titles.

- -

SIGN ME UP TO RECEIVE INSIDE ROMANCE
ABSOLUTELY FREE

(Please print clearly)

Name

Address

City/Town   State/Province   Zip/Postal Code

(098 KKM EJL9)   **Please mail this form to:**
In the U.S.A.: Inside Romance, P.O. Box 9057, Buffalo, NY 14269-9057
In Canada: Inside Romance, P.O. Box 622, Fort Erie, ON L2A 5X3
OR visit http://www.eHarlequin.com/insideromance

IRNBPA06R   ® and ™ are trademarks owned and used by the trademark owner and/or its licensee.

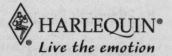

If you enjoyed what you just read,
then we've got an offer you can't resist!

Take 2 bestselling love stories FREE!

Plus get a FREE surprise gift!

Clip this page and mail it to Harlequin Reader Service®

IN U.S.A.	**IN CANADA**
3010 Walden Ave.	P.O. Box 609
P.O. Box 1867	Fort Erie, Ontario
Buffalo, N.Y. 14240-1867	L2A 5X3

YES! Please send me 2 free Harlequin American Romance® novels and my free surprise gift. After receiving them, if I don't wish to receive anymore, I can return the shipping statement marked cancel. If I don't cancel, I will receive 4 brand-new novels every month, before they're available in stores! In the U.S.A., bill me at the bargain price of $4.24 plus 25¢ shipping & handling per book and applicable sales tax, if any*. In Canada, bill me at the bargain price of $4.99 plus 25¢ shipping & handling per book and applicable taxes**. That's the complete price and a savings of at least 10% off the cover prices—what a great deal! I understand that accepting the 2 free books and gift places me under no obligation ever to buy any books. I can always return a shipment and cancel at any time. Even if I never buy another book from Harlequin, the 2 free books and gift are mine to keep forever.

154 HDN DZ7S
354 HDN DZ7T

Name	(PLEASE PRINT)	
Address	Apt.#	
City	State/Prov.	Zip/Postal Code

Not valid to current Harlequin American Romance® subscribers.

Want to try two free books from another series?
Call 1-800-873-8635 or visit www.morefreebooks.com.

* Terms and prices subject to change without notice. Sales tax applicable in N.Y.
** Canadian residents will be charged applicable provincial taxes and GST.
All orders subject to approval. Offer limited to one per household.
® are registered trademarks owned and used by the trademark owner or its licensee.

AMER04R   ©2004 Harlequin Enterprises Limited

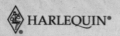

SPECIAL EDITION™

Welcome to Danbury Way—where nothing is as it seems...

Megan Schumacher has managed to maintain a low profile on Danbury Way by keeping the huge success of her graphics business a secret. But when a new client turns out to be a neighbor's sexy ex-husband, rumors of their developing romance quickly start to swirl.

THE RELUCTANT CINDERELLA

by CHRISTINE RIMMER

Available July 2006

Don't miss the first book from the Talk of the Neighborhood miniseries.

Silhouette®
BOMBSHELL™

The Marian priestesses were destroyed long ago,
but their daughters live on. The time has come
for the heiresses to learn of their legacy, to unite
the pieces of a powerful mosaic and bring light to
a secret their ancestors died to protect.

The Madonna Key

Follow their quests each month.

Lost Calling by Evelyn Vaughn,
July 2006

Haunted Echoes by Cindy Dees,
August 2006

Dark Revelations by Lorna Tedder,
September 2006

Shadow Lines by Carol Stephenson,
October 2006

Hidden Sanctuary by Sharron McClellan,
November 2006

Veiled Legacy by Jenna Mills,
December 2006

Seventh Key by Evelyn Vaughn,
January 2007

Page-turning drama...

Exotic, glamorous locations...

Intense emotion and passionate seduction...

Sheikhs, princes and billionaire tycoons...

This summer, may we suggest:

THE SHEIKH'S DISOBEDIENT BRIDE

by Jane Porter

On sale June.

AT THE GREEK TYCOON'S BIDDING

by Cathy Williams

On sale July.

THE ITALIAN MILLIONAIRE'S VIRGIN WIFE

On sale August.

With new titles to choose from every month, discover a world of romance in our books written by internationally bestselling authors.

HARLEQUIN *Presents*

It's the ultimate in quality romance!

Available wherever Harlequin books are sold.

www.eHarlequin.com

HPGEN06

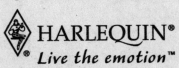

Life.
It could happen to her!

Never Happened just about sums up
Alexis Jackson's life. Independent and
successful, Alexis has concentrated on
building her own business, leaving no
time for love. Now at forty, Alexis
discovers that she still has a few things
to learn about life—that the life unlived
is the one that "Never happened"
and it's her time to make a change....

Never Happened
by Debra Webb

Available July 2006
TheNextNovel.com